DEEP
FRIED
FATE

DEEP FRIED FATE

A JANE ROBERTS MYSTERY

CAROL CHEN

This is a work of fiction. Names, characters, places, and incidents either are the product of the author's imagination or are used fictitiously, and any resemblance to actual persons, living or dead, businesses, companies, events, or locales is entirely coincidental.

Published by Carol Chen
41 Meadow Drive
Camden, Maine 04843

For Thomas Campbell and his Clan
on both sides of the pond

ACKNOWLEDGMENTS

For all your insights, feedback, or help, or all of the above, Thank You, Thank You! to Cheryl Ayer, June Bower, Cookie B. Breton, Thomas Campbell, Patt Chen, Madelene Cole, Naomi Gettle, David Hopkins, Kate Jackson, Barb Karl, Dorie Klein, Rick Kot, Jamie Landi, Kris Landi, Peter Michelena, Susan Raab, Cheryl Rogers, Marc Rogers, Meredith Johnson Sadler, Pat Shannon, Debbie Taylor, Renée Tondelli, Tim Whelan, the Maine Lobster Festival, the New England Crime Bake, and the wonderful book clubs who dare to dive in!

Special thanks to travel humour writer Simon Michael Prior for his helpful video on formatting MS Word for IngramSpark.

Taylor Curry is once again my book cover template hero!

DEEP FRIED FATE
Cast of Characters

Jane Roberts, Public Safety Officer on St. Frewin's Island

Helen Orbeton, PSO receptionist

Israel Tenner, Jane's PSO assistant

Storm Nosmot, homicide detective

Cissy Burkett, island local

Duncan, Cissy's son

Monica Tunny, local teen

Delphi, local teen

Faith, local teen

Oxford Monteith, author

Samantha Lloyd, Oxford's sister and island caterer

Nathan Herinton, Samantha's beau and island local

Sugar Betts, Oxford's friend on Ferguson Mountain in Plimpton, Maine

Konstantin Balankoff, Jane's beau

Torrance Balankoff, Konstantin's sister

John Leckman, island vet and doctor

Maggie Banner, owner of Grand Harbor Inn

Waikiki Banner, Maggie's sister

Ryan Young, bank loan officer and Maggie's beau

Chanson Pratt, summer resident from Texas

Salem Pratt, Chanson's husband

Zen-Beau Lovey Pratt, Chanson's son by Zen-Ti Smith

Zen-Ti Smith, entrepreneur

Zara Billings, island local, now in prison

Jerome Williams, manager of Calderwood Boatyard

Joe Miller, boat carpenter at Calderwood Boatyard

Bernie Pushaw, island local

Hansen Moody, Bernie's business partner
Sonny Mannix, State ferry captain
Captain and Mrs. Bryce, island retirees
Mary Bartlett, island orchard owner
Betty Dodge, island local
Beatrice Jenkins, island local
Abe Jenkins, Beatrice's son, owner of water taxi service
Dahlia Jenkins, Abe's wife
India Barton, island local
Fredly Tunny, island local

Board of Directors, Attorneys for Hallucinogens
Maxwell Dunham, Head of New England Drug
    Enforcement Agency
Calvin Ritter, FBI Science and Technology Branch
Alex Champus, FBI Agent
Harriet Buxton, Director of Human Resources, Maine
    State Police
Lieutenant Joseph Adderley, Jane's superior at Maine
    Crimes Unit-Central
Dr. Andreas Kerner, State Medical Examiner
Todd Chisolm, State Evidence Response Team
Sean Peters, State Medical Examiner's Office
Gail, Sean's girlfriend and employee at Maine Bureau of
    Human Resources
Dave Tower, Maine Drug Enforcement Agency Regional
    Task Force

Random Thayer, Oxford Monteith's abutter on
    Ferguson Mountain
Jamie, abutter
Turk, abutter
Chummy, abutter

a·but·ter
/əˈbədər/
noun
the owner of an adjoining property

1

JULY 22, 2022
Orion's Spit

Homicide Detective Storm Nosmot of Maine Crimes Unit-Central made one last call on the ferry terminal's public payphone before boarding the 8:30 PM water taxi to St. Frewin's Island. He hated making the call, even though part of him was relieved to be doing so. Jane Roberts, the island's Public Safety Officer, would have to be told, but at least it would come from Storm and he would be with her to help her through the tragedy awaiting them both.

The anonymous tip had been phoned in to MCU-Central two hours earlier.

....

Jane was stirring a pot of butterscotch pudding at a critical stage when the phone rang. She momentarily imagined not answering her phone, but that was never really an option. Not for a Public Safety Officer on a small Maine island with a year-round population of some 300 men, women, and children, where every home had a bottle of booze in the cupboard and a gun on the rack.

"Jane...Storm here. Have you heard any news tonight?"

"What do you mean by news? I'm in my nightgown, stirring a pot of pudding that's about to curdle. What are you calling me for this late?"

"OK...ah, I'm at the public dock on the mainland right now, and I'm getting the water taxi to St. Frewin's.

I'll see you shortly. And sorry, but you need to pick me up. This is work-related. I'll fill you in when I get there. And bring your big flashlight. Got to run."

Jane stared back at the phone as she heard him hang up. Now what? She had to get dressed? Pain in the butt! But at least she had a good half hour to finish with the pudding and clean up before meeting Storm at the water-taxi stand.

....

Jane got out of her truck and walked towards the town dock. It was past 9 PM, and all the soft evening light of late July had disappeared.

A vast, black cloak of silent velvet had descended upon the harbor, the cloak touching no one...its weight so close, but never felt...with small orbs of light pulsing tiny beams along the ocean's edge...from docks, garages, homes....

Jane saw Storm trudging up the wooden pier. He was a big man, always moving with ease as though he were walking on water. Not that he was Christ. More like Noah or Moses with the flowing beard...approaching the world with a calm, level bearing. But tonight his head was down and he seemed tired.

"Hey there, Mr. Nosmot. I'm dying to know what's dragged you out here in the middle of the night."

"Jane...good to see you. Sorry about this unexpected visit." Storm opened his arms wide to offer a hug.

"I gather you're not here simply for a social call...no midnight charmer routine? After all, we know you're a happily married man."

"It's a lot worse than that, Jane. There's been a murder apparently. In a cabin at the end of Orion's Spit. Can you drive us there?"

"What? Who? How come you know about this and I don't?" Jane complained as they got into her truck.

"An anonymous call came into MCU-Central about two and a half hours ago."

"Figures. I never get enough respect out here."

"Don't take it personally. The caller dialed 911 to report a dead body, so it got routed to me. No reflection on your abilities."

"Well then, I'm glad you're here. If it's a murder, I can always use the company." Jane gave him a bleak smile.

Storm said nothing. He could not bring himself to tell her. If he didn't say anything, she would hate him for it later. And if he tried to act as if he hadn't known, she would see right through it. Still, he sat there wordless.

Jane drove towards Orion's Spit. It was odd that Storm was unusually quiet, but she followed suit.

She thought back to the buzz now and then that would circulate about the cabin down on the point. The place belonged to the middle brother of the Tunny family, ne'er-do-wells who were known to throw game jacks and gash point screws on the road in front of their house. Flat tires for day trippers motoring by were the Tunny idea of fun. So was chaining young family members inside closets. But again, it was all just now and then...just rumblings.

Jane drove past the Tunnys' worn-out, multi-gabled heap that must have been a solid residence once upon a time, when adults were adults and worked hard to earn an island living. Nowadays, however, the Tunny offspring tended to let even simple, seasonal jobs at the island boatyard escape from their grasp. The sagging structural lines and worn, naked clapboards of their home and the spilled guts of rusted machinery and dead household appliances flung about the starving grass in the yard reflected the hearts and souls of the people who dwelled within, who clearly didn't give a damn.

The cabin was another building altogether. The cabin was special...notorious. A hangout where the middle brother and his buddies would gather and drink, especially during hunting season, or so Jane had heard.

She drove slowly down the narrow way, her truck jolting cock-eyed as she swerved to dodge potholes as wide as half the road. Then they saw the log structure in her truck headlights. She couldn't remember how she knew the way. She must have been down here at some point, but she had never been inside.

It was completely dark out...beyond dark. Black in the way rural Maine was on a moonless night. Too dark to tell if one's eyes were open or shut. Too dark even to feel the air or to take the next step with any confidence.

Jane turned off the engine. "So what do you say, Storm? Spooky enough for you?"

"If we use our flashlights, we'll manage." He felt helpless. He should say something...get it over with. But he couldn't.

They stepped out of the truck and started walking towards the cabin's front porch.

....

Storm swept his flashlight like a wand around the cabin's main room...tracing wide circles of light over the log pole walls, looking for the reason the anonymous caller had dialed 911. Jane did the same. She could feel the night breeze blowing freely through the cabin.

Jesus Christ.

Perhaps the fresh circulation was helping to flush out the stench to some degree, but Jane wouldn't be surprised if she passed out within seconds.

Jesus Christ.

If not from collapsed lungs, then from the extreme effect of pair upon pair of dumbfounded eyes staring down at her from the cabin wall in the thin roaming beam of her flashlight. Eyes set in time...set by death...so many haunted, grieving gems. And the incisors, all the little fangs, jutting out like ivory punctuation marks in the gruesome, withered smiles.

Jane's sanity was urging her to leave immediately. But curiosity made her hold her flashlight steady to take inventory of the cruel spectacle before her...to identify what kind of animal head, in each instance, was nailed to the wall....

"Oh God, Storm. Raccoon, skunk, squirrel...."

No discriminating between wild and domesticated...*a cat!*, turkey, deer, fisher, mink, chipmunk. Head after head, walls of wildlife voodoo.

"What is this?" Jane grimaced as she spoke. "Trophies? Shockers? Conversation starters?"

Storm hacked hard to clear his throat. "I'd say it's a hunter's decapitated harem."

"What are you thinking?" Jane looked to Storm for some kind of anchor, some kind of sanity.

"I'm relieved to see it's only animal heads. We're OK, Jane. Just take a deep breath."

"Are you kidding? My nose hairs are falling out. I'd spray them with bleach right now if I didn't plan on using my nostrils again."

"I hear you. Let's just take a look in the rest of the cabin, and then we can leave. Maybe this has all been a prank...at least on the part of our anonymous caller."

"OK. I'll look to the right. You check out the left. Does this goddamn hut have any electric lights anywhere?" Jane griped as she walked towards a small alcove off to the side.

She stepped into the alcove and automatically felt on the wall for a light switch, while aiming her flashlight into the interior. Her left hand slapped something that felt like fabric...damp fabric? Something solid and long and slick. And she was vaguely aware of a tackiness under her left sneaker.

She swung her flashlight to the left. A leg in pants? "Storm! It's a body!"

Jane heard the sticky sound of both her shoes, the tug of something gummy as she shifted and aimed her light higher. Storm had reached her side. They both looked upward.

Ten Days Earlier

2

JULY 12, 2022
Tired Kittens

Receptionist Helen Orbeton was gazing at the dust specks floating in the sunlit air that summer day in the main room of the Public Safety Office on St. Frewin's Island.

She was thinking about her late husband and about her true love, Dr. John Leckman, the island vet and MD. How their three lives together and apart had played out year after year and then her husband was gone. She was thinking about her son, Josiah, in prison up in Warren. Twenty-five years was a long time, but now he had some twenty-three years left to serve. Someday, one day, he'd be back home.

The ringing phone drew Helen from her thoughts. "Good morning, Public Safety Office."

"Helen! It's Cissy Burkett. I don't know what to say. It's simply crazy!"

"What's crazy, Cissy?"

"Well, you know we got that new puppy, Jack. And he just got his balls chopped off. And the vet sent me home with a bunch of sedatives and pain killers."

"That should help him, Cissy. Is there some problem?"

"I probably shouldn't even tell you, Helen. But I've got to tell someone in case it ends up bad."

"You can tell me, Cissy. Go ahead."

"OK...my son, Duncan, you know Duncan...my middle boy...he's got a job on the mainland now. But he's home for the week. I mean it's summer...best time to be here, right?"

"And about the dog?"

"So, yes, right. So I go to give Jack his pills this morning, and do you know, every last one of those pills was G...O...N...E. Bottles all empty, Helen. Empty!"

"What do you think happened?"

"I'm not saying Duncan took them. But the damn dog sure didn't."

"Well how many pills are we talking about?"

"Three pills twice a day for nine more days."

"This new puppy...is he a big dog?"

"He's a Bernese Mountain Dog, Helen. Paws the size of frying pans."

"So his pills are geared to his weight," Helen said, thinking aloud.

"That's right. And my son Duncan, he's a half-pint."

"OK...here's what we do, Cissy. You call Dr. Leckman and tell him what happened. He can help you with more medication for the dog. And he can also advise you about Duncan. Is Duncan home right now?"

"He's passed out on the couch."

"Passed out! Oh, Cissy. Definitely call Dr. Leckman right away. He'll probably want to come check on Duncan. And if you want to keep the new dog meds here at our office, you could drop in each morning and again before we close at 5:30 PM to get Jack's doses for the day. Or maybe you can keep the dog meds at a friend's house. Whatever works best. Good luck, Cissy. Call Dr. Leckman right now."

Helen hung up and got back to work. She hesitated a moment, and then she herself called Dr. Leckman to report Cissy Burkett's news. His phone line was open; she told him everything. And then she wrote down the event in the PSO daily log book. Jane would want to hear about this.

....

Later that day the front door of the Public Safety Office flew open, and three young teen-age girls rushed in, their thin arms and legs whirling in pastels and urgency. Israel Tenner, assistant to the Public Safety Officer, and Helen Orbeton looked up from their desks. Helen was about to ask the girls if she could help them, when they all began waving their hands and talking at once.

"Mrs. Orbeton. We have an emergency!" One Monica, per her name tag, started shushing the other teens.

"There's a tire out in the ocean filled with kittens! We don't know how it happened, but it happened."

"We were just hanging out at the beach when this tire started floating past us. And then we heard lots of crying, and we could see these little heads squeaking and peeking out of the tire," said the girl with a name tag of Delphi.

Israel spoke up next. "Girls, this sounds serious. But let's slow down. Where are these kittens in the tire? Where in the ocean?"

Name tag of Faith spoke up. "At the beach in front of Penobscot Inn."

"And how many kittens?" Helen asked.

"At least three!" said Monica.

"OK," Israel said, taking charge. "Helen will call the Penobscot Inn. I'm going to drive us over there to try and help save those kittens. How did you get here anyway? Did you run over?"

"Connor Mulroy from the Pub gave us a lift."

"Great. We may still have time." Israel herded the girls out to his car, hoisted his kayak on top of the roof and secured it. "All right, team. To the kitten rescue!" And they started off for the Penobscot Inn.

A few guests were standing around on the beach at the Inn. They waved at Israel as he and the teens jumped out of the car and unloaded the kayak.

"None of those babies has jumped yet. But you better hurry!" said one of the onlookers with binoculars in hand.

Israel told the girls to go get some towels and a laundry basket from the Inn staff. He carried his kayak down to the water and slipped into it and his life jacket. Lucky for all of them, there was little breeze to spin the tire out to sea or upset its flotation. As Israel started paddling, his kayak left the shore and moved towards the black ring of rubber.

"What a classic rescue mission," an inn guest remarked. "An officer racing out to save those little critters. You got to love Maine!"

Another bystander made a slight face. "In another country, it would be refugees out there hanging on to tires. This island is so sheltered from the real world."

His companion admonished him. "Lighten up, will you? We're on vacation!"

Israel started making kissing sounds as his kayak neared the cruising kittens. He could see their soaked bodies starting to scramble madly atop the tire as it swayed in the waves. He added some pssst, pssst noises to get their attention.

"Rub a dub, dub. Are there three of you in this tub?" The kittens did a panic dance as Israel approached them.

"OK, you hairy little pirates. You hang on one more second." Israel took a bungee cord from the well of his kayak and hooked it to the tire and the kayak so he could tow the tire in with him. He then started plucking each little wet evacuee off the tire without hesitation and stuffing them one by one inside his shirt. He had to beat them to it before they skittered from the tire for good. One, two, three...four! Not just three. God almighty. Who would do this to something so helpless and cute? Sick human beings.

Israel began paddling back to shore with the kittens squirming inside his shirt, climbing up his chest, and two of them spilling out of his shirt and crawling towards his neck.

The intense, limitless sun warmed both man and little fuzz balls and brought pure clarity to the air and sky around them. A Maine blue sky in July, defying any paint box in the world...so breathable, endlessly blue, infinite and free, high above the ocean. Nothing like it.

"Hold tight, maties. We're in the home stretch." His two wobbly mini co-pilots almost hit ejection mode as they shifted their weight and dug their baby barbs into his shoulders while his arms slowly drove the paddle heads through the water. He half expected to see a furry body go flying into the ocean with every stroke that cut under the dark surface.

People on the narrow beach couldn't help grabbing their cameras to take pictures of the blond Sundance Kid approaching with his juvenile cargo. Everyone was laughing or exclaiming or cheering as Israel neared the shore. The girls ran into the water towards him with the towels and basket as he tried to balance himself and his midget passengers when hoisting his body out of the kayak. Two of the girls pried the kittens off of Israel and put them into the towels, and then placed the little bundles in the basket Monica was holding.

Israel looked at the girls with great seriousness and told them to bring the kittens into the Penobscot Inn and keep them there inside until he got back to them within the hour. "Don't take no from anyone. Tell them that's an order from the Public Safety Office. Got that?" Their heads bobbed up and down.

Israel smiled at everyone and couldn't help laughing out loud. Another day, another good deed.

....

"Israel," Helen said, once he was back in the office. "You are the absolute talk of the town. The phone's been ringing for the past twenty minutes. You're everyone's hero!"

"That's exactly why I love this place, Helen. What a nutty day. And to think Jane missed it all. But I have three questions. Do you know why those girls had on name tags? And do you know who those girls are?"

"Haven't the faintest, Israel. As for who they are...I think Monica is one of the Tunny kids. Maybe Faith and Delphi are relatives or summer pals of Monica? I don't really know. And your third question?"

"Did you take any messages for me?"

"Nothing while you were out."

"OK, thanks. And Helen, when you say Monica is one of the Tunny kids, you mean that family down on Orion's Spit? The guys are kind of a wild bunch?"

"Exactly. Those Tunnys," said Helen. "You must have heard about them."

"Yes, I have. Too bad for Monica...she seems like a good kid. Anyway, I've got some calls to make and then I'm heading back to the Penobscot Inn to try and find homes for our tired little survivors."

"Tired? Oh, please...spare me," said Helen, volleying it right back at him with a crooked smile.

One Year Earlier

3

APRIL 2021
New Abutter

I am a frozen cave woman, a troglodyte in worn out flannels poring over the New York Times *bestseller list and knowing I'll never, ever get near that god damn list. And I am sick and tired of silk liners and thermal layers and Polartec and Gore-Tex and whatever else the NASA space program has bequeathed to us ordinary mortals who do not live in Florida.*

Author Oxford Monteith jammed a corn chip into her tomato salsa and took a crunchy bite before chomping on another mouthful of roast beef sandwich. She was more than ready to uncurl and soar from the clenched holding pattern of Winter in Maine. Anything to loosen its grip. Correction. She was ready to jump out of her skin.

Maine didn't really have spring...more like a raw, overcast Pleistocene epoch with three or four squirts of sun and warmth thrown in as torture. And storms of heavy, wet snow bordering on slush that smothered everyone's daffodils and any wilted foxglove leaves daring to push through their icy sweaters.

And then, boom! Suddenly it was 70 degrees out...until it plunged back to 40.

But at last...finally...springtime was poking its nose into the calendar and sniffing around the edges of unmeltable snowbanks lying around like gritty beached whales. It was about time. Oxford was done with the Arctic quartet of Darkness, Cold, Ice, and Snow.

And yet, despite her loathing the survival mode in this moment, Oxford did celebrate the wintry closed-in, tucked-in warmth of her Lincolnville home in JanFebMar when the wood stove pulsed with orange heat. She loved stepping outside to find herself in the magical, irrational whiteness of snow; loved walking on white and being belted by whipping, snow-spattering winds that blurred her sense of control and reminded her of forces beyond anyone's control.

During the recent dark months, in her flannels and her thermals, she had cried, too, at odd moments when thinking about her late husband's profound loss. Never mind her loss. He had lost more than everything...there would be no more tomorrows, no more future.

Oxford was now letting go of the exhausting memories...the months she had struggled to help her spouse hold on to his dignity and stay upright, while his final illness tore him down. How painful it had been to witness the crumbling of this enigmatic human being who asked her every morning if she thought he would get better, until the day he looked at her with empty eyes and said "I *will die.*"

She understood the well-meaning, heartfelt comments from friends. She wanted to appreciate those comments. The truth was, and she tried to assure people, she sensed very little grief or loneliness now.

What she felt was a showering down of relief and freedom...thankfulness that it was over. "It"—only two letters from the alphabet—all that was needed to encompass a lifetime...to set it free...into nothingness.

Nothingness. Relief and freedom? How could she be feeling these things? Was it too soon? Was it wrong of her? Was she heartless? She hoped not.

Oxford rose from the kitchen table and stuck her head outdoors to breathe the cold, cutting air. She noticed a message on her phone. Click. She carried the phone to the deck outside to listen to the recording while she took deep breaths.

"Hi. This is Random Thayer. I bought the house on Ferguson Mountain that's next to you. I need to buy some land from you. So please call me. We should talk."

Well, there you go. Son of a gun. Oxford shook her head. She knew exactly why this new abutter was calling. His well waterlines were located in part on her property.

Oxford owned a large piece of vacant land on Ferguson Mountain in Plimpton, a tiny town several miles north of Lincolnville, Maine. And with the change of ownership, this new owner, Random Thayer, no longer had the legal right to have his waterlines on her property.

Last summer, Sugar Betts surprised her old friend Oxford with the hot real estate news. Sugar owned a camp on Ferguson Mountain near Oxford, and she had seen the for-sale sign going up. Oxford's longtime abutter on the mountain was finally selling his house!

After peeking through windows and studying the real estate listing online, Sugar declared the house needed a total gutting—due to a sinking foundation, an interior left a shambles by frozen pipes that burst one winter, no working utilities, and scarcely more than a quarter acre. A nightmare waiting for love and salvation, and priced at over $300,000.

Oxford had often wondered how all this would unfold. Especially because of those encroaching waterlines. And now she had a new neighbor. OK!

....

Oxford spent the afternoon on Ferguson Mountain with Random Thayer, a lanky, young man, whose hair was a mess of dark roots interrupted by blond half way up. In his late 20s? Maybe early 30s?

And he had a brother, Jamie—his so-called human Swiss Army knife. Because he could do anything! Jamie with the silvery brown hair and an engaging smile of strong white teeth, and eyeglasses he removed when he shook hands with Oxford.

Oxford could feel a haze coming over her. Being around two men she had never met before and talking tons of details overloaded her senses. She tried to stay alert to what they were saying, but her brain felt like when she had stared at the sun too long.

Lots of comments about the failed well and the need to fix it before winter. And look how the road leading to the house was gutted by such deep gullies. Random would bring in a bunch of gravel fill to build the road bed back up. But what was it with all the surveillance cameras on every other tree? Random was going to talk to the other camp owners. Why would Random and his three brothers want to be all over the internet on those cameras?

They tramped over to the old well and got a rough idea of the strip of land Random and his family would need from Oxford. Maybe she could throw in a few more feet so they could add a small porch off to the side?

When their site walk was done, Random insisted on driving Oxford back to her car, which she had parked a little ways from the house. As they trundled along the camp road in his utility terrain vehicle, she asked him, "So, what's your line of work?"

"I'm in sales and now also real estate," Random said. "I like to find just the right luxury items for my clients. In some cases, that can take a long time. In fact, I finally sold a specialty piece three years after I first found it, and that's the day I decided to call you—because I sold that piece." He was grinning.

Oxford found that endearing. "So, Random, you'll hire a surveyor to pull it all together for us...a picture and a description. And then we'll wrap it up. I guess that's everything for the moment. So nice to meet you!"

4

APRIL 2021
"iAbutter"

Back at home, Oxford could feel how energizing her day on the mountain with those two new male abutters had been...ripples were starting to curve their way through her.

Three hours she spent with these total strangers who had stepped into her world, talking, laughing, analyzing details together. She had looked at them close up...their eyes, their skin, their arms; she had listened to their intensity. It had all drawn her out more than she would have imagined.

She had not had the distance to see how far she had sunk into her sense of loss these past few months, burrowed into her own emotional winter. But that was about to change. It was changing.

Oxford sat down and typed in her Google search words, "Random Thayer, Graniteville, Maine." Random had said he and his brothers were living in Graniteville until they tackled the Ferguson Mountain house enough to move in and continue with their renovations.

Who didn't search people these days? Just a look-see. You never knew what you'd find. Oxford felt the surge of the hunt for information revving up inside her. The chase was on...the rush of curiosity bubbling over.

But Oxford found nothing of substance. It was a slight disappointment...it was a relief!

Later that evening, she was standing somewhere between the oven and the refrigerator when an imaginary caboose of sensuality slammed into her. So ultra-unexpectedly. What was this?

It was a notion of Jamie. And this notion told her she would love to sleep with Jamie. Jamie! For God's sake?! That's blunt! Where did this surge come from?

She got back on the computer. Nothing that made any sense came up under "Jamie Thayer." How could that be in this day and age? As a means to learn more about Jamie, her only avenue was to dig deeper about Random. She wanted more, felt as ravenous as a she-bear exiting hibernation in spring, on the lookout for a whole cow to eat, at least.

Random had mentioned he had a duplex in Graniteville? She brought up the Abenaki County Registry of Deeds website and searched his name and found one residential property. When he bought this property, the deed into Random stated he was from Fall River, Massachusetts. OK. Let's google that.

She input "Random Thayer, Fall River, Mass." Amidst the duds and blind alleys her search kicked out, one startling article froze her in front of her computer screen. Oh *no*. Whoever said "There's no going back" had clinched it. She had crossed the Rubicon and landed on a rap sheet.

Oxford's eyeballs started to roll. This was insane! Please God, let this all be a coincidence. That's what it was…it had to be two people with the same name, same age range, both living in Fall River, Massachusetts. And the innocent Random Thayer had moved next door to her land. That wasn't asking too much, was it, God?

....

"Sam! We have to talk. You won't believe what's happened. Or what could be happening? I just can't believe it."

"Oxford, slow down. What are you babbling about?" Samantha Lloyd was on the phone with her sister. And Samantha was surrounded by 300 fried shrimp toasts looking back at her and waiting to be frozen in advance of an upcoming golf club event.

Samantha was the tough, impeccably organized, well-oiled catering diva, who was capable of feeding however many whomevers partied at the grand estates each summer on St. Frewin's Island. And she kept stomachs happy at the island's yacht and golf clubs.

Oxford barreled on. "The Ferguson Mountain property. That's what I'm calling about. Remember how the abutter's well waterlines encroached onto my property forever? Well, the abutter finally sold the place, after all these years. And the new buyer's been in touch with me to buy a strip of land from me to correct the problem. But get a load of this. The new guy may have a history of trouble with the law!"

"Look, I'm not going to stay on the phone if you don't calm down and slow down. I'm busy wrapping up a bunch of food. I'll put you on speaker phone. Try to be clear and succinct. Try to make sense!" Samantha snapped.

"OK, OK. So I started googling my new abutter. Oh boy. Never google your abutter, Sam. Although of course everyone googles everyone these days."

"That's not necessarily true, Oxford. I don't google everyone who crosses my path," Sam said.

"Anyway, his name is Random Thayer and he lives in Graniteville but used to be from Fall River, Mass. And what crops up under his name on the web, but a 2010 news item about an arrest in Fall River involving burglary, possession of stolen goods, and possession and manufacturing of controlled substances. Hah! Controlled substances...why don't they just say drugs?!"

"Oh, Oxford. You're not kidding, are you?"

"What do you think, Sam? Is this all a coincidence? Or is there going to be an article in *The Plimpton Times* when Random Thayer gets caught some day making meth on Ferguson Mountain? I can see it now. 'Thanks to the sale of land from abutter Oxford Monteith, the criminals were able to create a meth lab on the property and commence the illegal manufacturing of controlled substances, blah, blah, blah.' Tell me what you honestly, seriously think, Sam."

"Oxford, listen. If I understand the crap you just blurted into the phone, chances are there is no coincidence. How many Random Thayers could there be in one town?"

"Fall River is a city, Sam. Not a town."

"Oxford...cut it out. Try thinking straight."

"That's the problem. You think too straight, Sam. You're hung up on convergent thinking. I, however, know how pleasant these guys are. I have a good rapport with them."

"These guys? There's more than one?" Sam said.

"Random has one of his brothers helping him. Jamie's his name. Random said to me, 'Jamie's my human Swiss army knife. He can do anything.' Is that a loaded description or what? Jamie also has this very sexy, wavy tattoo on his arm," Oxford said. "And, umm...."

Sam heard Oxford's long, pregnant pause, about as pregnant as an elephant expecting quadruplets...in the Serengeti...7000 miles away from Sam's 300 fried shrimp toasts waiting impatiently.

"I think I'm nuts about Jamie," Oxford added.

"Oh, my God, this is going from bad to worse! You just met these people. Are you out of your mind? Why do you want to go near these guys? Why are you selling even one inch of your land to take care of their waterline encroachment problem? Don't get involved. Let them come up with their own solution."

"Neighbors, whether or not they're gangsters, need water to drink, wash, and flush, Sam."

"But have you stopped to ask yourself why you're drawn to such a potentially messy, if not risky, situation?"

"Hey! They're nice people. They're appealing. And Sam, maybe Random's on the mend, criminally speaking, IF he's a criminal. Maybe he's trying to pull together a new life in Maine. Besides, he's so gentle. It can't be him! I can't imagine he has a violent side to his personality."

"Sunny-Side-Up strikes again," Sam said in exasperation. She let out a hot sigh from Maine to South America.

"Listen, Oxford, contrary to what you think, someone in the criminal drug world could definitely have a very dark streak that wouldn't hesitate to push meth on current and future addicts. And turn their skin to sallow rags. And leave their teeth looking like stubbed out cigarettes. All for profit. These pushers and traffickers are capable of real damage—evil. You've seen enough movies and read enough in your lifetime to have an idea about these characters. They can be really appealing, and they can be monsters. All in the same package."

"You're so negative, Sam. That's unhealthy," Oxford cautioned. "It's going to cramp your world outlook. You know, just the other night, when *Public News Hour* played a newscaster's speech to some college graduates, she encouraged the students to get to know people who are not like the students, people who are different."

"Well, sure, Oxford," Sam said, "these guys sound like a bunch of felons. And you're not. So that would work perfectly, and Walter Cronkite would be proud of you. But seriously, I've got to go. These shrimp toasts cannot just sit here acting as though they're vacuum-packed and germ free. I have got to hang up. Let me call you back in an hour."

....

"Hello?"

"Oxford, it's me. We can pick up where we left off if you promise to speak only in sane sentences, OK?" Samantha said.

"Listen, Sam. Random is just the half of it. His brother, Jamie—he's the real gem in all this rough stuff I'm digging up. And you know what? When I first met him, he took off his eyeglasses while walking towards me and Random. How about that? I think he did that for me. He wanted to look good for me. Oh! I'm in love!"

"Oh, no you don't. Don't punish me with one of your over the top, over-the-phone routines, Oxford. I do not want to hear it. And don't forget—you're a relatively new widow. So shouldn't you act like one?"

"Look, believe me, Sam. I don't know why or how Cupid's arrow skewered me, and I'll be the first to admit it's absolutely irrational. But my heart is in my nostrils!

"Only my sister..." Sam said.

"It's amazing to feel passion again. I had forgotten all about it. Two days ago I was a widow, totally unaware of what a bone-dry life I've been leading all winter. Flat...White...Neutral. And now? Real blood is rushing through my veins instead of that watered-down slurry of widowhood. And I don't even know Jamie!"

"Just out of curiosity, what does this Adonis look like?"

"I wouldn't go that far, Sam. He's, well, not a face that would sear itself into your memory. He has bangs, doesn't have any fat on him, looks on the young side of forty, definitely has some intriguing tattoos on his arms. He wears glasses like I said, and I'm guessing he could have Irish in him?"

"You know what I think? I think you're kind of crazy right now, Oxford. And I don't think we should talk any more about this Jamie until you've had forty-eight hours to cool your spigots."

"That's ridiculous, Sam. Even if it amounts to nothing, I've actually met someone who has set me on fire. That's a good thing, right? And I never saw it coming. I want to make this man happy...in every way a woman can make a man happy. You know what I'm saying. I'm not going to stoop to verbs!"

"Oh, please don't." Sam weighed her next words and decided to let loose. "You know, Oxford, the way you act when you're high on love...it drives me insane! You're bombarding me at eighty miles an hour with your hormones flaming, and I'm supposed to stand here and *not* get scorched by your explosions of dopamine and oxytocin? You would drive Esther Perel and Dear Abby to drink," Sam said.

"Come on, Sam. Don't you like to feel on fire? Why don't you ever come out with foaming hormones? I know what's fueling your lackluster attitude. And I've suspected this for some time now. I bet you don't get ten percent of what you really desire out of your—tut, tut, Son of the American Revolution, Nathan Herinton. I bet he needs to crank up his GPS to find his way around when you two are in bed."

There was a moment of silence.

"Oxford, I'm hanging up. Talk to you later."

5

MAY 2021
Flying Dutchman

Jane Roberts was on the PSO phone, but she quickly scribbled a note to Helen Orbeton on her scratch pad..."Please listen in on this call. I can hardly understand the man!"

Helen picked up her phone and gently punched into Jane's line to join the call. Jane walked back to her desk with the phone clamped to her ear.

"Like I was sayin', Officer Rawbitts, ain't no way I'm gettin' any closah to that stinkin', bobbin' mess out theyah. Prubbly need ta cuss god."

"I understand, Mr. Carleton. I do understand. But I don't understand why you need to curse God. Let's not worry about Him right now. Can you tell me one more time when and how you happened to find the boat in your cove?"

"OK...fuhget ta cuss god. Listen up. This mornin' at 4 a.m., I sees somethin' big hangin' out in ta wattah. And I'm thinkin', what's that elphant doin' floatin' in Walker Cove?"

"4 a.m.,...good...I'm listening," Jane said.

"So's I pull on my rubbah boots and head down ta my dinghy on the dock. An' I puttered out ta see what's what. And do you know, that there fancy boat smelled so much ta high heaven, I couldn't get no nearah than ten feet."

"I hear you. Tell me more."

"Smelled damn near like a war trench graveyahd. I know somethin' about a war trench 'cause I was in Viet Nam, right? And I says ta myself, no way Honor Carleton's steppin' foot on a runaway boat that's smellin' like ta My Lai Massacre. No way."

"Excuse me, Mr. Carleton. Did I hear you correctly? Your first name is Honor?" Jane asked.

"That'd be me," Mr. Carleton said.

"What an elegant, classy name. Your mother and father must have been quite something."

"That they were, Ma'am."

"OK...one last question and then I'll meet you at your place in about twenty minutes. I'm bringing my assistant, Israel Tenner. Do you have any idea where this boat came from?"

"Well, like I says, I didn't board ta tub, but most our currents around heyah in Penobscot Bay run southwest, you got that? So maybe this death boat, she's comin' from somewheres notheast. How's that for shahp thinkin'?"

Jane hung up with Mr. Carleton and called out to Helen, "Thanks, Helen. I think I got most of what he said finally. But what was all that about cursing God?"

"Jane, Mr. Carleton was talking about getting the Coast Guard. And he has a point. We should call the Maine Marine Patrol or the Coast Guard to check on that boat. That's the correct procedure."

"Oh come on, Helen. It's just one boat in a dinky harbor. It's not like it's a yacht or a cruise ship on the high seas. And we're not busy at the moment. Israel and I can go check...save the taxpayers some money. Easy."

Helen shook her head. "You're in charge. You can make the mistakes."

"Look, the boat is floating around. That sounds like it's either been abandoned or anyone on board is not doing too well. Doesn't sound like we're going to have to tackle people or arrest them immediately, right?"

"Like I said, Jane, it's your call," Helen shrugged.

Next Jane rang up Bernie Pushaw. Then she and Israel got in her truck and headed first to the office at the Environmental Fields septage recycling site.

"Bernie has some hazmat suits in his office. Since this is an emergency, we'll use his gear so we can get on some stinking stray boat over in Walker Cove."

Israel looked askance at Jane. "Why is it stinking?"

"We're going to board and find out."

....

"That's some kind of a catamaran, isn't it?" Jane said to Israel as they neared the mystery boat that had floated into Honor Carleton's view at dawn. They had borrowed Mr. Carleton's dinghy to motor over and board the intruding hulk.

The craft was floating aimlessly within the confines of black-blue water in the granite-collared cove. Stiff clusters of spruce stood guard atop the shore of chunky slabs and mounds, angular blocks, sprawling futons and loaves and pillows of granite piled upon granite.

Bright white paint on the vessel's double hulls and the immaculate fabric of its sails said very clean and very expensive. The accompanying dinghy was suspended at the stern and shaded by a horizontal solar panel rigged above.

Israel scanned the boat with his binoculars. "No sign of anyone on board. No movement. Very strange. But

I'm having second thoughts, Jane. Shouldn't we get the Marine Patrol out here?"

"Come on, Israel. You're as bad as Helen. Not everything has to be done by the books. Why drag the Marine Patrol way out to St. Frewin's Island. This is just one boat. We don't need the Ghostbusters."

Jane trimmed the motor as they neared the craft.

"Can you smell rotting flesh?" Jane asked.

"Jeez, Jane. Why so blunt?" Israel frowned at her.

"Well, Mr. Carleton said he didn't board the boat because it smelled like the My Lai Massacre. That kind of sums it up. But I don't notice anything right now. Do you?"

"No, but I'm not sure if I would know what rotting flesh smells like," said Israel. "Maybe the gusty wind is moving things along.

"Oh, you'd know what it smells like. Better keep your mask handy. We'll board and see what's going on. Can you get the fenders? I'll pull us in closer here." Jane put the dinghy engine in neutral, and they glided towards the stairway built into the back tail of one of the hulls.

As they stepped carefully up the narrow access stairs to the cockpit, Jane braced herself. Chances were, one or more people were on board somewhere on this cat, and probably not in good shape at this point. What would that mean? Jane almost didn't want to know.

She feared the worst, and she hated that feeling. Death and its handiwork perhaps waiting, poised, right around the corner, and Jane knowing she would have to walk straight in and embrace Death professionally...and ultimately personally. Personally, because she didn't yet have the psychological brakes to keep her emotions at bay.

God knows what was happening to her usual snappy curiosity...that open eagerness to plunge into trouble. Maybe it was wearing off. Maybe she wasn't cut out for dealing with Death after all. But Jane was a PSO now. And in that world, Death was a working partner.

She looked around. "OK...nothing up here on the deck. Let's go through this door."

Jane and Israel entered a glossy teak interior, where the navigational station was centered between the galley and the salon. Some opened packages of crackers and cheese, several plates and silverware, and half-finished bunches of grapes and a few apples must have slithered off and come to rest on the seats of the banquette that ringed the salon table. Two empty bottles of champagne were slowly rolling around on the floor in tune with the shifting of the boat.

"Looks like the party snacks slipped off the table, after a small celebration maybe?" Jane wondered aloud.

She slowly descended the interior stairs to the cabin in the starboard hull, while Israel stayed above and opened galley cupboards and looked around the navigational center cubbyholes.

"It's a bit narrow down here, Israel," Jane called up from below. "In fact, pardon my palaver, but I just don't get it. Why do people spend time and money on these floating camper trailers? I feel so cramped, like I've stepped into what would happen if you crossed a Hobbit house with a rubber ducky."

Jane began opening the door to the cabin...but before she saw and smelled what was left of a man and woman who had likely been dead for more than twenty-four hours, Israel rushed down the steep stairway.

"We've got to get out of here right now, Jane," he insisted. "I found something that looks like drugs in the galley. And this boat has probably been drifting because no one is alive any longer to steer it. I think everyone on board may have overdosed on something out of their control."

"But that's why we have these hazmat suits, Israel. Let me just check this cabin...oh, no, you're right about people being dead. I just found two. Oh, God...."

Jane snapped her head away from the forms on the bed. It was nearly unbearable. The human shapes were slightly inflated, and their skin color had turned to grayish green. Every nauseous gas in the cabin poured through her flimsy mask.

"Jane, listen, we need better gear if we're going to keep looking. We need respirators and taped gloves. Better yet, we should leave now and call this in to the DEA squad. They'll have the proper equipment and expertise."

"But Israel, how do you know everyone on this boat has OD'd on something? Let me just take a quick peek in the other hull. I've got my face mask on securely, and I'm going to hold my breath when I can. Just give me five minutes."

"Why aren't you listening to me, Jane? If there's fentanyl on this boat, all it takes is an amount on the tip of a pencil to kill us. But if you won't listen to me, then I'm coming with you. If we drop dead, we drop dead together," Israel said with annoyance. He stomped up the stairs towards the other set of stairs leading down to the other hull.

"That's the spirit!" Jane sassed back.

She went up the stairs to the galley and then down the port side stairs to join Israel. He said he would check the one cabin while Jane took care of the other.

Israel slowly opened the door. If there were poisonous residue within, he was trying not to disturb it. He looked inside. One man, still alive! Though hardly. The human wreck looked straight at Israel and began whimpering through jagged intakes of breath. "Is...Israel...." The man could not finish...his thought...his sentence.

Israel stood like stone, watching the dying man gasping, "Is...Is...." He was too far gone for Narcan, and Israel had none on him to administer.

"What is he saying?" Jane was suddenly at Israel's side and asking as the breathing dwindled to nothing in the near corpse of the man.

"Jesus, Jane! Don't creep up on me like that."

"He was trying to ask a question, Israel. Asking 'Is...something or other.' This is horrible. We'll never know what he wanted to say."

Israel looked away. He did not share with Jane anything the man had been trying to say.

"Jane, look, I am leaving right now. If you don't, believe me, you are a dead woman. So we're going....right now."

"Well, FYI, there are two more dead people in the other cabin," Jane said hurriedly.

"All the more reason we're leaving." Israel grabbed her arm and yanked her into the hallway and shoved her towards the stairs. She got the message, and they both ascended quickly back into the galley and salon area.

"Let's get off this boat entirely. I have a really bad feeling about everything. Let's go," Israel said angrily, in a mood Jane had never seen before. She listened this time, and they rushed across the cockpit area to exit by the stairs they had first ascended.

....

They jumped into the dinghy, untied the fenders, and Jane started the motor. They headed back to shore, towards Honor Carleton's dock.

After a few minutes, her shock purged by the sun and the fresh air, Jane spoke in a curt voice. "What the hell was that all about back there, Israel?"

"Jane, what are you? A control freak? I have a brain, too. And I could tell something was very wrong. Why doesn't my analysis make sense to you? Can't you see we were probably in real danger on that boat? Those people are dead...didn't you hear me say I found some kind of drug in the galley?"

"I heard you, but we have hazmat suits and face masks."

"Yah, but they're not good enough if some really bad shit is all over the place. Like on the counter tops, on the door knobs, on the floor. We're talking just a few lethal milligrams, Jane. In fact, we should wash our hands and hose down our shoes and this boat when we get to Mr. Carleton's place. And dispose these hazmat suits and masks as hazardous waste."

"OK, OK. Relax, Israel. I'm totally on your wave length. You're right. Best to be cautious. But you have to admit. It's just so freaky. I mean, we're out on the gorgeous ocean right now, returning to our home island in Maine. How could this be happening? I can't imagine dropping dead without warning!"

"Jane, sometimes you astonish me. And don't touch your face until we're all cleaned off."

6

JUNE 2021
Sublimate

"Sam, it's Oxford."

"Can I hang up and pretend I didn't pick up?" Sam put the phone on speaker and continued rolling out her pie crusts.

"Come on. We need to talk."

"You need to talk. I need to work. This new golf club account has me pulling fourteen-hour days on a quiet week!"

"Why so busy? What's giving those golfers such ravenous appetites?"

"Oh, the usual type-A retiree infighting that goes on in any social entity. The goal is fun and sporting games but tribes inevitably form and face off. And suddenly your social club is mired in very conservative Irish Catholic Republicans from the Midwest crossing swords tipped in gin with very conservative East Coast Republicans obsessed with lineage."

"That's all?"

"That's just the beginning. So what's up?" Sam was starting to relax.

"I know you don't want to hear about Ferguson Mountain...."

"That's right...no want to hear," Sam said.

"But I just have to share my thoughts with you. OK?"

"OK." Sam's experienced arms rolled her annoyance at her sister into the expanding circles of pie dough.

"All this swooning over Jamie has helped me understand that I was starved for love, Sam...starved for love in my marriage. And now that it's over, I realize everything in my brain convincing me I was content to be single again, to pursue my writing, to pursue my interests, whatever, whatever, was really masking all this white space in my brain lying fallow and empty—whereas I am really dying to fill that white space with 10,000 details about someone I could love, who would want to love me back."

"Uh huh," said Sam, who was busy patching broken areas of dough.

"Did you even get half of what I just said?" Oxford huffed. "Or is your head buried in the pie crust in the sand trap at the end of the fairway?"

"Go on. I heard you. Your brain faked you into assuming you were alone and well. But now you realize you're alone and hungry for a guy, especially since your marriage had a love deficit. Simple."

"God, you can be so cut and dry, Sam. But I'll forgive you if you'll just hear me out on my new neighbor and everything I'm trying to figure out about him."

Sam laughed. "Hit me. I'm your target."

"So, I'm starting to think maybe, just maybe you're not off the charts to suppose my new neighbor might be a felon...or maybe a former felon. Because when I met Random at his house, he worried repeatedly about the propane truck being able to get down into the property during winter. I'm thinking to myself, why so much talk about the god damn propane deliveries? Then I thought, google meth and propane. Logical next step, right? And do you know what I found?"

"They go hand in hand."

"Right! Emptied propane tanks are handy for storing ingredients when making meth."

"OK. Wait. Instead of giving me your blow-by-blow criminal forensics, why don't you simply ask your new neighbors if they're criminals?"

"Oh, sure, Sam. I can't do that. That's like asking someone, are you gay? Or, are you still beating your wife?"

"Yah, yah."

"So, item number two: Random says his business is luxury sales. He holds on to choice pieces for quite a while until he finds just the right buyer...something like that. Well, sure he holds on to them for a long time! Because he needs the trail to go cold after the Cartier diamond-paved bracelets have been stolen, right? And then he dishes them out and makes a killing."

"Oh, Oxford."

"Item number three: Random said he's thinking of adding a porch on the shady side of the property that has no great view of the valley. So I ask myself, why build a porch on the boring side of the house? And you know why? To have discreet, out-of-sight windows for tubing to vent his meth fumes. But of course!"

"Whoa, you've really been burning the midnight oil."

"It doesn't take much. And all this talk about renovating the house before winter for him and his brothers? Maybe that's a front. Just an excuse he's parlaying to make me hurry up and sell him the strip of land so the meth kitchen can get cooking."

"I can see the possibilities of a parallel universe here. But maybe you're obsessing too much about all of this?" Sam said.

"Obsessing? You're the one who said to back off from the fire. Now you're questioning my closer scrutiny? Might I add that there's also the issue of all those security cameras. Random counted like fourteen of them, and they're getting on his nerves. Why? Because he doesn't want his little meth pavilion on YouTube, that's why!"

"Well, good job, Oxford. But I suggest you go easy. Slow down. Relax. In fact, after my summer catering rush is over, why don't we tootle on out to Ferguson Mountain and bring your new neighbors a welcome basket? Some cheese, fruit, cookies. That'll give us an excuse to look around, look more closely at what's going on. Then maybe we'll have some real clues, instead of me listening to you distorting facts through your amorous, thrill-seeking kaleidoscope. You might even get a look at your sweetie, Jamie. How's that sound?"

"I knew I had a real sister buried in all that pie crust, Sam. Welcome aboard! Love your idea. Let's go for it!"

"And meanwhile, Oxford, it's so obvious what you should be doing. Start putting this all down on paper for your next mystery. It's staring you in the face, isn't it? Juicy ingredients that have fallen into your lap because of a waterline encroachment. What luck! Start spinning your tale of illicit shake and bake and see where it takes you."

7

METHAMATICS
by Oxford Monteith

The small lightbulb is shaped like a flame, casting a faint glow over the deep blue black of his tattoo. Inky waves and chains drape and ripple over the muscle rising along his left forearm—primitive, tribal, the might of oceans etched onto a single human drumstick. He could be a warrior descended from the Maori.

She leans down to kiss the smokey coils...touches the waves and links with her tongue...salt. She licks along the arc of his muscle while his eyes hold her in place, her tongue feeling the resistance of the arm hairs as she forces them against their grain.

He draws her face closer to his eyes. His voice tumbles out like the first time she heard it...that gravelly "Come hither"...a low warble wandering in the back in his throat. "Come hither."

"Don't think I didn't read everything you wrote about me in your book...how you couldn't even toss parmesan into linguini without me looking up at you from inside the pasta bowl. Come on!"

She kisses him on his forehead, in the middle, where his silvery brown bangs part on their own. She's been wanting to do that for a very long time. She mustn't spill her emotional beans. She can't let on that she's wild for this guy—madly...one bite short of rabies.

"It's pure fiction, Jamie. Didn't you read the disclaimer?"

"Disclaimer? Hah. How's this for a disclaimer?" He pulls her towards him, her choppy, coppery brown hair sliding over his face and into the tiny spaces between their shoulders.

They are so close now, he is whispering. "And when you felt like your heart was in your nostrils and you were snorting buckets of carbonated champagne hormones, that was never true?"

She's delighted. "No comment."

"Well, maybe you can fool your readers, but not me. And in case you're still wondering, Oxy, *I want you.* Every part of you. But I also want to know...after all your pounding on the keyboard about us, did my feelings ever occur to you?"

"Occur to me? Your feelings? I don't know...." She's hesitating. "Your buddies told me you were Jamie, The Loner...maybe your heart buried up in the tundra? Chewing on permafrost?"

"Don't. Just be quiet, OK? Be nice. It's time for our denouement."

"*Denouement?*" Her head pops up from the pillow. "You know that word? How do you know that word?"

....

Outside, an old stand of lilac bushes in full, pendulous bloom shields the intruders from anyone's sight inside the house. A steady munching sound infiltrates the quiet night air. Turk, the head honcho, jabs Random in the arm. A handful of peanuts in and out of shells flies out of Random's hand.

"Cut the friggin' cacahuates," Turk whispers low. "You're gonna alert our author bitch and her whole neighborhood with your crackin' and chompin'!"

"The dame's got it coming to her either way, Turk. Who cares if she hears us?" Random says as he bends to feel for his nuts in the grass.

"Since when did the element of surprise go out the window?" Turk hisses. "Besides, Jamie's in there with her, the fuckin' traitor. I don't want him to catch wind of us. I wanna see his eyeballs bust straight out the back end of his skull."

....

His big white smile is making her crumble. He challenges her, his arm slung round her neck possessively. "Denouement? Now you're questioning my vocabulary? God, you've got some nerve. You said it yourself in your novel. I could be the 'Christopher Hitchens of hoodlums.' Word power is a classy part of my charm."

"What are the other parts?"

"You're about to find out."

"And then?" she asks, her question turning into a deep kiss along his throat.

"You're going to get edited."

8

JUNE 2021
Requiem

"Jane, why don't I make two copies of this DEA report about the stray catamaran you searched. That way you and Israel can go over the details more easily," Helen Orbeton said as she walked towards the copy machine.

"Thanks, Helen. From the little I heard, it sounds like Israel's instincts were right on," Jane admitted, without adding that she sort of had Israel to thank for saving their lives. No need to get melodramatic.

....

Jane and Israel sat at the PSO long-plank table and read through the DEA facts and conclusions on the Lagoon 470 cruising catamaran and its five occupants, all of which had floated into Honor Carleton's realm the month before.

"This report would be shocking enough about the excess fentanyl adulterant in cocaine pills that killed all five people on board..." Jane was saying, when Israel interrupted her.

"...But then we have the bombshell about the dying man you and I found alone in his bed," he said.

Jane shook her head in disbelief. "Exactly. He was one of our own...Dave Tower...Head of the Maine Drug Enforcement Agency Coastal Task Force. For the district that includes our own Abenaki County."

"Pretty depressing," said Israel.

"I just don't get it," Jane said, staring at Israel. "This guy was with the Maine DEA for years. He should have, and would have, known better than to lift some drugs from a recent bust...and invite his friends along for a joy ride...on his fancy catamaran. What a fool! And how could he afford that catamaran?"

"Maybe he had family money?" Israel guessed.

"No idea. Did you know him?" Jane asked.

"Not at all," said Israel.

"I wonder what the DEA has found out about Tower's finances. I'd love to know how he paid for that cat...even a used one."

"Maybe we should leave this incident to the DEA and not try to excavate to the very bottom ourselves. You don't want to get too distracted by all the minutiae when we have our own work to do, Jane."

"Hmm...I guess you have a point. But some things don't make sense. Tower snatching the drugs. Tower having so much dough. Don't you smell even a tiny rat?"

9

OCTOBER 2021
Love Thy Neighbor

"Oxford," Sam was giving her sister that "I know better because I'm the older sister" look. "I'm guessing you want to go racing and singing through the woods and jump into Jamie's unsuspecting, tattooed arms, but I really think we should approach this whole mission with polite restraint."

"Oh, Sam, there you go again. Miss Safety and Propriety. Caution at every corner. But, look, I've already met my abutters. They know me. And they're so happy that I didn't charge them an arm and a leg for that strip of land for the well and waterlines. We're good."

"All I'm saying is let's walk in a measured pace when we get near their property. We'll cut through your land down onto their road and saunter on over...just a neighborly pop-in." *Without warning, and heaven help us if we bump into something we're not supposed to see,* Sam thought with a shudder.

....

"Hellooooo," Oxford started crooning as they walked towards the house. Sam looked nervously around her, remembering all the tree cameras Oxford had mentioned. Could anyone see them? Would anyone recognize them? She was definitely having robust second thoughts.

No one came out of the house to greet them. It seemed empty, but Sam thought she heard something like a radio. She made the quiet sign to Oxford and motioned for her to follow Sam to a nearby window.

Sam tiptoed up to the window with her head below the sash. She stepped to the side and peered in slowly. A man inside the house had his back to Sam. He stood at the kitchen counter and went about making a sandwich.

Sam watched his short, thick fingers open a bag of bread and a jar of mayonnaise. He took a piece of bread, bent it slightly, shoved the whole piece into the mayo, and then swirled the slice around to coat the exposed side of bread with mayo. Sam's heart almost stopped.

He withdrew the slice, put it on a plate, and added a piece of what looked like liverwurst. Then he baptized a second slice of bread exactly the same way and patted it on top of the sandwich. Sam was transfixed and revolted. Food was her universe, and she had never seen such a spectacle. She stepped aside, her face contorted on purpose.

Oxford frowned at her, paused a moment, and then quickly walked up to the door and started knocking. Sam stepped away from the window.

"We've come all this way. We're not going to gain anything by not trying to visit," Oxford said out loud to Sam.

"Hey there, what's up?" A man behind the women was speaking. Oxford and Sam both jumped at the voice of the live male person who had crept up on them.

"Oh, my goodness, hi!" Oxford laughed. "We're here to see Random and Jamie. Are they around today? I'm the person who owns the land over there, and we just wanted to drop by with a welcome basket."

Sam stared at the man. He was a pot-bellied, older fellow in need of a shave on his lumpy face covered in

facial fuzz...like a stubbled, salt and peppered cauliflower.
He wore a stained sweat shirt with cut-off arms and
bow-legged jeans. Sam could feel her guard going up.
What had Oxford gotten them into?

Oxford put out her hand. "Hi, I'm Oxford and this is
my sister, Samantha."

"Well, we're mighty surprised to see anyone up here
this time of the year, generally speaking. I'm Chummy,
by the way," the pot belly said.

"Chummy, do you know," Oxford asked, giving it a
second shot, "if Random or Jamie are in? And would
they be your brothers?"

"Why don't we go in and you can ask them yourself?"
Chummy grinned. Sam frowned down at the ground so
he could not decipher the "Asshole!" bursting onto her
face.

Chummy took them inside the house. Both women
were shocked to see the sprawling mess before them. It
had been months since Random purchased the property,
but clearly the place was not yet a "Des Res." *House
Beautiful* was a long way off—even Fred Flintstone's
family cave was a long way off. Chummy didn't seem to
notice or care.

From the bare concrete floors up the un-sheet-rocked
walls to the bare ceiling, a scramble of rough framing
boards, electrical wiring, and plumbing pipes snaked
along the walls and ceiling overhead. Haphazardly
stapled plastic sheeting over unframed windows and
doorless doorways gave a ghostly curtained effect to the
entire first floor. The kitchen area Sam had viewed
through the window seemed slightly more finished,
though still disorderly.

"Random! Jamie!" Chummy called out. "Two kindly dames are here to give you some cookies."

Oxford and Sam heard footsteps coming from what appeared to be the area of the new side addition Random had mentioned as a goal...where Oxford fancifully worried the brothers would place their ventilation system for meth production fumes. She chided her inner self. Time to stop thinking like that.

"Whoa, Oxford. What a surprise! You should have called first. We would have dug out the vacuum cleaner and tidied up for you. And this would be?" Random asked, pointing to Sam.

"Oh, Random...and Jamie, this is my sister, Samantha Lloyd. She was the one who encouraged me to bring you a welcome basket. We filled it with cookies and some fruit and cheese. Part fun, part nutrition!"

"Damn, that's sweet of you," Random said as Oxford handed him the gift. Sam stood by smiling weakly, hoping her misgivings weren't jumping off her face and plowing into the three men who stood there staring at the women somewhat awkwardly.

"Hi there, Jamie," Oxford attempted a slight wave of the hand. He nodded, but didn't respond. She held back on the gigantic, leaping smile she had intended to plaster him with. He seemed distant today, not engaging as before.

"Well, Ladies," Chummy said. "This is very kind of you, but unfortunately, as you can see, we have a lot of work ahead of us, so we probably should get back to it, though no insult intended to your kindness."

....

"Well, that was as exciting as a flat tire! I can't believe they just took the basket and we left. What kind of Welcome Wagon was that?" Oxford was fuming as they settled into Sam's car and prepared to drive back towards the coast.

"Wheel-less Welcome Wagon, my dear," Sam said. "And I agree with you...something did seem fishy. That guy Chummy, while articulate, did not project the friendliness you claim to have found in those other guys."

"I know! It was like another planet, though Random seemed himself. But Jamie? Jamie? He was bland, almost faceless. No resemblance to the man I first met. I admit I am really disappointed. He took the intensely hot air out of my emotionally vulnerable balloon. In fact, I'm pissed," Oxford said.

"Besides the men's lack of interest, there was something else bizarre. Did you happen to notice that room full of electronic equipment way off to the left in the house? With all the plastic sheeting hanging in the way, it was hard to tell what was what. But I think I saw lots of machines and blinking lights and screens. That was very weird, Oxford. Way too high tech for a house in the woods maybe?"

"What am I? A detective? I just got the cold—well, make that neutral—shoulder from someone I thought I wanted to spend the rest of my life with. Of course I didn't notice any electronic contraptions in that house wreck."

....

Once the women were gone, Turk appeared from another room. Short and boxy all over, he was wound up tight like a fat wet rag rung dry. "What was that that just blew in and blew out?" His mouth was full of liverwurst sandwich with a flourish of mayo lip gloss.

"And did I hear something about some kind of fuckin' Welcome Wagon? If I recall correctly, Jamie, you were supposed to steer Random to buy in a secluded location. Now look at us—you two just had two goofy Girl Scouts cooing at you with chocolate thin mints in their sticky paws."

"Turk, easy. We'll take care of it. Don't worry. We've got this under control." Jamie said.

"Yeah, don't mind that Oxy woman, Turk," Random added. "We've got this."

"Oxy? You're calling Oxford 'Oxy'? That isn't funny, Random," Jamie shot back.

"Hey! Cool your jets, man. I'm just having fun. Shortening her name to Oxy, of all things. What a hoot," said Random.

"That's enough, both of you. Get back to work. And those goody-two-shoes better not show their faces here again. You make sure about that," Turk said as he walked away from them.

"You know, she's an author," Random said. "And she's absolutely bonkers over Jamie."

"Zip it, Random," Jamie said, pointing at him.

"You should have heard her go on and on about Lover Boy here. All this female loop de loop!" Random was cracking up.

"Shut it down," Jamie yelled as he waved a fist at Random.

"Christ! Could we have a worse combination on our hands?" Turk turned and strutted back towards Random and Jamie like a male dog intent on doing damage. "You mean to tell me this Oxford, Oxy, whoever, is some high-spirited dame who may just keep popping up here, drooling over Jamie?"

"Maybe you'll have to throw some serious cold water on her to dampen her enthusiasm," Random suggested.

"And you're sure she's an author? She told you so?" Turk asked.

Random nodded yes.

"Shit. You give that kind of woman any kind of slack and she's liable to start blubbering it all on paper for the whole world to see. And remember, my colleagues, none of this is going to help us in our real efforts."

Chummy added his two cents just then. "Colleagues, I like that. Those gals think we're brothers."

"Random, you've got that Oxford woman's number?" Turk said.

"Yah...we've spoken by phone."

"Then log it." Turk bit into his liverwurst sandwich and walked away.

Random called out after him, "I already did, the day Jamie and I first met her."

Back to the Present Year

10

APRIL 2022
Secret Agent

"Welcome, Everyone, to our OCDETF conference. In the war on drugs, New England is cleaning house starting today!" The Speaker opened his arms wide for emphasis. "And the real work will begin right here at home!" He brought his fist down to the podium in a show of force and confidence.

Applause. Applause.

Officer Jane Roberts felt a hot pulse fork through her. An acronym already? It was only 9:00 AM—Keynote Speaker, introductory remarks.

She thumbed through the "Key Terms" section of her conference handout and found the OCDETF entry: "Organized Crime Drug Enforcement Task Force." *Got it.*

The man at the microphone and his fellow presenters on the dais were some of the few stately adults in the room. Maxwell Dunham's expensive-looking suit encased his good posture, and his polka-dotted tie was the male adornment of the man at the helm of the New England Drug Enforcement Agency. The polka-dots reminded Jane of oxycodone pills. Didn't anyone take time to think through these fashion gaffs?

By and large, the attendees ringing the tables on the floor fell into two categories: Lots of jowly, uniformed bacon pulled out of the precincts, and lots of raggedy undercover types pulled off the streets and crowned with backwards baseball caps.

"We're going to touch on some SWGDRUG and SAMHSA first thing, but our main focus will be CPOT, meaning not only NHI and NMI, but also the massive, constant flood of fentanyl," Chief Dunham informed them.

All Jane could jot down quickly was CPOT. Her "Key Terms" told her that meant "Consolidated Priority Targets." Got it!

Jane ran her hand over her throat and looked at her companion next to her. "Sorry, but could you take notes while I run out to the hall for some air. I don't feel that great."

"Jane, it's just started. Can't you hold on another twenty minutes at least?"

"Not sure. I've got this laryngeal stenosis thing going on in my throat."

"What's that?"

"It's like, uh, an unnatural constricting of the throat due to ambient circumstances."

"Ambient circumstances? Bull shit. It's always something with you, Roberts. What is it now?"

Some attendees at their table started clearing their throats as a signal for Jane to quiet down.

"Look, it's all these acronyms they're lobbing at us. They're constricting my throat, OK? I'll be back in a minute." Jane pushed her chair delicately and took off.

....

"Sam, can you hear me? I'm down in Boston." Jane was whispering into her cell phone in a side hall of the Drug Enforcement Agency's conference room.

"Boston? What for?" Sam gazed down at the five wedding cake recipes fanned out before her.

"Can't go into details now, it's work related. More later. But I have to let off some steam. Guess who the bosses stuck me with down here?"

"Why do you say 'stuck' with whoever this is?"

"Why do you have to answer a question with a question?"

"OK. Just say what you want to say, Jane. But be quick. Remember, it's April, and I've got half the female population of the Eastern seaboard out in my front yard, down on their knees, begging me to help fix some kind of screw-up in their upcoming DIY wedding menus."

"Can you still hear me, Sam?" Jane asked.

"Sort of. But what's all that buzzing, Jane? Oh...let me guess. You're using your cell phone that came over on the Mayflower."

"Hardy har har. OK, so this is the problem. You know who's here with me? Finn Gallinen of all people! Why him? Why me?"

"What's so bad about Finn? I thought you guys kissed and made up," Sam said.

"But he's still such an automaton. So stiff. You can't get a laugh out of him, unless he's laughing AT you. And this conference? It's turning into fifty percent acronyms. They drive me crazy!"

"That's idiotic, Jane. Why do you let them get to you?"

"Sam...just think about it. Our parents spent hundreds of thousands of dollars to get us to articulate and write like intelligent human beings. And now people can only communicate in wordless capital letters? Pretty soon everyone's brain will be reduced to a byte. Is that progress? I don't think sooooo."

"Jane. Did you ever imagine it's you and not the world that's inside out and backwards? Sociologically speaking, you get sandpapered with heavy grit every time you step out the door. Why is that? I think you should give it some thought."

"And here I was hoping you would commiserate with me. Forget it, Professor. I'll hang up and go rub up next to some extra coarse true grit."

"You know, Jane, sometimes you remind me of my sister, Oxford. Like two manic-elative peas in a pod. Can't shut you up. Can't shut you down."

"Gee, thanks, Sam."

....

"Ms. Roberts? Mr. Gallinen? Could you come this way? Chief Dunham wants to speak with you privately."

Jane looked at Finn. Her twisted face was trying to telegraph, "Did we do something wrong?"

The suited messenger led them to an office down the hall from the conference room. Inside on one of two office couches sat Chief Maxwell Dunham. He immediately stood up when Jane and Finn entered the room and then looked towards his office companion.

"Come right in, Ms. Roberts and Mr. Gallinen. I don't think you need any introduction to...." The coiffed, liver-colored hairball slowly turned to face them. Jane's laryngeal stenosis took a giant leap for mankind. Before her stood a slimmed-down version of Harriet Buxton, smiling and looking far more stylish than Jane could have imagined was possible for the battle-axe head of Human Resources of the Maine State Police.

"Jane and Finn! So glad you could make it to Boston," Harriet Buxton grabbed their hands and greeted her two employees with atypical bonhomie.

Jane smiled back at Harriet. "Look at you, Mrs. Buxton! So swish and lovely!" Harriet laughed lightly and bent her head towards Jane's ear. "It's all about two words, Jane: Joseph Adderley." Lieutenant Adderley...of course...of course...Jane's superior officer and Harriet's new flame.

Everyone sat down and Dunham began.

"So, Jane Roberts and Finn Gallinen...we have a problem." Chief Dunham and his oxycodone-sprinkled tie sat very straight. "We've looked at the statistics, and they don't lie. Way too many undercover drug stings in Maine have failed these past few years. And they're still failing."

"I had no idea," Jane said. Finn nodded.

"We suspect Maine law enforcement personnel are getting their hands on highly confidential plans for drug raids. And feeding those plans to the very targets of those raids."

"And the targets are?" Finn asked.

"Maine drug dealers and manufacturers of illicit drugs...from home-cookers on up to the milling operations," said Dunham.

"In other words," Harriet leaned forward, "the criminals know precisely when the police are about to swoop in. So the producers and the pushers and all their paraphernalia slip away before we can pounce."

"Repeatedly," Dunham emphasized.

"Why are you telling us this, Chief Dunham? Do you want our help?" Jane began to feel a flush of trepidation because she had no idea what good she and Finn could do.

"Precisely, Jane. In two areas. First, you and Finn will be part of our anti-corruption team. Second, you will also be our eyes and ears on the ground at your posts."

"In what way?" Finn said.

"OK, concerning your posts, both of you work on remote, inhabited islands. We already know the tiny inlets and coves on your islands are parking lots for the 'shadow boats' and 'ghost boats' that transport drug cargos destined for the mainland. It's been a problem for years, but now it's accelerating. So as gorgeous as it is, the brave coast of St. Frewin's Island is a super magnet for these 'shadow boats' to unload their illegal cargo onto vehicles in the dark of night. Those vehicles then cross by ferry to the mainland where the drugs are distributed throughout the state...with no one the wiser. Same goes for Finn's island."

"This sounds like an episode from *Poldark*," Jane blurted out. "What are we supposed to do? Conduct midnight stakeouts along the shore?"

"No, no, nothing that fancy...yet," Chief Dunham said. "For now, we just want you to be aware of the potential situations and to pay attention to the possibilities. As for our anti-corruption team, you will both be officially privy to our top-secret, confidential investigative measures on that front."

"If we do discover some boat is up to no good, what do you want us to do?" Jane said.

"Call it in to the United States Coast Guard right away. And if you find any local people who are involved with the shadow boats, you should report it through the usual channels," Dunham said.

"And corrupt personnel...how do we handle that?" Finn said.

"Any suspicions, any questions, come directly to me or Harriet Buxton. If we're not available, you can contact Alex Champus at the FBI."

Alex Champus?! Jane stifled a desire to yell, "You have got to be kidding me!" Instead, she nodded agreeably.

At the end of Dunham's spiel, Jane walked out of the DEA office, feeling perplexed and lonelier than if she had woken up cold and starving on top of a barren mountain in the middle of an unknown, uninhabited continent. Either that or Pluto...didn't matter which one.

She looked at Finn with a sour face. "You know, that's the problem with Top Secret/Totally Confidential," Jane said. "Now that we're in on it, we're going to be isolated and alienated from the rest of the world while everyone else and their grandmothers are sprinkling cocaine on their morning oatmeal. What fun is that?"

"Stop grousing, Roberts. And quit joking. This is serious stuff. It's an honor we've been chosen to help. Keep your eye on the overdoses, not your peeves."

Jane was not entirely ignorant of the problem. She recalled what a taxi driver told her about losing family and friends to drugs and alcohol..."I've been to more funerals than the years I've lived, and I'm thirty-seven."

And she had been volunteering in a food pantry during her police academy training when she found a customer in the back of the storage area, in a puddle of urine, passed out against a shelf of canned vegetables, a needle in his neck.

After that episode, she learned how to administer a dose of naloxone when needed. But she knew she wasn't looking forward to the next opportunity. She wasn't comfortable, wasn't inspired to get so close to that sort of life and death drama.

....

Jane and Finn made their way to the Boston DEA cafeteria. Finally...lunch! Food! A blessed reprieve. She had visions of clam chowder and a lobster roll....and maybe, just maybe, a piece of Boston Cream pie for dessert....

They paused at the cafeteria entrance to read the menu. The offerings ranged from BLTs, BLATs, BECs, CBOs, PB&Js, and PCSs, to ICSs.

"Not that big a selection. Just sandwiches," Finn said.

"I don't get it!" Jane whispered to Flinn. "Can't the United States government afford the fucking ink to print out the fucking names of these sandwiches?"

Finn frowned at her. "Enough already. Just have a BLAT...before your windpipe shuts down."

....

"Excuse me a minute, Finn," Jane said as she put down her Bacon, Lettuce, Avocado, and Tomato sandwich. "I see someone I want to say hi to. I'll be right back."

She made her way to the beverage station and caught up with a slim, wiry man whose wiriness was sheathed in a buzz cut, white shirt, and black suit. She knew a G-man when she saw one.

"Champus! Alex Champus. Ha ha!! I knew I'd bump into you again somewhere, somehow, you conniving, scheming traitor. Remember me? Jane Roberts? St. Frewin's Island? New Year's Eve raid?"

"Is this a confrontation?" he said, looking Jane over from her billowy hair to her black, V-neck T-shirt, down past her khaki cargo pants to her Merrell sneakers.

"I hope you realize you owe me one, Champus. After leading me into the dark and leaving me in the dark at the Pratts' New Year's Eve party. You really did string me along with all your reconnaissance bullshit."

"As I recall, Roberts, you were disrespectful at first and soused in the end. Not a reliable combination."

"You only got what you deserved. Now, listen. I have a question for you, because I hear you've got lots of dope on this scene. Do you have any idea why Finn Gallinen and I are really here and getting groomed for this hard ass surveillance effort concerning corrupt Maine cops and drug lords?"

"Based on what I hear from the higher-ups, you are not supposed to breathe a word of what you just said to Anybody. Do you hear me? Nobody."

"Right, but isn't it obvious at this point in time that our government drug enforcement throughout the United States...no, make that the world, is one seriously leaking ship? And in my opinion, I bet you're one of the biggest drill bits in town. No offense."

"You know, you don't rise to the level of a hot mess...yet, Jane. But you're close. Why don't you just toddle on back to your lunch table and pretend you never saw me today?"

"Champy, as I said, you owe me one. And I have the evidence I need to stew your rutabaga for good if you don't give me some info."

"Where does that garbage come from?"

"Well, Mr. FBI. I know about you and Howdy Doody McGill and that illegal Chinese gold the Russians sent over to St. Frewin's Island for Senator McGill's Christmas stocking a few years ago."

Jane could see Alex Champus' shoulders twitch...just a whisker. Whether or not he would admit to the stocking stuffer, Jane knew she had him by the balls.

And to be sure, she added, "And I know you tipped off Senator McGill about the Feds coming to get him at the New Year's Eve party. That's how Senator McGill slipped away."

"OK. Fine. I love making women happy. So I'll make you happy, Jane. Just this once. Listen up, because I'm going to walk away when I'm done. And I never want to see you again."

Jane smiled at him. He was so pompous...so naïve.

Champus motioned Jane towards a nearby quiet corner of the cafeteria. He bent his head and began in a low voice. "So, Maine's particular problem with sting operations started around 2015. Then the problem seemed to die down around 2019, when you and Finn got hired. Lately however, Maine's drug raids are failing again. And why? The working hypothesis is focused on people with long careers inside the system who might have become disenchanted with their measly paychecks. Said dissatisfied individuals apparently began to sabotage Maine's official efforts against drugs, presumably in exchange for kickbacks from the drug networks."

Jane's eyes started to widen.

"You and Finn haven't been on board long enough to hold a grudge. Which is why you two are clean and innocent and perfect to play the internal stool pigeons, if you follow what I'm saying. And that's all I'm saying." Alex Champus started to turn away.

And then Jane's memory served her...it circled back to the summer before. What had Champus just said? "People with long careers...who might have become disenchanted with their measly paychecks...." Isn't that what Champus said? Could it be Dave Tower was a round peg who had fallen into that round hole? Had kickbacks from drug traffickers to Dave paid for Dave's fancy catamaran? Ultimately his floating coffin?

"Alex, wait! Just one more question. What's Harriet Buxton got to do with all this?" Jane asked.

"Use your brain, Jane. Harriet Buxton is the head of Human Resources. She is the keeper of all employee applications." Champus began ticking items off on his fingers, "and resumes, cumulative performance reviews, disciplinary records—in short, every individual's work persona. Dunham's had her going through all that paperwork with a fresh eye to flush out any suspicious characters. Harriet's the one who cleared you and Finn for your fancy, new roles. And now, I've paid for my sins, so it's Adios to you."

Jane let him go. She had enough to work with for the time being. And besides, Senator McGill's Chinese gold fiasco she had reminded Champus about could hang and quarter Champus professionally any old day. He would never be off her special hook. If he thought this was catch and release, he was gravely mistaken.

11

MAY 2022
Phantom on Ice

"So are the United Nations and the World Health Organization taking good care of my Mr. Balankoff?" Jane held the phone close to her ear. A heavy dose of static bombarded Konstantin Balankoff's voice, which was beaming in from the Pacific Ocean.

Jane was madly in love with this man, but he was gone from St. Frewin's Island more than he was there...with Jane. Gone more than she had ever anticipated. What kind of romance was absentee romance? Her heart was not growing fonder.

"Are they taking good care of me? Best not to ask, Jane," Konstantin said. "I'm not going to ruin your day with details about the rotten food and the slime and roaches on this carcass of a boat."

"Did you know about the condition of this ship before they sent you out to do the inspection?"

"Well, the higher calling and prestige of trying to bring justice to the ever-exploding world of fishing empires gone rogue in international waters is an honor I just can't pass up, Jane, no matter how wretched."

"You long-winded masochist!"

"Thank you, my dear. And from what I can see, just about everything out here is illegal...the type of fish caught, the enormous number of fish caught, the horrendous treatment of this crew, the decrepit condition of the boat, the record-keeping, the

67

compliance checks, where the boat fishes. If this is the norm, I wouldn't be surprised if the whole world runs out of wild seafood in another decade."

"Oh, great. More uplifting news. We're using up the planet, aren't we? Anyway, please promise me you'll take care of yourself out there, Konstantin."

"Of course. I'm not worried, and you shouldn't be," he assured her.

"At least I have the leisure of my own clean, dry bed (but empty, Jane thought) at night, even if there's hardly anyone around I can bounce things off of concerning this top-secret team I'm on."

"But didn't you say Finn was part of your team? Why not talk things over with him?"

"I guess. But it annoys me to have to coordinate with someone like Finn."

"You've got to relax around your colleagues, Jane. Try not to take offense just because someone has an entirely different world view."

"I know; I know. We're driving up together to one of our top-secret meetings in Augusta next week. I guess I'll try to bond with the guy. Bond. Such a loaded word...Jane Bond. No, Jane Bonds. But will she or won't she?"

....

Jane was seated next to Finn and supremely on edge at the Augusta conference. She could not wait to rant at him about everything they were hearing once the meeting was over.

Cyber spying! PEGASUS! PHANTOM! Thank God she and Finn would be together in his car on the drive back to the ferry terminal. As it was, she kept nudging his arm every time another shock wave hit her.

She was particularly bowled over by the so-called Unit 8200 in Israel. Unit 8200—so mysterious...evocative.

The speaker was explaining Unit 8200 was the heart and soul of the Israeli cyber-empire...the fertile hothouse for the creators of "Pegasus," Israel's unparalleled surveillance spyware.

Jane often had to watch herself when it came to high-powered afternoon meetings like this. Her brain could get a little sleepy and droopy right after lunch. But not today. No chance in hell. She kept squirting eye drops into her eyes to keep up with how much they were popping out of her head.

"What I'm about to tell you cannot leave this room, cannot be discussed with anyone but those of you present."

The speaker was from the FBI's top rung—a man by the name of Calvin Ritter, standing before them like an American flagpole, locked tight in his career-climbing, gun metal suit. He looked like the Federal big cheeses always tried to look...maybe like Ronald Reagan or Pierce Brosnan, bronzed gods fresh off the Caribbean beaches.

And Ritter, to Jane's astonishment—in that he had traveled to frumpy Augusta, Maine, to be with them— he, Calvin Ritter, commanded the FBI Science and Technology Branch.

"Pegasus and Phantom. Pegasus and Phantom. Why are these two names deemed so outrageous worldwide? Because these spywares enable the user to take over your cell phone. Knowledge of its location. Absolutely all of its content. And many of its capabilities. Like a monkey on the back of your cell phone itself—a *genius* of a monkey.

"Now, Pegasus works all over the world, except on US cell phone numbers. And Pegasus is illegal in the United States.

"The same goes for Phantom, the junior offspring of Pegasus. But Phantom is different. Phantom can hack into US cell phone numbers. Phantom is also outlawed in the United States.

"However," Calvin Ritter said...Jane sensed the American flagpole was about to toss a grenade into his audience. "The Federal government has decided to permit a very small, very contained trial run using Phantom spyware here in Maine...and only Maine."

Growly, throaty noises bounced around in the room in reaction to Ritter's announcement.

"Hold on. Hear me out," he said. "This is an isolated mission of limited duration that is currently on ice. But it will be deployed in the near future. We will track its effectiveness in pinning down corrupt members of your own force."

"Where in Maine?" a voice from the group called out.

"I can't give you those details," Ritter said.

"When will it start?" another person asked.

"Again, I'm not at liberty to say." Ritter said, looking slightly apologetic.

Jane grabbed her glass of water and quenched what was left of her tightening throat tissue. The grenade, or make that a bomb, had landed.

They've turned us into outlaws under the sanction of our own government. How much weirder can it get? How guilty are we simply for sitting here and listening to this crap?

Jane's head was spinning. The most powerful cyberweapon in the world was about to gobble up cell phones in little old Maine where most people routinely went undercover in highly covert search of fresh lobster rolls, deer to hunt in November, and winning lottery tickets. As Maine goes, so goes the nation. Would nation-wide Phantom surveillance be next?

....

On their way home, Jane took out her cell phone and looked at it in a new light as Finn drove them towards Route 17-East. She thought about all her personal comments and idiocies typed and talked into her phone and what it would be like to have unintended readers or listeners of the same. Would she feel foolish or furious? How much would it matter?

"Finn, I can't believe what we heard in there. They're going to unleash the Phantom spyware in Maine. Are we living in a sci-fi movie? What do you think?"

"I was surprised to hear the news, Jane. But how harmful could it be to the ordinary, law-abiding citizen? If you're not doing anything wrong or illegal, chances are the law is not even thinking of hacking into Jane Roberts' cell phone, right?"

"But the problem is Who decides Who is doing something wrong...and what is Wrong? That's already a problem in other countries using Pegasus. And we know the FBI has had its own share of flaws over the decades...going after gays, civil rights activists, and people deemed subversive at any given point in history."

"Well, there's always going to be a balancing act in law enforcement," Finn countered.

"Finn, that's a stock line and a lame line, and you know it. Just look at how cell phones have taken over our lives by our own choice. It's very easy to imagine something like Phantom spyware becoming routine. The slippery slope of the iceberg of the invasion of privacy could melt into a bottomless lake."

"Jane, you're an alarmist half the time. Can you think of an equally effective way to interface with the drug world? They're gaining all the time."

"But it's the overarching concept, Finn. Cell phones are our alter ego. Your cell phone is practically your adjunct brain. The only difference is that you don't need a password to access your own brain. And now users of Phantom won't need a password either, in effect. It's not just about fighting crime. It's about Americans' human expectations of human privacy. Can't you see that?"

"So don't use a cell phone. That's a solution. You're always trumpeting that philosophy on St. Frewin's Island where you have no cellular or internet connection. What's changed for you since I first met you?"

Jane thought back to the island's decision to ban wireless communication technology years ago because of a tragic car accident involving a cell phone, where an entire family was wiped off the face of the earth.

"You're right. But now I do use my cell phone off island on a regular basis. I'm not saying it's become essential for me...but the camera is really helpful. Fortunately, my camera can take pictures on the island, even though there's no connection."

"So, why do you need more out of your cell phone if your camera works?"

"Well, I take pictures and then I send them to people when I'm on the mainland...I need the cell phone for that. It's helpful for work, or when things break and need repair, for home maintenance, sending tick bite photos to my doctor, stuff like that."

"OK, but the Feds and Phantom could care less about your failed fridge or your Lyme disease scares," Finn said. "So I don't think of it as a personal assault. The big issue I see is the age-old question...should illegal drugs be legalized?

Finn slowed down for the turn onto Route One. "If people are determined to try and feel better with drugs, even if drugs can hook them and kill them and ruin the lives of others, should drug users be allowed that freedom? Like alcohol users? How much harm should society be willing to sanction? It's always going to be a can of worms."

Jane thought for a moment. "In other words, should people be free to pursue drug addiction? Isn't that opening the door to a long, slow, painful, and inefficient suicide? And as far as what role free will plays, once you're addicted, it's the warped, addicted you who's now running the show...the old you, the real you, has been kicked off stage by your fucked up brain and neurons. You have become a very sick person with a serious medical condition, and then the question becomes more complex and more lethal. Do we want to hand out freedom of self-destruction to people who are no longer their real selves?" Jane could feel herself running headlong into the impossibility of the whole topic. She needed to change course.

"But, Finn, if you don't mind, could we put all this aside for a minute? Can we talk about today? Did you see anyone in that room you know? I don't think I recognized a single person."

"That's true. I assume they're like us, people who have received clearance to be on the corruption task force."

"Which means other people we know, like Storm and Lieutenant Adderley, or Helen and Israel, may be under suspicion?" Jane said.

"Let's not jump to speculations and conclusions just yet, Jane. We're not going to solve this overnight."

....

A few days later, Jane went looking through all her desk drawers and then pulled all the drawers in Israel's desk. Nothing. Where could it be?

"Helen, do you know where Israel put this past winter's deer harvest data? I have to review it now and then forward it to Inland Fisheries and Wildlife."

"Why don't you call him over in Vermont, Jane? He's on a little break, but he won't mind if you take a moment of his time."

"OK...no problem. I'll dial him and get my answer."

Jane flipped through her rolodex and rang up Israel's cell. No answer. Why wasn't he picking up?

She was due over on the mainland for a dentist appointment after lunch. She could stop in at the ferry terminal internet cafe and google the phone number for Israel's family in Stowe, Vermont. She'd track him down one way or another.

....

Jane returned later that afternoon from the dentist and detoured into the internet cafe. She input "Tenner, Stowe, Vermont." Nothing came up.

That's curious. He has all those relatives in Stowe. That's who he's visited during Christmas breaks. What am I missing here?

Jane got back in her truck, drove onto the ferry, and returned to St. Frewin's Island.

"I still can't get Israel on his cell phone, Helen," Jane said, once she was back in the office.

"It's not the end of the world, Jane. Just call Inland Fisheries and Wildlife and tell them you'll get the report to them next week. Israel will be back soon, and then you can finish your task."

"You're right. No reason to sweat about it," Jane said. But it nagged at her all the same. Why couldn't she reach Israel?

....

"So, how's it going out there on Catunk Isle? Are you settling in?" Jane was on the phone with Finn, who had officially taken up his new post as PSO on Catunk Isle.

"Hey, Jane. Thanks for calling. I've finally moved into my little rental out here. The digs are pretty simple, which suits me. Now I've got to get up to speed on keeping the locals out of trouble, but other than that, it's all been straight forward."

Jane looked over at her door to be sure it was closed. "Any news on the anti-corruption front? Any pirate ships coming on shore on your island, full of pills and contraband?"

"Nah. It's been peaceful as far as I know. I haven't seen anyone misbehaving."

"Ditto out here. The tide comes in; the tide goes out," Jane said.

"Anyway, got to get back to work. Hope you're staying sane, Officer Roberts."

"Sure, Officer Gallinen...you, too!" And Jane hung up. Finn wasn't really that bad. She should lighten up towards him. It wasn't his fault he had the personality of a broom closet. Who cared if his charisma was right up there with powdered milk. She should be less judgmental.

12

LATE MAY 2022
Cat Out of The Bag

"I really think the book has come together, Sugar," Oxford Monteith was catching up with her old friend by phone. "These guys who moved in next to my land out there have been the wildest trip I've ever taken where I went nowhere."

"What's that supposed to mean?" Sugar asked.

"Meaning they're kind of mysterious, intriguing, a little rough around the edges, I'm crazy about one of them, and I've written a semi-autobiographical mystery about all of them!"

"Oh boy, sounds like you're cooking, Oxford. Do I get to take a peek before it comes out officially?"

"Well, maybe, but don't pass it around, OK? Keep it under wraps. And I want to hear all your questions, complaints, anything that bothers you about the story as a whole."

....

Sugar Betts pulled on her hiking boots and added a heavy flannel shirt infused with tick repellent. She went out the door and started tramping towards Oxford Monteith's land.

It had been a week since Sugar had finished reading Oxford's manuscript, first in the comfort of her year-round home, and then at her camp. She had sat inside reading Oxford's work while the sun's rays rose higher and higher in the sky, even as the warmth of each day remained interfaced with chilling swaths wandering among the hours.

Sugar loved the thrill of reading the book just several lots down from where the real action was taking place. It made her feel racy. And sure enough, her curiosity got the better of her. By early June, she was ready for her mission. She wanted to see this Ferguson Mountain Gang for herself.

Sugar made her way carefully down a rocky embankment towards the front of the house. She could see four men sitting on the outside deck. Straight out of Oxford's book. Right before her.

"Hi there!" Sugar called out. "I'm your neighbor from down a few camps. A friend of Oxford Monteith's. You know...the author?"

"God damn it. Now what?" Turk grumbled to Chummy. "Are you two young dick heads the ones responsible for this blonde go-go chick showing up?" he said, looking at Random and Jamie with irritated disapproval.

"She's coming towards the deck, Turk. What do you want us to do?" Random asked.

"Just stay cool. Let her do the talking. Don't any of you go on about anything. Keep it simple."

Sugar walked towards them, taking confident strides in her blue jean leggings and hiking boots, a big smile on her face, and the manuscript clutched in her painted nails.

"Welcome to Ferguson Mountain! I've heard all about you from Oxford. We go way back." She extended her hand and greeted them one by one. "I'm Sugar Betts, by the way."

The men looked at her as if she were a female Martian crashing through their cosmic barrier.

"Mind if I sit a moment? ...There," she said as she took a seat and shimmied into one of the outdoor lounge chairs. "Now I'm comfortable."

"What brings you here, Ma'am?" Random asked.

"Well. You mustn't let Oxford know that I dropped by. And you can't tell her why I dropped by. But I have a surprise for you!" Her apple cheeks and fuchsia lips nearly mowed the men down.

"We're all ears, Ma'am," Chummy said.

"Did you boys know you're the inspiration behind a new mystery novel Oxford's writing? I swear to God." Sugar rolled her eyes and thrust her long, golden tresses behind her ears and shoulders.

"No, we did not know that," Turk said, reddening from his neck up. He was going to throttle Oxford Monteith if he ever saw her again.

"If you promise to behave as I've asked, I'm happy to hand over this precious manuscript to you for your own reading pleasure. You will get such a kick out of your descriptions! And from the looks of you, I'd say Oxford is spot on! This is so funny!"

"Why thank you, Ma'am. And our apologies that we're standing up now, but we have work to do, and I'm sure you want to get back home before the woods get too dark," said Random.

"Oh, oh, so soon? Well, OK, then. I'll say goodbye for now. But I'll be back at some point. You can count on me to be a good neighbor. Always ready to help...or party!" Sugar got up and walked towards the steep hillside she had cut down to reach the house, all the while looking back and waving. She could see the oldest one of the bunch aiming a theoretical gun and shooting at her in jest. What devils....

....

"Give me that damn thing," Turk said as Jamie started leafing through the manuscript. "What'd I tell you? That Monteith dame's gone and scribbled it all down to expose us and make us look like a bunch of fools. That's what I'm betting." Jerking the manuscript away from Jamie, Turk stomped into the house and slammed the door behind him.

"Who knew we'd have all these women problems, on top of everything else we're juggling?" Jamie looked at Random and started shaking his head and coughing in laughter.

....

"Well, Turk's done reading all he's gonna read, he says," Random told Jamie and Chummy as he walked into the kitchen with the manuscript two hours later. "But it sure sounds like he's havin' kittens after seeing what Oxy put in her book."

"Let me have a shot at it next...you guys can wait. I want to see what the fuck Oxy, as you call her, wrote about me," Jamie said.

"Sure, man. Go for it. Can't be all bad," Random said.

....

"This isn't the end of the world, you guys," Jamie said as he caught up with the other three men after he skimmed through everything Sugar Betts had handed them. "I say we get Oxy to make a few changes here and there, sweeten it up to boost our egos, and then let 'er rip. We could buy a carload of copies to hand out to the guys in the Boston and D. C. offices."

"That's a very positive outlook you've got, Jamie," said Random. "But first we all have to read the book and then we go see Oxy for changes."

"Wait a minute. I know I'm the one who said sweeten it up, but what if she won't?"

Turk scowled at Jamie. "She doesn't get a choice. She's just the author. We're the fuckin' content."

13

METHAMATICS
by Oxford Monteith

"Psst, Turk...Random," whispers Chummy some twenty feet away from them and the house, his eyes signaling towards the second floor. "The upstairs light's off now. Ready to go in?" Heads nod yes. All three men—Turk, Random, and Chummy—bend low and run for the entry. They know it will open, no problem. They've already done their homework. People on St. Frewin's Island don't lock their doors at night.

....

Jamie and the author, the human bacon and the human egg sizzling in the frying pan of passion in this lovely summer cottage on this beautiful summer's night on St. Frewin's Island. She is certain this is love. He is certain he wants to make love. The Great Divide. But it's a start, isn't it?

The sound of the front door smashing open blows these tender feelings out from under the bed covers. Jamie grips the author to his chest. They hear voices they both know. He jumps up. The author leans towards the nightstand...grabs her phone. She dials her sister, drops the phone.

And they run....

The gunmen tear into the room and blast away with their big, fat pistols where the lovers' warm impressions linger, sculpted into the bedding. The lovers' thoughts, their delight, and utmost joy at coming together against such great, weird odds should now be a million red dots horribly adorning two walls. Their laughter and their denouement should run crimson on the hot sheets and the cold floor.

The goose down from their gunned pillows and comforter becomes airborne like snowflakes on wings. White is the only color below. The gunmen see nothing but white.

14

EARLY JUNE 2022
Summer Visitors

"Jane? I've got some juicy news for you." Helen Orbeton walked into Jane's office several days later, waving a fax in her hand. "Maggie Banner sent over one of her 'Ruckus Reports' to give you advance warning."

Jane rubbed her hands together. "Bless that Maggie! If she smells trouble on its way to her inn, she makes sure we know about it. What have we got?"

"Maggie says she has two upcoming sets of exotic guests at the Grand Harbor Inn to alert you about, just in case the inn's neighbors start hollering. First off, the national organization, Attorneys for Hallucinogens, has booked a retreat next month, that's the second week in July."

Jane straightened up like a length of 2 by 4. "The Attorneys for Hallucinogens? As I live and breathe...those people.... You know, Helen, I read somewhere that their goal is to sort of massage the legal system to better accommodate the use of hallucinogens and psychedelics. Now I know there's lots of research out there about the chemical benefits for troubled individuals. But how many more mind-bending concoctions are really going to improve life on this planet? Talk about thinking outside the envelope and wandering off the reservation...all rolled into one joint."

"Are you trying to be funny, Jane?"

"OK...OK. Sorry."

Helen continued reading Maggie's memo. "After that, J.T. Karl's Wild Open has their camera crew and models coming to the Grand Harbor Inn for a week to shoot their upcoming catalog."

"No kidding," Jane said. "I bet Zara Billings will be here with the J. T. Karl crew. What an evolution she's been through. Zara Billings—Inn owner one month, charged with the death of her husband by fentanyl, then widow and prisoner the next month, and now, a year later, a feature prisoner and model for a clothing line in a major emporium's catalog. I still can't believe Chanson Pratt used her muscle on the J. T. Karl Board to pull that off for Zara. My life should be so boring. I'm jealous!"

"Well, it isn't, and you shouldn't be," Helen counseled.

Jane remembered something else. "Don't forget. We also have the *Princess Marjo* cruise liner and her 3,000 guests docking the third week in July in the main harbor, so we better brace ourselves for that onslaught as well."

"And you were worried it would be dull around here, weren't you, Jane?" Helen puckered her mouth at Jane as she returned to her desk. Jane blew her kisses.

....

Israel Tenner entered the office an hour later. "Good morning, ladies!" He leaned down to take off his muck boots and put on his regular work boots.

Jane came out of her office. "You're in a good mood. How did the shellfish survey go?"

"I'm happy to say not many juvenile clams, and no pregnant lobsters stuffed inside anybody's haul. But I did pick up the latest stink."

"Meaning?"

"Really, it's more daily nuttiness. Nowhere but on St. Frewin's. This big news is from over at the graveyard."

"The graveyard?" Jane said.

"Yes. Betty Dodge is bound and determined that she and her late husband are having only ONE headstone—not two. So she's added her name to the existing headstone resting over her late husband, and she says her kids can add her dates when she's gone."

"That sounds reasonable," Helen said.

"That's right," Israel continued. "And Betty doesn't see any problem with it. But the cemetery director, who's her cousin by the way, is insisting on one headstone per family member. No doubling up allowed, he says. So Betty has been drumming up support and racing around polling everyone she lays eyes on about the simplicity of one headstone for a married couple. She says her children all say 'Do what you want.' But her cousin is ready to shoot and bury Betty himself—under her OWN headstone of course, if she keeps up with her campaign."

"Now that's what I call utter nonsense. Betty should do what she wants. In fact, I know for a fact that Agatha Christie and her husband share one tombstone. So what's the big deal?" Jane said.

"The passions are running high on this one, Jane. You can't underestimate family feuds about dealing with the dead. And graveyards? Their contents may be cold, but they're definitely hot beds of controversy," Israel said.

"You're probably right, Israel," Jane said. "I'm the worst at being sensitive towards things other people think are a huge deal. And with people more and more explosive about their differences these days, it's too much conflict for me. I tend to turn away, but you pay attention to others' feelings. You see the undercurrents and acknowledge them. That's an important skill."

"Takes all kinds to make a good team, Jane. I'm here to round things out. How's that?"

"Perfect, I.T.! And by the way, I'm a little curious about one thing. I tried to call you the last time you were in Vermont and I wasn't having any luck. So I googled your last name for Stowe, Vermont while I was at the ferry internet cafe and again no luck. I thought all you Tenners lived in Stowe."

"Oh, sorry about that. They actually live in North Calais, which is a small village a little way from Stowe. I just say Stowe all the time because everyone's heard of Stowe and all the skiing out there. But let me give you my parents' cell phone number for next time. They don't use a landline any longer."

"Thanks, Israel. That's good, just in case."

15

JUNE 2022
Island Chatter

It was Saturday and Jane was enjoying the leisure of standing around schmoozing with Sam in her work kitchen. Jane watched Sam whisk together the cheese and eggs and milk for her Southern Macaroni and Cheese bake. It was a lucky ladies' book club who would sink their teeth into that dish later in the day.

"I tell you, Oxford is a walking, frothing carnal mousse," Sam said to Jane. "And of course she has nowhere to plant her imaginary ecstasy nor her criminal fantasies about her neighbors' manufacturing drugs. I told her to rework her passions into fiction for her next book. Obvious idea, right? And she's done it...in a semi-autobiographical way. Meaning you and I appear in the book, Jane. Hah!"

"And you were saying one of the men swept her away simply by ending a few of her sentences for her while they spoke?"

"Yah, that's all it takes for Oxford to think 'intimacy' and she goes wild. It's some guy named Jamie...according to Oxford he's a trim, tattooed, bespectacled, alleged Irish-American of vague visage with bangs, who may or may not cook meth."

"Vague visage?" Jane said.

"You know, when you can't quite recall a face because you're so distracted by the whole person to begin with? Something like that."

"And more meth? God...why so much meth?" Jane started pacing. "How did the world ever get so screwed up and unhappy? Do we need to talk about it? Should we sweep it under the rug? Or maybe have a public seminar about it on the island? How about that for public safety?" Jane was warming to the topic.

Sam nodded at Jane and sprinkled some Colby cheese over the first layer of macaroni.

"Just look at the numbers, Sam. Year after year, no matter how many billions of dollars and human bodies we throw at this drug tsunami, it gets bigger. People everywhere are in compromising positions with needles in their veins...if they're not in coffins. Even in some public libraries, there's meth on the toilet paper rolls...and on the books! Think of that...meth on *The Cat in the Hat!*"

"*The Cat in the Hat?* That's sacrilegious," Sam said.

"What I don't understand is this. If the whole world knows by now that these drugs will kill you, why do people continue to put anything in their mouth unless they've peeled it, boiled it, baked it, pulled it out of the earth or off a plant?"

"Except a marijuana plant or a poppy...or a magic mushroom," Sam noted.

"Well, OK. Right," Jane said. "It's insane." She knotted her hair up behind her head and then let it all jump free.

"I have to admit, I don't pay much attention to the topic," Sam said as she put the Southern Macaroni and Cheese into the oven. "Work is so busy now that I've got the new account at the Golf Club. Have to keep the conservative stomachs of my Republican and Catholic golfers happy."

"You're always going on about the Republicans and the Catholics. Don't you have any Democrats or Protestants?" Jane asked.

"I don't worry about my Democrats, Jane. They'll eat anything I put in front of them."

Sam began tidying up near the sink. "Anyway, while Nathan and his gang from the *Synchronicity* yacht drink as people do in social settings, he doesn't wolf down drugs. And my helpers here on the island are all fairly sober, reliable types, so you're asking an ignoramus. But, sure, why not have a drug info seminar for the public? You had that talk about dogs on drugs a while back. Why not the human version?"

"Hmm, the more I think about it, the more I can envision it, Sam. We could have an impromptu civilian drug panel. Maybe call it 'Drugs Are Us.'"

"Oh, that will bring in the crowds, Jane," Sam frowned.

"Did you know Zara Billings is going to be in town in July? She could give a spiel on the why, the how, and the aftermath since she managed to kill her husband with fentanyl."

"Wouldn't that be a bit outrageous, Jane? Should the PSO showcase someone who managed to kill her husband?"

"Well, we could balance out the panel with your sister...you just mentioned she's writing about drugs in her book, right? And it would probably help to have an addict join us, too."

"Who would that be?" Sam asked.

"Well, maybe a recovering addict. But I don't know a recovering addict. Do you?" Jane said.

"I don't think so. What about a DEA person? You're in law enforcement. That should probably be part of your pitch with this panel, right?"

"You know, for the addict part"—Jane was brainstorming—"we could ask for audience participation. It's a sad fact that too many families are dealing with this. Maybe people would be willing to share their experiences.... I know! We could schedule the drug panel to coincide with that big, visiting cruise ship. It's the same time Zara will be here. There's bound to be lots of people from the cities and the suburbs with nightmares to share. How about that?"

Sam looked skeptical. "You think people are going to want to sit down to chat about such personal tragedies while they're in Maine on a cruise vacation? That's crazy, Jane. But if you're right, St. Frewin's is really going to rock. And wait until Trudy Moody hears about your idea. Get ready for the backlash."

"Thanks for reminding me," Jane said. "Trudy keeps shoving her nose into anything remotely civic-related. Why we would need the blessings of our retired Town Clerk is beyond me.

"Though I guess I can see your point about people not wanting to talk about their own struggles with drugs. Too sensitive a topic. What I'd like to know more about is why people ever start on drugs. Maybe I can ask around and find a recovery counselor to discuss why people turn down the dangerous path in the first place."

16

METHAMATICS
by Oxford Monteith

"Jane, I've got Mrs. Beatrice Jenkins on the line. She's needs to tell you about something strange walking along the road." The PSO Receptionist, Helen Orbeton, put the call through to Jane in her Public Safety office.

"Yes, Mrs. Jenkins, this is Jane Roberts. Helen tells me you have something to report?"

"That's right, Officer Jane. Now I don't know what you'd call it. But I think I'm havin' some kind of biblical moment. And it's goin' on right outside my kitchen window. Like Adam and Eve hitchhikin' or somethin'. They look—what's that detective word? They look *furtive*."

"Please don't take this the wrong way, Mrs. Jenkins. But have you taken any medications today?"

Beatrice Jenkins laughed and coughed into the phone. "You mean like somethin' my nephew might have left behind by mistake and not somethin' my GP gave me? Child, I'm eighty-two. Party drugs wouldn't work on me. But at my age, if they did, I'd swallow a whole honking chug of 'em because I'm too old to live any longer. It's high time for me to die."

"But don't you still look forward to things?" Jane asked.

"Like what?"

"Well, a beautiful day, a funny moment, your next meal."

"You hain't had my cookin'."

"Maybe I could copy some recipes for you to try, so you could have some variety."

"Don't bother. I can google *Bon Appetit* all I want."

"You know how to google, Mrs. Jenkins?"

"Sure I do. How else am I gonna keep up?"

"Wow. I'm impressed."

"Well you should be. You know, I was a beta tester for *Candy Crush* back in the day."

"The video game?" Jane's mouth fell open.

"That's right. Paid real well. And now I'm testing *Call of Duty's* new stuff."

'That's incredible, Mrs. Jenkins! I hardly know what to say."

"You betcha...and the best part of it? It drives my daughter-in-law bananas. She's jealous as all get out. Hah!"

"Sounds to me like you really aren't ready to die yet," Jane said.

"Well, you got a point. The good Lord keeps handin' me rain checks. And them video places keep sendin' me real checks. So if that's what God wants, I'll keep takin' 'em."

"OK. Let's go back to Adam and Eve for a minute. You said they're hitchhiking outside your window? Could you describe them to me?"

"Well, as you know, Adam and Eve means they ain't got much of anything on 'em. But these two...they're coverin' up with all kinds of branches. Looks pretty leafy...and fruity, if you know what I mean. And if anyone's on drugs, it must be the two of them, 'cause the guy keeps callin' the woman Oxy. Now, what's that all about? Callin' her one of them pills?"

Oxy? Jane felt the frisson of the lightning bolt hit her squarely in the think tank in her head. "What's your address, Mrs. Jenkins? I'd better jump in my truck and come take a look."

....

"What's that you're reading, Jane?" Israel Tenner asked Jane Roberts, when he looked into her office during lunch break.

"This? It's Oxford Monteith's latest novel, *Methamatics*. She's Samantha Lloyd's sister. You know her books?"

"No, I don't," Israel said.

"Well, you can get your paws on it when I'm done. But you have to leave me alone now so I can read a bit more before lunch is over. I'm deep into it."

Israel snuck closer. Jane could see a devilish grin spreading across his face.

"You look like you're really enjoying that book, Jane." He leaned over and grabbed it from her hands, then sped off into the main room.

"You little shit," Jane said under her breath. "Give that back to me!" she yelled as she jumped out of her chair and ran chasing after him.

17

JULY 2022
Garden of Eden

Helen Orbeton walked towards Jane's office. "Jane, maybe you should run over to Mary Bartlett's place. She just called to say she's got strange people climbing the trees in her yard...and hugging them."

"Wait," Jane stood up from her desk. "Can I talk to her first?"

"She hung up. Sounds like she's hopping mad."

"Great. Tree climbers. Tree huggers. A monumental threat to public safety for sure." Jane continued to make dismissive noises and mumble to herself as she walked out of the PSO.

....

It was an absolutely beautiful day on St. Frewin's Island. The kind of day where every leaf, every fir tree needle was vibrating back and forth as if deliberate and sentient. Long, broad knives of sunlight lunged off the ocean waters across the fields and through the tree branches into Jane's eyes.

She thanked God for it all for the millionth time as she drove her truck through the soft summer air, along the narrow lanes, past one white clapboard house after another...each one differing in their angles and sheds, the color of their front doors, the lives of their occupants...their secrets. And all around, the live presence of peacefulness, without the roar of the mainland highways and the relentless scurrying around.

DEEP FRIED FATE

Wait a minute. There's Israel in his truck, driving in the opposite direction. Jane flagged him to slow down and she did the same. "Tenner! What's up?"

"Hey, Jane. I finished checking on that loose dog down at the Pub, and then I ran into Bernie Pushaw. He said Captain Bryce's wife is all hot under the collar about naked tourists dancing on the rocks in front of their house. So I'm headed over there to investigate."

"Captain Bryce, as in the retired navy commander? You know, I bet he doesn't realize he's probably hosting some of those Attorneys for Hallucinogens who are here for the week. I think I've got some of their lawyers hanging out in trees at Mary Bartlett's," Jane said. "OK...you look into the dancers in the buff, and I'll meet you back at the office in a bit."

Jane drove off from Israel and pulled up to Mary Bartlett's house five minutes later. The fruit was beginning to set in Mary's front yard orchard of varietal apples—Golden Russet, Black Oxford, Suncrisp, and Sundance. All of them Jane's favorites when late October arrived...she loved their names!

Mary Bartlett had lovingly pruned and maintained her varietals over the decades. The tree branches showed deliberate restraint, like kabuki dancers bending and swaying close to the earth. Nothing about the trees was towering or branching. Their bounty sprang from bowing low towards the earth, wings clipped to yield the eventual perfection of sweet and crunchy rounds shaped by God for the human hand.

Human bodies were now hugging and hanging from these sacred trees of Mary's...human bodies who surely had higher degrees—BAs and JDs and maybe even some

MAs thrown in, which didn't seem to do much to distinguish these low-hanging jurists from monkeys.

Jane started waving at the adult tree ornaments. She could see Mary Bartlett opening her front door, her face a merger of frets and scowls.

"Don't worry, Mary. I'll talk to them," Jane said as she walked towards the fruit trees.

"You better do something quick, Jane," Mary said. "They're about to ruin half my crop!"

"Welcome to St. Frewin's Island. How's everyone today?" Jane greeted the tree creatures.

"We seek to flow within the Garden of Eden!" said one of the men closest to Jane.

"Are you folks by any chance connected to the Attorneys for Hallucinogens group on the island this week?"

"Board of Directors!" the swinging orangutans chimed in unison.

"Impressive," Jane called out as she approached more closely. "We're so glad you're getting a chance to visit St. Frewin's Island. And you're so lucky to have discovered our own local Garden of Eden."

Jane projected a look at Mary Bartlett that tried to communicate "patience."

"We're wondering," Jane elaborated, "if you could help Mary Bartlett here with her upcoming harvest of apples. These trees are setting fruit right now, and that means the fertilized ovules are becoming seeds and the ovaries will start to develop into the flesh of the apple."

"Oh," said one of the lawyers suspended upside down, "it sounds as though the womb of Mother Earth is hard at work and we might be interfering with Nature's procreation?"

"Yes! Brilliant. Something like that," Jane went on encouragingly. "The less stress on the infant fruit and branches on the arms of the trees right now, the better the crop. And I appreciate that you're very sensitive about communing with Nature's miracles. We don't want to botch her harvest."

That seemed to sink in. Slowly, gingerly, three dangling women and two dangling men drifted down off the branches and landed on the grass in front of Jane and Mary Bartlett. The psychedelic directors looked as if they had tumbled out of an Alex Katz painting—sleek, stark, angular faces, and the women's lips painted bright red…East Hampton dolls, now bathed in a mystical state of consciousness.

Jane looked at Mary, and Mary looked at Jane. The incongruity of the moment caught Jane's imagination. She wondered what miracles it would take to turn her and Mary Bartlett into haute babes. Red lipstick alone wouldn't cut it. They'd have to plane their cheekbones and jawlines and iron their hair for about two years—while getting rid of all their frumpy clothes—reasons enough to start frantically stuffing their faces with psycho fungi.

"So, would you folks like a ride back to Grand Harbor Inn? Or maybe the nearby lobster roll shack?" Jane looked over the shaky group.

The board of directors gathered themselves and brushed off leafy debris. Jane could not bear to alarm them and tell them about the possibility that they had rubbed hallucinogenic shoulders (and arms and legs) with the toxic, itchy brown tail moth caterpillars, who loved apple trees even more than the mystical visitors. Jane knew Maggie Banner had all sorts of remedies and creams back at Grand Harbor Inn. She and her staff could minister to the rash-ridden, if necessary.

"Oh, we're fine drinking in the beauty of this day," one of the women said. "We'll just trip on out of this Paradise and be on our way. We're heading to the Town Hall now for our Annual Meeting. We're a bit late, but we'll be fine."

Jane motioned them towards her truck. "Seriously, come with me. The Town Hall is nearly a mile from here. I'll drive you all there so you don't have to run in this heat."

As they set out, Jane said to the group, "Could I ask you why you promote psychedelics?"

One of the women spoke right up. "The well-being of humans is our guide. We strongly believe in supporting the trinity of body, mind and spirit, and hallucinogens have proven beneficial to all three."

Jane glanced into the rear-view mirror at her passengers. "I know this may sound bizarre, but I'm just wondering if any of you have ever tried to find an answer in something less controversial, something that's not challenging the drug laws."

"And what would that be, Officer Roberts?"

"Well, maybe something like needlepoint? I mean, I know those canvas mesh grids and all that wool may not deliver a completely consciousness-expanding trip, but needlepoint is pretty amazing."

"The warp and weft of life, Officer Roberts?"

"Right, exactly!" Jane said.

"But all that colorful wool...the striking imagery? It takes forever to get there, don't you think, Officer Roberts? We want bursting floods of visions and rainbows all at once, up front and knocking us over. We don't do one stitch at a time."

....

"So, Israel, you may as well start with your report on the naked beach revelers. Anything worth writing in our log? Any procedural points of law enforcement that need dissecting?" Jane bent over quickly and started laughing in front of Israel and Helen back at the PSO. "I'm sorry. I just can't believe this is part of our job. Go ahead. Bare it all to me."

Israel sat down at the table and motioned to the two women to do the same. He pulled out his notepad.

"OK, our disrobed visitors on Captain Bryce's shore claimed they had, and I quote, "partaken of ayahuasca to reach beyond their consciousness and reality," Israel began. "When I found them, some were bowing to the ocean; others were sitting on the rocks and opening themselves to the Universe. I tried to keep the bolder ones from entering the Bryce lawn, but do you know how hard it is to manage five naked people who are determined to find their primal selves by rolling around on someone else's grass?"

"Where were Captain Bryce and Mrs. Bryce while all these mushrooms were expanding their caps?" Jane asked.

"I think Mrs. Bryce might have been hiding inside. But to tell you the truth, Captain Bryce didn't seem to be in a hurry to chase away any rof the visiting flesh. Probably made his day!"

"He stood there and gawked?" Helen said.

"Well, he went up to several of those pieces of toast and started what seemed to be a lively conversation.

Something about maybe trying marijuana to reduce his glaucoma-induced eye pressure."

Jane rose up from the office table. "Wonders never cease. You know, Israel, if you add this event to your rescue of the kittens from that tire in the ocean, you're building up quite the PSO portfolio."

"No kidding," Israel said. "And when I was leaving I could see Captain Bryce posing with several of his unclad female invaders for their selfies. I heard him yell out, 'You can post the damn things anywhere you want!' "

....

"Hi, Jane. I thought I'd check in to see how you're all doing out there." Storm Nosmot was on the phone. "St. Frewin's Island's murder rate has plummeted all year so far, and I'm starting to get worried."

"You think you're funny, don't you, Storm? And I suppose you're swimming in dead bodies at Maine Crimes Unit-Central?" Jane said.

"Actually, it's been pretty quiet on our end, too. Nice to see people aren't snuffing each other out. But none of us likes sitting around when we're so highly trained to track down killers."

Jane was itching to bring up the police corruption issue, but she held off. She had to behave and keep quiet.

"I've seen a lot of your favorite colleague up here in Augusta lately," Storm said.

"What do you mean?" Jane asked.

"Finn Gallinen."

"Finn? In Augusta? He's supposed to be stationed out on Catunk Isle."

"Well, he's been at the Human Resources Office lately. Meeting with someone I guess. I don't know anything else."

"Hmm. Neither do I. Maybe I'll ask him the next time we're talking."

"So that's all. Just wanted to check in."

"Maybe Harriet has taken him under her wing. But why would she do that?" Jane asked.

"There could be a hundred reasons why he's been hanging out in Augusta. What do you care?"

Jane still felt she should not elaborate about the anti-corruption team, but she was miffed. "I just want to know what those two are up to. Makes me feel left out of whatever it is they're doing," she said.

"Look, you don't even know Finn is with Harriet. We don't know anything. And besides, you can't stand Harriet Buxton, last I heard. And you can't stand Finn. So why would you not want to be left out of whatever two people you can't stand are up to?"

"Ha! Have you thought about syntax recently, Detective Nosmot?" Jane laughed.

"Sin? A tax? What's that supposed to mean?"

"Oh, please. Listen, I think it's time for us to hang up, Storm. But I'm glad you called. Seriously. We all miss you. Maybe Fate will send us a murder soon!"

"Jane, hush! Take care of yourself, and please give Helen and Israel my best."

"Will do. Thanks, Storm. Ciao!"

Jane hung up the phone. She was annoyed. What was Finn doing up in Augusta? Something to do with the anti-corruption team? If so, why hadn't Jane been included? Was he even going to update her?

Come to think of it, what about hiring Israel...the other important decision in which she had been given no part. What about Israel? Not that she didn't think he was perfect for the job and, yes, she loved working with him. But how the hell did he get chosen for her office on St. Frewin's Island?

No one asked Jane for her input at the time. No one sent her a folder of candidates to review. What was she? Wallpaper? Didn't Harriet Buxton have a thoughtful bone in her body? Not a word from her in advance of Israel's arrival. Hmm. And now maybe Finn was meeting with her...and without Jane. Hmm!

18

JULY 2022
I Spy

"Hey, Oxford. It's Random here." He was calling Oxford at the guest cottage she was renting on St. Frewin's Island from Konstantin Balankoff. "We're wondering if you wanted to get together for a barbecue at our place on the mountain?"

"Well, Random, thank you for asking. That's a nice invitation, but I'm out on St. Frewin's Island for the summer and it's not all that convenient to come back to the mainland right now. Maybe we could think about another time?"

"Uh, hold on a second, Oxford. Turk wants to talk to you."

"Hello, Oxford? This is Turk."

"Yes, Turk. How's life on Ferguson Mountain?" Oxford said.

"Never mind that. Now, listen. This may come as a surprise to you. But some of our book-wormy buddies came across your new novel and noticed a distinct resemblance to our operation, I mean, our family house out here on Ferguson Mountain. And some people think it's time to get together with you for a little editing. Tighten up the book some so it reads better. You get my drift?"

"What do you mean 'reads better,' Turk? It reads exactly as it should."

"Look, Darlin', so you say. But our image is on the line here. We'd love to buy a couple pallets of *Methamatics* to hand out to our business associates, but we need you to make a few changes first. And we can see you published this independently, so it will only take you a few clicks on the keyboard to smooth the way for our big order. What do you think?"

"Well, when you put it like that, maybe I could be accommodating, Turk. I'd like to think about it and get back to you. How's that?"

"Don't take too long, Darlin'. Think about your profit margin. You might even get on one of those bestsellers lists if I give you a boost." And Turk hung up.

....

Oxford reached for the pitcher of lemonade. The obvious question came pouring out with the lemonade into her glass. Did those guys just call her out here on St. Frewin's Island? That was strange, right? How would they know she was out here? How did they get the telephone number for Konstantin Balankoff's guest cottage?

This called for action. She stood around, sipping lemonade and plotting that action in her head. Then she dialed the mountain house.

"What?"

"What? What kind of a way is that to answer the phone?" Oxford asked.

"Yah, I said 'What.' Who's this?"

"Ah, this is Oxford Monteith. Does it sound as if I'm talking to Chummy?"

"You got it. You wanna talk to Lover Boy instead?"

"Sure." *Lover Boy? What's Chummy doing calling Jamie—I'm guessing—Lover Boy? How does Chummy even know to call him Lover Boy when I'm on the phone?*

"Hello."

"Jamie, is that you?"

"Yes."

"Hi! It's Oxford. Listen, Turk was asking about making some changes to my novel, *Methamatics*. And he has a point...even though the book was published last month, it is print on demand. Which means the printer only prints the book when someone orders it. So I could make a modest number of changes and submit them to my printer before Turk orders his copies. Does that work for you guys?"

"That should keep Turk happy, Oxford."

"Great! Could the four of you plan to get the ferry that arrives on St. Frewin's Island in the early afternoon on July 20? We can work on your changes all afternoon, and you can take a water taxi in the early evening to return to the mainland."

"Sounds good, Oxford. And by the way, I read what you wrote about me...."

"Oh, really? Well, listen, we can talk more later. I've got to run now. See you all on the 20th!" And Oxford hung up. She could not deal with flirtation right now...*because....*

To think the Mountain Gang wanted her to alter *Methamatics*! What a little Hitler that Turk was. But, yah, ha haa! Oxford would hand them the semblance of a rewrite. That's what she would do. She would pretend to tinker with her precious sentences as they wished. Then she would order an author proof for them to approve. But before going live with the rewrite, she would revert to what she, the author, wanted, and then she would hit the "OK to publish" button on her computer screen.

The Four Musketeers would probably never notice, and if they did, Oxford would improvise somehow. And the Four Musketeers might regret they had ever met Oxford Monteith. If they had intended to put a torch under her authorial butt, then she had caught fire. She was a flaming bonfire of indignation at this point.

Oxford got into her car and drove straight to her sister's work kitchen. Through the screen door, she could see Samantha slicing up a bucket of tomatoes. Oxford didn't bother to knock—simply walked in.

"Here we go again, Sam. This is unbelievable, except that I think I know what's going on. Tell me one more time about that electronic equipment you thought you saw at the Ferguson Mountain house."

"Come on, Oxford. Give me a minute here. You stomp in on me and my tomatoes and launch into some topic without any routine visiting etiquette or warnings, such as 'Hi, it's your wacko sister again.' "

"OK. OK, Sam. Looney Tunes is here. Now can you talk, for God's sake?"

"Yes...sure. And I think I heard you correctly, so here's what I remember. I saw a bunch of electrical lights on a wall of equipment at the mountain house. And that's it. I don't remember another single detail."

"Well, this is my problem, Sam. Something is not quite adding up. You tell me what you think. Random and Turk called me today on the landline, the phone at Konstantin Balankoff's guest cottage. How did they know where I was? How the hell did they get Konstantin's number?"

"Beats me, Oxford. Are you sure you didn't give them the number early on?"

"But why would I? I've only talked with them on my cell phone when I was in my Lincolnville house. This is the first summer I'm renting Konstantin Balankoff's guest cottage on St. Frewin's Island. On top of it all, Chummy referred to Jamie as 'Lover Boy.' Where did that come from? How does Chummy know about my crush on Jamie? They can't be seers."

"You're thinking it's the electrical equipment I saw?"

"What else could it be? They know too much, Sam. I think those slimy bastards have hacked into my cell phone. I think they've been listening to our conversations about Random and Jamie and whether or not they're all into meth cuisine. God damn it! I can't believe they've been able to cherry pick through my amorous frenzies!"

"Yes, but, Oxford. Wait a minute. You don't hesitate to publish your passions for public consumption, so what do you care?"

"Sam, I control what goes into my books and ultimately out the door. That's a big difference compared to the whole shebang coming off our phones and getting dumped into their spy machines for all of them to hee-haw over.

"So what are you going to do about it?" Sam said.

"We're going to come up with a plan. It's already jelling in my brain. I'll get back to you...but only in person. Sit tight, and watch out what you say on any cell phone call you make on the mainland. I don't know if they can infiltrate your landline, but I bet your cell phone could be next, if it isn't already compromised. OK?"

"OK," Sam said, taking up her knife once again. Tomatoes, tomatoes.

"OK. I've got to go now." Oxford left thinking *no more cell phones.* Face to face was key to protect her ultimate goal.

19

JULY 16, 2022
Panel Prep

Jane's impromptu planning committee for "Drugs Are Us" was meeting in a back corner of the pub. Samantha Lloyd started off. "I spoke to my long-time account, the Yacht Club, and they're enthusiastically on board to direct about fifty members our way for the panel discussion. My new account, the island Golf Club, estimates about thirty of their golfers will attend. So that's already eighty people to fill the Town Hall."

"Impressive, Sam!" Jane said. She flipped through her notes. "I asked the Abenaki County Chamber of Commerce about the cruise ship *Princess Marjo*. They report about a hundred people are interested in joining us, and some may be willing to share their family histories...how they've dealt with opioids at the dinner table. Can you believe it? One hundred people. That's fantastic. So now we're up to 180 people for starters, mostly from away."

Konstantin's sister, Torrance Balankoff, gave her report. "We've posted all kinds of signs, so local people know about 'Drugs Are Us.' As expected, I've heard complaints from people like Trudy Moody and, interestingly, Maggie Banner from Grand Harbor Inn. Neither of them feels the theme suits our world here...they say it's negative, such a downer, it will rain on people's vacation, stuff like that.

"I told them people can simply ignore the panel and act as if it's just another day. But I also said it's very cutting edge and important, that drugs are something that affect us all. Trudy Moody sniffed and said to me 'What happened to Vacationland?' She didn't think the Governor would approve."

Jane crossed her eyes and said, "Never mind about Trudy Moody. She's a post-menopausal leech. Besides, we can't please everyone all the time. Also, I heard from Zara Billings. She's prepping her presentation about killing her husband with a fentanyl overdose...why she did it, how she did it, what did she feel afterward, would she do it again. It'll be a powerful primer...she could be any of us."

Torrance laughed out loud. "Jane, you're nuts. Why would any of us want to kill our men?"

"OK. OK," Jane backed off. "Just kidding. But I think she'll bring a personal touch to the panel. We'll also hear what the Director of Rehab at the drug clinic in Graniteville can tell us about why people start taking drugs and why some people end up addicted when others don't bother to go near drugs."

"And finally," Sam said, "my sister, Oxford Monteith, will talk about her new book, *Methamatics*. It's a semi-fictional tale about new neighbors who turn out to be undercover agents pretending to cook meth in their home...to entrap drug dealers. Mostly she'll focus on the tell-tale signs of an illegal, clandestine drug lab. You know, suspicious activities people might see in their neighbors' back yards."

"God forbid," Torrance said.

"But God doesn't forbid these days. That's the problem," Sam added.

"Good. Let's bring this meeting to a close." Jane gathered up her papers. "I think that gives us enough to present a respectable panel for 'Drugs Are Us.' We're holding this event in the Town Hall because the number of anticipated guests has swelled. So we'll meet there at 9:00 AM on July 20 to set things up. The panel will commence at 10:00 AM and run for about two or three hours. Let's hope for the best!"

20

JULY 20, 2022
"Drugs Are Us"

"Sam! Sam, come here," Jane was motioning to Samantha Lloyd at the Town Hall the morning of the "Drugs Are Us" panel. "Guess what? Chanson Pratt just showed up with Zara, and do you know what Chanson has in her hand?"

"Jane, hurry up and tell me. We're running out of time. The panel is starting in twenty minutes."

"Chanson is holding the hand of her new little boy! Come with me. You can meet him."

"We haven't seen much of the Pratts this past year or two, have we?" Sam said.

"They were probably down in Texas most of the time, but they're here now at their summer house. There she is."

"Hi, Sam! Good to see you again! We wanted you to meet my little guy here," Chanson said, walking towards them, looking happier than ever...and even more at ease than Sam remembered from the past.

Sam looked at the child...Adorable! She felt an instant upwelling of emotion. He was the same color as Sam...the warm tone of a cherry wood chopping block, which came from Sam's Irish and Apache background. She flashed Chanson a beaming thumbs up. "What's his name?" Sam asked.

"This is Zen-Beau. And his middle name is Lovey, so he's Zen-Beau Lovey Pratt."

The little boy bent forward to hug Sam's leg. She picked him up and raised him into the air. "Oh, you little charmer, you!

"Chanson, forgive me," Jane said, "but may I ask you a blunt question? What does Salem think about this child you had with another man?"

"Oh, we're all so lucky. I think I can say we feel joy. Salem was great about embracing Zen-Beau straight into the family. And Salem and Zen-Beau's father, Zen-Ti Smith, are a team when it comes to bringing up our son. And our daughter, Geneva, and the Pratt family at large? They are Ec-Stat-Ic!" Chanson said, waving her hands in circles. "There hasn't been a Pratt male heir among any of Salem's siblings...until now."

The three women stood there smiling at one another, all their thoughts of what had gone on in their collective lives over the past two years now rolled into one wonderful, new human being...their own little miracle man.

Jane had long wondered how Salem Pratt, Chanson's husband, would take to an illegitimate son, even if the term was passé these days. Salem had made his millions in the semiconductor world, so he had to be a tough millionaire. But apparently he had a soft heart of gold as well.

Jane had also wondered who this Zen-Ti Smith really was. She had been able to piece together that Zen-Ti had commanded an urban group called the "Forbidden Fruits" in recent times. And Zen-Ti may have orchestrated the temporary disappearance of both Chanson Pratt and good old local Bernie Pushaw several years ago at Chanson's New Year's Eve pig roast. And now there was Zen-Beau Lovey Pratt.

How Bernie had gotten balled up in the escapade was beyond Jane. But she decided she didn't need to know. As for Chanson and Zen-Ti, that was the beauty of human math...one plus one could equal three...it just took a little time.

"Anyway, I've got to move it and help Zara get ready," Chanson said as she guided Zen-Beau back stage. "I'll see you guys later!"

"That's the other exciting news, Sam," Jane said. "When the management of J. T. Karl's Wild Open heard about Zara appearing on our panel, they put together a quick fashion show for her to promote the 'U Hauled Away' incarceration clothing line today. So we're tacking that on right before Oxford's presentation. It will be a colorful interlude. I bet the cruise ship crowd will eat it up!"

....

"Sam, maybe it's a case of nerves, but my throat is so parched. Do you have any lozenges on you?" Oxford asked as she swayed from one foot to the other in the shadows of the wing before joining Jane, Zara, and the Rehab Director at the table on stage.

"Sorry, Oxford. I don't have anything. But hold on a minute. I think I saw a bowl of hard candy on the stand in the hallway. Just a sec."

Sam returned and dumped into Oxford's palm a handful of candy in wrappers. "There you go. Suck on these."

"What are they?" Oxford asked.

"I don't know. Probably something generic the Town put out for exactly the reason you need them. Try at least one, and then off you go. Good Luck!"

Oxford popped three candies in her mouth and began pushing them around with her tongue. Chanson was pitching a spirited, final few words to the crowd for the "U Hauled Away" clothing line.

As Sam headed to her seat, she looked down at the remaining candies in her hand and began unwrapping one of the sweets for herself. She noticed some fine print and looked closely at the words.

Jane was now announcing Oxford's participation with a zippy introduction about her new book, *Methamatics*. She invited Oxford to walk out on stage, which she did.

Sam sat down and read the candy wrapper:

"Psychedelic Mongo Kryptonite
Courtesy of Sacred Valley Boomer Sweets"

Sam's mouth dropped. Psychedelic? Mongo Kryptonite? She watched her sister slowly walking and then uncharacteristically weaving her way out on stage. Sam quickly rewrapped the candy, put the sweets in her pocket, and held her breath.

"Well, Hello, Everyone! Welcome to St. Frigging Island! My name is Ox....ford Mon....teeeeeeth."

Oxford took a deep bow and stayed with her head flung down. She continued speaking...to the floor boards.

"And right, yes, Jane Roberts already told you that, didn't she? Ha ha!!"

Oxford struggled upward from her bow, followed by a very deep curtsy. Audience heads began to swivel nervously.

"So, why are we all here today? Why are we all here?" She took a second bow and popped another candy in her mouth.

Jane glanced towards Sam who had chosen a nearby orchestra seat. Jane tried to catch her attention with a questioning face, but Sam seemed to be vigorously burying her head in her hands.

"We are here today to figure out how the heck your neighbor bakes a pie full of scooby and pookie and speed! Sounds like we're talking about a hell of a good time, rrright?

"But, really, before I get into that, I have to say, that so-called fashion show you just witnessed? Holy Crikey! If you want to slink around in a boozy orange crushed velvet jumpsuit with a fake leopard collar and a fake leopard waistband and some kind of gummy bear cop ankle monitor, you go right ahead, you cruise ship stooges! But don't come near my wardrobe. No way am I going out to dinner looking like I escaped from (1) the prison issue of *Vogue*, or (2) a yacht!"

Jane rose from the speaker table and approached the author. "Oxford, could we hear some details about the tell-tale signs of someone cooking meth in their kitchen?"

"Cool your coconuts, Jungle Jane. I'm improvising."

"OK. Well, please try and stick to your topic," Jane said as she returned to her seat at the panel table.

Oxford clapped her hands together. "Now back, Baby, back to our topic! Drugs and pies. If you see fumes coming out of your neighbor's pies, that's a clue! Got that, Bo-Peep?

"And drugs? Well, it isn't just about being potty over Vicks VapoRub, is it? It could be guns or porn. It could be stamps! Or love!

"Now which of those four would you rather I talk to? I mean talk about. Well, of course I'm going to talk about addiction to love," Oxford said, grinning at several audience members.

"So, love. Well, I speak from personal experience. I am addicted to love personally, based on a whole lot of experience!" Oxford started pounding her chest with her fists.

Jane threw another imploring look at Sam that begged to ask, "What is going on? with Oxford?" But Sam appeared to be going to great lengths to disappear by locking her neck between her knees.

"What does that mean? To be addicted to love?" Oxford was pacing the stage and waving her arms at stunned audience members. "It means you are totally hot! hot! hot! for the Man with the Tattoos!

"I mean you can bake four and twenty black birds in a pie for all those golfers stuck up to their necks in their sand traps, but what about pies for those East Coast Republicans and their lineage? What are you going to give them? Cream pies? For Pete's sake! Are you crazy?

"And what about pies for those conservative Midwestern Catholics and their rosary beads?! Are you going to dump worm burners in their pies? Holy Smokes!

"Look at my sister over there, excavating under her chair. She must be turning purple. She's wanting to drag me and her pies and her duffers out of the rough and into the ocean! She thinks I'm putting one foot in my mouth, saying something, taking that foot out, and then putting in the other foot. When all I did was put three of her golf balls into my kisser!"

Sam stood up abruptly to bring her sister's spectacle to a close...or else strangle her. "Oxford, why don't you say a few final words about the meth?"

"The meth?" Oxford shouted. "I've been to the Meth!" and she began yodeling "Celeste Aiiiida!! Forma Diviiiina!!"

People were standing up startled and looking for the exit. Others spoke loudly among themselves, and several cruise ship passengers started to heckle Oxford.

"You're a nut case, Lady!"

"We didn't come here to listen to a horny fruitcake!"

Oxford seemed bewildered by the blowback. "Does anyone have any questions?" she asked.

"Yah! What size handcuffs do you wear?"

"Someone call 911!"

Sam turned to look at the audience. Half the people looked ready to kill; the other half looked as if they needed a sedative, quickly. Many faces were pink chunks of watermelon; other faces were staring in shock like white blobs of whipped cream piped on top of necks.

If Sam's lucrative catering accounts with the Yacht Club and the Golf Club did not evaporate into thin air after her sister's scorching performance, Sam would forever dedicate her life to God. If, if, if...it was time to get Oxford off the stage.

Jane scanned the crowd before her. How did this ever happen? She stood up and walked around the table to escort Oxford away. Sam joined them and they succeeded in convincing the author it was time for a break.

21

JULY 20, 2022
Revisions

"Hold it a minute, Sam!" Oxford was yelling from her bedroom. She had returned to her rental cottage after Jane and Sam pulled her off the "Drugs Are Us" panel.

Although she crashed for a twenty-minute power nap, her mind was in a fog. She needed a cup of tea. Something to bolster her before the Four Musketeers showed up whining and demanding changes to her book.

"Do you want any tea before you head to Ferguson Mountain, Sam?" Oxford asked as she added water to the kettle. "If you leave soon, that should give you enough time to drop our surprise little bomb on the mountain guys' house while they're on their way to St. Frewin's Island. And then you can get back to the island in time to join us for the charades party tonight."

"Oxford, I refuse to deliver any bomb to anybody until we talk about what happened to you at the panel this morning."

"What do you mean? I don't remember a thing," said Oxford, the tea kettle shrieking along in the background.

"You're joking, right?"

"No. Maybe that's not a good sign. But what are you talking about?" She poured her hot water.

"My God, Oxford. You flipped from the very first sentence. Everything that came out of your mouth was utter nonsense or total insanity."

"Oh boy.... Let me think a minute. OK...I had the usual for breakfast. Then I drove to the Town Hall. We got ready for the panel and I was about to go on stage...and then. OK...wait."

"I knew it!...It was the candy, wasn't it?" Sam said, rolling her eyes to the skies.

"That's right. I told you my throat was dry and you handed me those candies. And we didn't really know what they were. Let me check if I have any left in my bag."

"Don't bother. I opened one just as you were about to make your presentation this morning. Those candies are psychedelic sweets from Sacred Valley Boomers! Whoever that is. "

"Well, there you go," said Oxford. "And don't forget who handed them to me, Sam."

"How crazy candies got into the Town Hall is beyond me. I'll ask the Town Office later on. I've got to get going to Ferguson Mountain. But you should call Jane soon and tell her to grab the rest of those candies at the Town Hall so no one else goes off the deep end. Maybe she can get them tested."

....

"Hey there, Oxford," Random and Jamie greeted her together as they marched through the front door with Turk and Chummy close behind. The two younger men looked around inside, swiveling their hips and holding their arms out wide. "Huzzah, huzzah! This place is great! Island living. Very sexy...."

Just the lines these lean, wily bucks would come out with. "I don't know about that," Oxford said. "Did you have a good ride over on the ferry?"

"Great, just great," Random answered as he looked around the interior.

She led the four of them to the kitchen table in her summer rental. They all sat down. She was about to offer them a beverage when Turk heaved his shoulders up and lowered his head.

"So, Oxy, like I told you," Turk began, "we wanna buy a shitload of your books so long as you tighten up the language some, you got that?"

Oxford looked straight at Turk and lowered her head to meet his. "Yes, sir. You just tell me what's bothering you, and we'll fix it. No problem."

"OK. So, basically, Chummy and I don't really consider ourselves dumpy old guys with pot bellies. We're more like, you know, Ronald Reagan...or Pierce Brosnan, with nice brown tans from the beaches in Barbados. And we don't wanna sound like we don't know how to speak the King's English, or the President's English, or whatever it is."

"I think I can fix all that," Oxford assured him.

"And maybe you gotta add more tatts to our bodies," Chummy suggested. "Wha' do you think?" he said, looking at Jamie and Random.

"Sure," Random said. "Easier to do a tattoo in a book than on our skin."

"So do you guys want me to cover you with nude babes and anchors and roses, or special words? Here's some paper and pencils...each of you write down whatever you want me to plaster on your flesh."

"Great," Turk said, cracking his knuckles. "Now the next step is our intelligence. You gotta ramp up our smarts and cut anything that makes us look stupid or silly. All that's gotta come out." He made a knife-like slicing gesture with his hand.

Oxford gazed at the men, suspended in her thoughts. "I guess that extends to the chapter where I wrote that Chummy's boys probably aren't busting out of any Speedo size charts."

She looked at Chummy. "I bet you didn't like that."

"You're catchin' on fast, Honey." Chummy smiled at Oxford, probably for the first time. She tried not to count how many thousands were missing in his million-dollar smile.

"OK. This all sounds doable," Oxford said. "I can probably work on this over the next day or so and email you a revised draft from the internet cafe on shore. How's that sound?"

"Hang on. Not so fast," Turk signaled for her to sit back down. We came all the way out here for serious business. We'll wait while you make those changes, and then we'll get into the deeper stuff."

"Well, I'm sorry, but I have a party I'm going to tonight, and I've got to get ready."

"In that case, we'll tag along. We'll go as your friends from Lincolnville. You don't need to say more than that. And then we'll finish up when we get back here later."

"Later? You're coming back here? What for?" Oxford said. She could feel her face knotting up.

"Darlin', we gotta work with you on stuff like your dialogue. It's all over the fuckin' map. And we don't like how you drift into trite language." Turk made it sound so obvious.

"Yah. Plot structure's for the birds, too," said Chummy. "You gotta lotta dead ends in crucial sections."

Oxford told herself to just suck it all up, because ultimately, she was going to soak these bad boys in their own grubby hubris.

"Are you forgetting the undercover cop angle?" Jamie asked Turk.

"Son of a bitch, that's right. Listen, Oxy, you gotta scrub all mention of us as undercover cops. We didn't tell you that. So I don't know where that's comin' from."

Oxford looked at each of their faces, first from the left, then from the right. *Were they trying to protect their undercover identity? Or were they* really *felons? The Four Meth-e-teers?!?*

"Come on, you guys...I've got to have creative license here to spin a story with some guts and muscle."

"Sure, sure," said Turk. "We get it. Just not on our time. No wiggle room there. Do what I say."

22

JULY 20, 2022
Charades

Oxford handed Jane the rest of Oxford's Town Hall funky candies while they were in the kitchen at Konstantin Balankoff's main summer house, preparing a nibbles platter for the charades party that evening.

"Sam said she's going to ask the Town Office about these sweets she found at the Town Hall. Maybe you should chime in as well, Jane. If you open one up, you'll see it's a psychedelic candy. Of all things! On St. Frewin's Island."

"Oh, no! Is that what happened to you on stage this morning?"

"I think that's probably exactly what happened to me," Oxford said, frowning at Jane.

"I bet I know where these came from. And this explains the absolute garbage that came out of your mouth during the panel. I mean I'm not scolding you, Oxford...it was just so off the wall."

"So who put the suckers there, Jane?"

"I think they were probably left behind by the Attorneys for Hallucinogens...by mistake obviously. They held their Annual Meeting at the Town Hall in early July."

"Oh, God. Well, that must explain it. You really have to go over there first thing tomorrow and collect the rest of that candy."

"I will...definitely. Now, where is Sam and who are those guys you brought to the party?"

"Sam's taking care of some last-minute catering details. She'll join us in a bit. And those guys are friends of mine from back home in Lincolnville. They came over on the ferry for the day and decided to tag along to say hi. We won't stay too long."

Chummy stuck his head inside the kitchen and smiled at Oxford...as if to warn "No more details."

She grabbed the platter of bread, cheese, and grapes and headed into the living room. *What I haven't told Public Safety Officer Jane is that I'm now having second thoughts about my quartet of hairy friends. I mean honestly...are we about to play charades with a bunch of criminals? Meth cookers and dealers? Holy shit. I've got to warn Jane somehow....*

....

"So in charades," Jane was talking to Maggie Banner and her boyfriend, Ryan Young; Nathan Herinton, and Oxford and her guests. "To announce a film, you mimic a hand-cranked movie camera. For a book, you unfold your hands as if you're reading a book. For a song, you act as if you're singing into a mike. For a TV show, you sketch out a box with your finger."

Everyone looked around and nodded comfortably about Jane's cues. Oxford sprang up. "May I go first?" She wanted to try and telegraph her concerns to Jane through her charade choices. Maybe it would work.

Oxford cranked a movie camera. Gave the sign for one word. She began driving and moving forward as though in a car. She made the show of a hand on the horn, and then more driving. And she waved her arms as if to show the same concept far in either direction.

"My Mother the Car!" someone shouted.

"No way. She signaled a movie, not TV."

Oxford repeated her charades.

"Driving Miss Daisy!"

"Can't be. She said one word."

Oxford repeated the show of a driver, and then she moved an inch and repeated it again. And did that repeatedly.

"Is she trying to say something about traffic?"

"Taxi Driver!"

"No, what's that film about trafficking? Oh! It is Traffic! That's it! Traffic!"

Oxford yelled "Yes!" and tried to flick her head slightly in the direction of Turk and his crew while staring at Jane. But Jane did not catch any significance.

Oxford bent over in frustration and took a deep breath. "I want to do it again!"

"Fine by us," was the general reaction.

She next cued a movie, four words. Then she acted out a smooching...twice. Then aimed her finger gun and shot twice. She waited a few seconds and then repeated the sequence...two smooches; two shots.

"Kiss the Girls!"

Oxford shook her head no and acted out her clues again.

"Love and Death!"

"No, no, no. She said four words."

Oxford gave a hopeless sigh. She repeated her gestures...two smooches; two shots.

"Kissing....Kiss the Moon! But what about the gun shots?"

Oxford gave it one more try.

"Kiss, Kiss....."

Oxford shook her head yes! And pulled her hands apart to suggest stretching out the illusive title.

"Kiss, Kiss.....Kiss, Kiss, come on somebody. Help me out here."

"Kiss, Kiss, Bang....Bang!!! That's it!!! Kiss, Kiss, Bang Bang!"

Oxford jumped up and down, trying to catch Jane's glance...trying to use mental telepathy to hint at the Ferguson Mountain gang. Nothing from Jane.

"Give me one more shot!" Oxford yelled. Her four visitors were starting to squirm a bit uncomfortably.

"One more shot, Oxford," Turk said, "and then we're driving you back to your cottage."

Oxford seized the chance. She signaled a song, three words. She encircled her neck as though tightly with her hands, then let go and gently began making downward motions with her hands.

"What the fuck?" Chummy said.

"Is she strangling herself?" Random asked.

Oxford tried again. Slowly strangling herself, followed by the slow, gentle downward motion of her hands.

"She's killing herself and she's making gentle motions," Nathan blurted out.

"Killing....killing...To Kill a Mockingbird?" Maggie guessed.

"No. That's not a song. But killing...killing...I've got it!" Random shouted. "Killing Me Softly!"

Jane sat silent throughout the game. She had noticed something peculiar at the beginning of Oxford's charades. She was sitting at just the right angle, in just the right lamp light to see the tattoo on the left arm of one of Oxford's Lincolnville friends.

And what Jane was certain she was looking at was the number 8200 repeated over and over in a wave-like pattern on the man's left arm...as in Unit 8200, the molten core of the Israeli spyware industry. Unit 8200, which the FBI speaker had talked about at the top-secret gathering in Augusta months earlier. Amazing.

Jane felt a tinge of confusion. Oxford had waxed on about Jamie's tattoos, both in her book and in her mind-jarring presentation at the "Drugs Are Us" panel. Was this tattooed man Oxford's Jamie? Both in her book and as her real-life abutter?

And was Jamie somehow connected to the Israelis' infamous Pegasus and Phantom spyware? Or was this just a ball of coincidences and Jane was misinterpreting a generic tattoo symbol? But she reminded herself, in her profession, there were seldom coincidences.

23

JULY 20, 2022
Cutting the Cord

Sam drove slowly along the camp road and turned towards Random Thayer's house. She and Oxford hadn't even discussed what Sam would do if the building were locked tight. So much for intelligent planning. But caterers were always getting locked out of a mansion where they were expected to take over the kitchen and whip together a complete Beef Wellington dinner for eight, plus a sherry-infused trifle full of exotic creams and out-of-season fruits, all without a key to the premises. Successful caterers never got locked out twice. So Sam came prepared with her lock-pick set, in addition to her carpenter tool bag and a duffel bag holding her tools of destruction: hand clippers, pruners, loppers, wire cutters, and a garden machete.

What she would do if someone were there guarding the house, or if someone came upon her and proceeded to grab her neck and break it, Sam had not quite figured out.

She walked up to the front door and found it unlocked. What a bunch of doofuses these guys were. Did they think they were living in a bubble? She walked back to her car and brought her cutters and tool bag into the main room.

That's when she heard the toilet flushing. Flushing?
Someone flushing?
Shock! Panic!

She looked towards the bathroom door. She could feel the hooves of adrenalin slamming into her heart. Her normally cool head took a back seat.

Come on, Sam. Think. Think! Sam looked in her tool bag, pulled out some rope, ran to the door, and began tying the rope to the door knob. She could hear a second flush of the toilet, then running water. Not much time left!

Sam pulled the knotted rope tight and looked where to tie the rest of it taut. Right there. Thick electrical cables were draped and stapled along the bare, raw wall next to the door. Sam wrapped the rope around the cables and knotted the rope firmly. Whoever was in the bathroom began to open the door to leave.

"Hey...what's going on?" She could hear the man inside the bathroom calling out and shaking the door knob. "What is this?" he yelled. "Turk? Chummy?"

Sam ran back to her tool bag, pulled out her hammer and some nails and returned to the electrical cables. She took two of the many pieces of scrap wood lying around on the floor and quickly nailed one into the rough wood wall on either side of the electrical cables...covering the ropey ends of the knot, to make sure the rope knot stayed secure.

She then grabbed thin pieces of trimmed wood scrap scattered about and started shoving them under the bathroom door to wedge it tight.

"Who the hell is this and what the hell are you doing?" came bellowing out of the bathroom.

Sam wondered if she should respond to her captive. But she thought better of it. Say nothing.

Her captive felt differently. "Listen up! This is Alex Champus. You should know you're dealing with the FBI here! Open this door now, or you're under arrest!"

The FBI?! Sam realized she no longer had the leisure to take her time. He might figure some way to get out. He might arrest her!

She walked quickly towards the wall of electronic equipment in the room off to the side, which she had noticed the day she and Oxford first visited the house. Various little lights were glowing or blinking back at her from the black metal boxes and rectangular screens stacked four pieces high atop a metal table. It was a bit like a skimpy *NCIS: Los Angeles* set, hardly sleek, and much more haphazard. Still, business was up and humming. Which made Sam realize she should turn off the circuit breakers before she made any cuts.

Mr. Champus continued exhorting vehement, clamorous pronouncements about the power of Federal agencies and long-term imprisonment while Sam darted around until she found the electric panel. She opened it, flipped off all the breakers, and then brought her tools into the side room.

Sam took in the room's hardware a second time. The complexity of it all and the reality of the equipment, of what she was about to attempt, halted her momentum. What was she doing here? Was this insane? Was this more of Oxford's insanity?

Sam took an unusually deep breath. She was in up to her neck. Something had to give. Should she turn around and walk out the door? Just leave and forget this place?

She felt in her pocket for those ridiculous psychedelic candies she had saved from "Drugs Are Us." Here was a possible solution. Temporary. Take the dive and recover later? She inhaled to her core again. Time to take one? More than one? No better time. Do it.

She picked up her garden clippers and started snipping wires, cords, and cables. Where lines proved too thick or tough, she switched to her loppers or her machete. Cut. Cut!

Like shearing the rubbery mane of a monster...Cut!

Sam started yelling her head off. "Here I come, Medusa! Gotcha now!" CUT!

"Serves you right your hair got permed into vipers!" CUT!!

Sam transmogrified into an avenging Samurai, twirling her pruners and spinning around, swooping left and right with her machete. "Banzai, Baby!" CUT! CUT!

Blinking lights went dark; various beeps went silent. The curtain rose to *2001: A Space Odyssey*. The interstellar mainframe on Sam's star ship started misbehaving. High time to give those smooth-talking digital brains a lobotomy. "No more funny stuff on my space ship, Hal!" CUT! And SEVER!

Wire after wire, cord after cable. Sam switched to ripping out some lines by hand for a change of pace. It went quickly. Chefs and caterers knew how to work quickly with their hands. Especially when high as a kite.

The finishing touch came to Sam in a flash. She went into the kitchen and found a kitchen knife and the jar of Hellmann's. She pulled a gallon jug of orange juice from the fridge and returned to the electronics room.

Aiming for ventilation gratings and control panels, Sam poured and splashed orange juice over the equipment, as if soaking a giant metal pound cake with a zesty tropical syrup. Then she dunked the knife into the mayonnaise jar repeatedly as she spread the creamy goo in pale, greasy swirls over the face of the electronic great wall. Perfect glaze. Perfect ending.

"You mother-fucking son of a bitch! Let me out, now!!" Alex Champus was warming up to another colorful volley of screeching. "You're looking at twenty-five years in prison, easy, you cocksucker!"

Sam's compassion was touched. She walked over to the booming voice and spoke to the bathroom door. "Listen up, you whining imbecile. I'm leaving you a pie for when the Four Bozos return. Make sure they give you a piece for all your suffering."

"Fuck You, Evil Woman!"

Sam hissed back "Thankless bastard" and started scooping up her gear to stash it in her car. She returned to the house with one of the many open-face, blueberry pies she was supposed to deliver to the Yacht Club once she was back on the island. After looking into several kitchen cabinets, she found the right ingredient and doctored the blueberry pie to her satisfaction. OK. Time to head home for the charades party.

24

JULY 20, 2022
Major Intersection

Jane heard the knock on the door of Konstantin Balankoff's main summer house. "Israel! I'm glad you could make it. Come on in." They walked into the living room where everyone was taking a break from charades and tackling the appetizers. Jane made the introductions.

Then she asked Oxford to join her in the kitchen. Random trailed behind them, forcing Jane to refrain from peppering Oxford with questions about Jamie's 8200 tattoo. They made small talk instead. After dithering a few moments over half-empty plates of appetizers, Jane returned to the living room. She noticed Israel talking to Jamie.

"So how's life going on Ferguson Mountain?" Israel said.

Jamie had a confused look on his face. "I'm sorry. Have we met before tonight?" he said to Israel.

Turk, Chummy, and Random turned their heads towards Israel.

Was it Jane's imagination, or did Oxford's Lincolnville pals seem to freeze in that moment? Her brain was crowded with hesitant questions. *What did Israel just say about Ferguson Mountain? So are these guys Oxford's infamous mountain abutters?? And possible meth cookers? And Israel knows these guys? How does he know them?*

That quantum instant in time when everything becomes tense and lethal was nose-diving straight at the charades party. Like those frozen micro-seconds before a fight breaks out, or someone pulls a gun, or a dog attacks, or a wife sees unknown, lacy female bikini pants shot through with peekaboo holes come tumbling out of the sleeping bag her husband used last weekend on his camping trip with the guys....

That kind of moment in time was poised to seize Jane's guests when Samantha Lloyd knocked and walked into Konstantin Balankoff's summer house.

"Whoa, whoa, whoa! If it isn't our wild and crazy abutters. What are you doing here?" Sam called out as she caught Turk in the act of plunging a triangle corn chip back and forth in a bowl of guacamole to forklift half a cup of dip.

"Look at you!" Sam said, laughing out loud and lightly grabbing his wrist. "There you go again! You are such a big dipper, Turk. We need to have a talk about party etiquette."

Everyone stared at Sam. In a few sentences, she had obliterated their tense and lethal moment, had broken the uncomfortable spell, and answered the unasked questions, all without realizing any of it.

Turk yanked his paw from Sam, stuffed his fistful of guacamole into his mouth, and said to her, "You're total batshit, woman." He stood up, and brusquely motioned for Jane to join him in the pantry off to the side of the kitchen.

In the dark space between wall-to-wall cupboards, Turk leaned like a wild animal towards Jane, looking as though he might sniff her. "I think I know what you're thinking. We know you're on the federal anti-corruption team. We've been keeping track of you. And you need to know we're part of that team."

Turk's startling words rained down on Jane like rubble coated in syllables. She summoned her composure and managed a dispirited smile...no twinkle in her eye. She punched back at him verbally.

"And I now realize you're the gang next door to Oxford Monteith on Ferguson Mountain. And not some pals from Lincolnville. But why should I believe that you're on the anti-corruption team? How do I know you're not really up there on the mountain spinning cotton candy all day long?"

"How about the name Harriet Buxton? Does that satisfy you?" Turk said.

"Harriet? What's Harriet got to do with you?"

"Her Human Resources office orchestrated our crystal crib on Ferguson Mountain for the DEA. Arranged the house purchase, made it look like a meth lab to attract the drug world. Her staff planted the articles on the web to give us an internet history as burglars and felons."

"You're kidding! Like in Oxford Monteith's book...."

"Sort of."

"Are you the ones with the Phantom cyber-surveillance equipment?" Jane was reeling, but trying to make sense of Jamie's 8200 tattoo she had seen earlier.

"No comment," Turk growled.

Jane could see how quickly he might rip someone's throat out. She wished she had a muzzle she could offer him.

"OK. I know the Phantom stuff is all hush-hush. But you're telling me you're the good guys, and Harriet helped you stage the whole undercover scene?"

"You heard me, Honey."

"Don't call me Honey," Jane said. "That's not appropriate. So what should we do about Israel? Do we question him right now?" Jane asked.

"No, let's sit tight. He should not have let on that he knew about us. Big Mistake. But we were already tracking him. And we haven't found anything incriminating on the cell numbers we have for him."

"More than one number?" Jane said.

"Yah, that's one way we know someone may be shady. They're using more than one phone. Capisce?"

"Sure, capisco," Jane said. "But, you know, maybe you don't have all his cell numbers."

"Are you trying to make my job harder?"

"Forget it. What about Israel's safety?" Jane asked. "There's no way he was supposed to know you, or that you're from Ferguson Mountain. So in effect, he's just blown his cover as a member of the corrupt crew. He could be in danger now. I think we should do something about that."

"Look, let's keep this simple. No one but present company heard what Israel said. But just to be safe, we'll bring him to the mountain house with us. He can stay there until we get the FBI and DEA up from Boston to interview him about his role in the corruption."

Turk could read Jane's hesitation. "We're Federal undercover agents, for Christ's sake. How much safer could Israel be?"

"Let me explain this to Israel, OK? I need to assure him he's not in any danger from anyone."

"Go ahead," Turk said. "I'm heading back into the living room. But don't take too long. We have to leave soon."

....

Jane waved Israel in towards the pantry so they could talk with some privacy. "Israel, I know this is going to sound pushy, but please bear with me. Those four guys from Ferguson Mountain...how do you know them?"

"Do you mind if I don't answer that, Jane?" Israel said.

"What's that supposed to mean?"

"Look. I fucked up. I don't know why I did. I shouldn't have let on that I knew where those four guys are staying. I don't know what's going to happen now."

Israel was scraping through his hair with both hands. "I can't go into details, but I'm terrified other people are not going to be happy I goofed. They're liable to do whatever they want with me if they find out."

"OK. Listen, Israel. You're going to be safe. These mountain guys are actually Federal undercover agents. You can go with them to Ferguson Mountain. They'll protect you until someone from the Boston FBI and the DEA come to interview you. The more you cooperate, the better off you'll be. They won't let anything happen to you. You can relax, OK?"

Jane had to talk the talk. She had to believe this was, at least temporarily, the solution to the deathly snag Israel had created for himself. She raced through in her head what Turk had just told her. He knew Harriet! Of course Harriet had pulled together the honey pot on the mountain...to lure in the drug trade...so the FBI and DEA could then catch any corrupt cops trying to infiltrate the masquerading meth cookers. How could Turk's explanation not be legit? How else would he know Harriet Buxton?

....

By the time Jane cleaned up at Konstantin's main summer house and returned to her own home, she had framed all the questions she hadn't had time to ask Israel before he left with the Ferguson Mountain men. How did he get caught up in the corruption in the first place? Why? Who were the bosses? Of course the Feds would grill him officially, but Jane wanted to hear it from Israel for herself. All she could do now was to go to bed worried. Worried about Israel's safety, worried about the truth, worried about how all the pieces that came tumbling out tonight would fit together.

25

JULY 20
Cabin Fever

"Hey! Hey!! Let me out!!" Alex Champus began hollering wildly and pounding on the bathroom door when he heard the men entering the house. "I'm stuck in the fucking bathroom!"

"Jesus Christ," Chummy said to Turk as they walked towards the yelling. "This is the kind of flimsy muscle the FBI sends us for compliance oversight shit? How could the joker get stuck in the can? And why don't the lights work? Random, Jamie—flashlights, now!"

Once they had flashlights, they saw the rope contraption Sam had created to imprison Champus inside. "What the fuck?" Turk said as he looked at her handiwork. "Random, Jamie, get a knife quick."

Turk scowled at Israel who had accompanied them back to the house. "You go sit down and don't ask any questions until I have time for you."

Jamie went into the kitchen and came back with a knife. "You know...there's a blueberry pie sitting on the counter in the dark."

"I don't give a fuck about blueberry pie! Somebody cut this rope and get Champus out of there," Turk said. "And Jamie, go check the breaker panel and get us some lights back." Turk then headed for the kitchen.

Chummy and Random rescued Champus and they caught up with Turk in the kitchen. The lights came on when they flicked the switches. Alex Champus related what had happened—his imprisonment, the female voice, the insane shrieking about Greek goddesses and space ships, the pie.

Random and Chummy looked at the pie, then looked at Turk. They all had the same thought at once. No one brought them goodies except Oxy's crew. The bitches.

Jamie walked into the kitchen. "Boss, you gotta come see this. We've got a major disaster in the control room."

"Nobody go near that pie," Turk shouted. "I want that preserved as evidence if we need it for some reason. For all we know, these witches are out to poison us."

The four mountain men headed for the electronics room.

Champus stayed behind in the kitchen. Turk the Jerk couldn't tell him what to do. Champus was the FBI. He was starving. And that freaking woman said he could have a piece of the pie. So he, the FBI, was going to have his pie.

He got a fork and plate and dug out a hunk of pie onto the plate. He started shoving pieces into his mouth. Then he began gagging...and screaming.

And the mountain men began screaming.

....

What am I going to do about all this while I'm stuck out here on St. Frewin's Island? Jane was fretting at 50 miles an hour the next morning. *Who can I hash things over with who isn't corrupt? Could I talk to Helen Orbeton? She's our office receptionist, for crying out loud. She can't be corrupt. But can I be sure?*

Her office phone rang.

"Thought I should check in and see how you're doing, Jane," said Finn Gallinen. "I'm on the mainland today for chores."

"Oh, Finn. You're just the person I need to talk to," Jane said with relief.

"Well, why don't I catch the ferry and swing by your office so we can catch up?"

He's been vetted...they told us so. And at this point, I almost don't give a damn. I've got to let off steam about Israel's situation. And Konstantin is wandering in the oceanic ozone today, so Finn's my lucky guy.

"Sounds good, Finn. If you can pick me up, we can go to lunch at the pub."

"OK. See you around 12:30."

....

Jane raised her hand to catch the waitress's attention. "Hi there. Thanks. Could I please have more tartar sauce?" She looked down at her fried clams and back up at Finn.

"Whenever I see you eating, Jane, you're eating fried clams. Or something equally saturated in fat," Finn said matter-of-factly.

"Hey, mind your own plate. I live in the Deep Fried Capital of the State, and I like to celebrate that fact, OK?"

"OK."

It amazed Jane that she might actually be warming to Finn's factory-made persona. He was pure, out-of-the-box American male, and she was starting to see the advantages to his unemotional, level stance towards life.

They ate their lunch while Jane filled Finn in on the Ferguson Mountain group and how Israel surprised everyone by knowing about the mountain men.

"Oh, right. Those guys," Finn said.

"I'm really scared for Israel. I don't know what will happen to him if the corrupt members of our force realize he's blown his cover as one of them. At least, that's what I think is going on. Israel says his life is now in danger. And I'm not going to challenge him on that."

"Jane, first of all, we should update Harriet. She'll know how to handle Israel's situation."

"I can do that."

"No. I'll take care of it. I need to talk to her about some other stuff, too," Finn said.

"Uh, speaking of which, could I ask you about something? It's about your recent meetings in Augusta. Storm Nosmot says he saw you up there quite a lot in the past month or so. Have I missed out on any anti-corruption training? I'm probably being too nosy...."

"Oh...that. Not a big deal. Harriet wanted to talk about Catunk Isle and how everything is going out there. It's the first time a PSO has ever been assigned to that island, and she wanted some experienced officers to go over various procedures with me about island policing. Nothing to get yourself worked up about, Jane."

"Sorry for poking into that...I'm the insecure type sometimes," Jane said. *But was he telling her the truth? And wait a minute. Did I hear him say 'Oh, right. Those guys.' when I mentioned the Ferguson Mountain men? Is that what Finn said?*

....

Finn took a slight detour to get gas on the way back to Jane's office. Jane waited in the car while he went into the package store to pay.

While Jane sat there, she turned to look around in Finn's car. A blazer lay crumpled on the floor behind the driver's seat. *That jacket's too nice to be left on the car floor. Men! So often so messy...must be a chromosomal thing.*

She stretched to pick up the jacket and hung it over the back of Finn's seat. *What's this?* Three cell phones were on the floor of the back seat where the jacket had been. *Three?*

Jane pulled her phone out of her bag and took a picture. *Why am I doing this? Why three cell phones? What can this mean?* She rushed to throw Finn's jacket back on top of the cell phones...and remembered Turk's comment at the party about people owning several cell phones. *Am I listening to my paranoia again? Am I being overly suspicious?*

Finn opened the car door and sat down. "OK. I got hold of Harriet on the store phone. She says I should go bring Israel home. She doesn't think it's necessary to put him through the ringer with the Feds just because he knew about the Ferguson Mountain gang."

"But how could he know about them? What does that imply? Is he part of the corrupt network or not? And is he now in danger for blurting it out? And why shouldn't the DEA and the FBI interview him?" Jane asked.

"Well, Harriet thinks whatever Israel said, it's not as if it got broadcast to the rest of the world. He was just at your party. So what? She doesn't want to attract more attention to him. She wants the corrupt group to keep on trying to accomplish whatever their next big move is...so the Feds can then cast a wider net...that's her thinking."

"I don't know, Finn. I don't know what to think. I guess we have to follow her instructions. But I'm not going to rest easy."

"Sounds just like you, Jane," Finn said with a laugh.

26

JULY 21
Seeing the Light

After lunch with Finn, Jane was on the phone to Turk. It rang and rang. Finally, on the ninth ring, someone picked up.

"Hi, Turk? This is Jane Roberts. May I speak to Israel Tenner?"

"Saints preserve us," Turk said. "Is this one of the estrogen monsters from the coast?!" he bellowed into the phone.

"Jeez, Turk. What's all that? I just want to speak to Israel."

"You listen to me, Missy PSO. I know what you and your girl friends have been up to. And we're going to flatten all three of you with the full force of the law."

My God. This guy is a seething human Brillo pad. "Turk, I have no idea what you're talking about, so cut the threats. May I please speak to Israel?" Jane said.

"*Cut* the threats? Oh, darling, that's rich. You are fucking witty." Turk turned towards Israel. "Get over here, kid. Your mama's on the phone."

"Israel...is that you?" Jane asked.

Israel walked to an empty room with the phone in his hand. "Jane...I'm so glad to hear your voice. It's a shit storm over here. You wouldn't believe it. All of these guys' electronic equipment—incredibly complex stuff—has been gutted...chopped up...dead. Turk is totally ballistic."

"Oh my God…electronic equipment? Complex? Could it be the Phantom equipment?" Jane guessed aloud. "No, wait…. You didn't hear me say that."

"That's the least of my worries, Jane. I'm sorry if I sounded like a wimp at your party. You've probably started to figure things out. What am I going to do if the rotten apples on the force come for me? I haven't told you guys much of anything, but the creeps don't know that."

"Can I ask you a few questions, Israel? Or do you still refuse to answer?" Jane said.

"Jane, you're killing me. I love working with you. But I've been compromised by all this shit. And the ridiculous spin on all of this is that the corrupt gang wanted to get hold of the Phantom system for their own use."

"Oh my God! How?" Jane said.

"I can't tell you that, Jane. But now this whole god damn operation is a moot point. Everything is kaput. There is no spyware left on the mountain for anyone to get their hands on. But the creeps won't let this slow them down—you wait and see. Which means my life is still on the line. What if they think I'm the one who sabotaged their goal? Don't let anyone know what's going on, Jane. Please don't tell a soul."

"Israel, maybe you're exaggerating? Finn and I both received clearance from Harriet Buxton's office. So I've gone over everything with him. In fact, he came by for lunch today and we discussed your plight. He called Harriet and she thinks you should come home. Her advice is not to make a big deal out of what happened."

"Jane! What are you saying? Finn? What proof do you have that he isn't also corrupt?"

"Look, the FBI explained that both Finn and I were too new to be corrupt. In fact, the FBI and the DEA teamed us up to help fight the corruption scheme."

"But look at all of us, Jane. I'm new, too. Like you and Finn. But the bad guys found their way to me and forced me to become a part of their group. So how can you be sure Finn is safe to talk to? What if he's already corrupted? You really don't know for sure, do you?"

Jane thought of the recent, odd things about Finn...Storm saying he had seen him in Augusta for several days, yet Jane wasn't included. The extra cell phones in Finn's car....and did Finn already know about the Ferguson Mountain gang?

But where would that put Harriet on the game board? Jane was simply not comfortable imagining Harriet at the heart of a major corruption scheme within the Maine State Police. Harriet Buxton? The formidable Head of Human Resources corrupt to her core? That would be like, well, like eating steak smeared with toothpaste. No! Harriet had sat there with Maxwell Dunham, the New England DEA chief, and explained the whole problem to Jane and Finn. Harriet had to be clean.

"Look, Israel. Let's not waste our time going round and round on this. I'll let you go for now. I just wanted to be sure you were OK. Hang in there. Things will calm down in a few days. First Finn will get you back to St. Frewin's safe. Let me know what ferry you're coming back on, OK? You can talk to the DEA and FBI once you're home. One thing at a time."

"OK, Jane. I appreciate you trying to look out for me."

....

Shit. Israel's paranoia is now my paranoia. But let's look at the facts. That's the dispassionate approach, right? Professional. Sensible. Not always my approach, but here we go.

For months, it had irked Jane that Human Resources, aka Harriet Buxton, had not involved Jane in interviewing candidates for the post of Assistant to the Public Safety Officer on St. Frewin's Island. Presumably Human Resources and Harriet Buxton hand-picked Israel Tenner and that was the end of that.

And when Jane had not been able to reach Israel on his cell phone in Vermont at one point, she could not locate a single phone number for all those wonderful relatives he spent Christmas with in Vermont. What did that mean?

It meant something was not right and Israel was not entirely who she thought he was, though she tended to agree with him that he wasn't safe now. Most of all, Jane was beginning to suspect Harriet might have a role in Israel's present dilemma. Jane felt a wave of enlightened panic bubbling up inside her...Harriet could be guilty. Maybe Harriet was guilty. What had seemed so impossibly far-fetched earlier in the day now had its own logic. Eating steak gravied with toothpaste was not so far-fetched after all. Jane felt a knot building in her stomach...Prime Rib with Beurre au Crest coming right up.

....

"Turk, this is Jane Roberts."

"My, my. If it isn't the estrogen monster again! What makes you think I should keep talking politely to you on the phone, rather than swim right over to your fucking island and wring the necks of you and your author and your catering buddy?"

"I still don't understand all this rancor, Turk."

"Yet, did Israel not tell you how some genie blew in here and decapitated very special, very important equipment—electronic spyware, to be exact—worth millions of dollars?" Turk hissed as he spoke. "And you're acting like you're totally in the dark about this fucking massacre?"

"Look. I'm really sorry to hear about your equipment. Sorry for you, the Federal government, the taxpayers, the FBI, the DEA, the legitimate members of Maine law enforcement, whoever. But I had no hand in the destruction, Turk. And it's your problem if you don't believe me," Jane said.

"All right. Just say what you have to say and then leave me alone for eternity, OK?"

"Turk, please listen. Do not let Israel Tenner out of your sight. Make him stay put until the FBI and the DEA arrive to interview him and get him to safety. "

"That's been our plan all along. Why are you boring me with this crap?"

"Because either Harriet Buxton or an officer named Finn Gallinen will try to convince you to let Israel go with Finn. And Finn is on his way right now to pick up Israel at your house. I'll say it again. Finn Gallinen is under instructions from Harriet to bring Israel home to St. Frewin's Island. But I'm telling you that would be a very bad idea, so don't let Israel go. OK? And please deliver this same message to Israel. He should not go with Finn Gallinen. Israel should stay with you. OK? I don't want to be talking about a dead man."

"Sounds as if you're not telling me everything, Jane."

She tossed a coin in her mind and it came down on sharing her concerns with Turk. Which she did...about the possibility that both Harriet and Finn were not straight players; were in fact, deeply involved in criminal activity.

Turk let out a huge sigh. "Fuzzy wuzzy, huh? Well, it wouldn't be the first time this kind of shit has dropped on my plate."

....

"Jane, Lieutenant Adderley's on the line. I'll put you through to him," Helen Orbeton said.

"Well, hello, Lieutenant Adderley. Good to hear your voice. Long time no talk," Jane said. Because she didn't know if she could trust him....

"I'm calling to put your mind at ease, Jane. You've worried enough about Israel. There's been a change of plans. He's going to sit tight with the men out on Ferguson Mountain until the Feds have a chance to interview him. So you can quit obsessing about your assistant. It's a waste of your time, OK? We need you to focus on all your regular work."

"Thanks, Lieutenant. I understand. And I appreciate your reassurances. I am really worried, but I'll get back to work, sir."

"Sounds good, Jane. Enjoy the summer...and your job." Adderley hung up.

Could she trust Adderley, even though he was romantically entwined with Harriet? He wouldn't lie to Jane, would he? Not Lieutenant Adderley....

27

DÉJÀ VU...JULY 22, 2022
Orion's Spit

Homicide Detective Storm Nosmot of Maine Crimes Unit-Central made one last call on the ferry terminal's public payphone before boarding the 8:30 PM water taxi to St. Frewin's Island. He hated making the call, even though part of him was relieved to be doing so. Jane Roberts, the island's Public Safety Officer, would have to be told, but at least it would come from Storm and he would be with her to help her through the tragedy awaiting them both.

The anonymous tip had been phoned in to MCU-Central two hours earlier.

....

Jane was stirring a pot of butterscotch pudding at a critical stage when the phone rang. She momentarily imagined not answering her phone, but that was never really an option. Not for a Public Safety Officer on a small Maine island with a year-round population of some 300 men, women, and children, where every home had a bottle of booze in the cupboard and a gun on the rack.

"Jane...Storm here. Have you heard any news tonight?"

"What do you mean by news? I'm in my nightgown, stirring a pot of pudding that's about to curdle. What are you calling me for this late?"

"OK...ah, I'm at the public dock on the mainland right now, and I'm getting the water taxi to St. Frewin's.

I'll see you shortly. And sorry, but you need to pick me up. This is work-related. I'll fill you in when I get there. And bring your big flashlight. Got to run."

Jane stared back at the phone as she heard him hang up. Now what? She had to get dressed? Pain in the butt! But at least she had a good half hour to finish with the pudding and clean up before meeting Storm at the water-taxi stand.

....

Jane got out of her truck and walked towards the town dock. It was past 9 PM, and all the soft evening light of late July had disappeared.

A vast, black cloak of silent velvet had descended upon the harbor, the cloak touching no one...its weight so close, but never felt...with small orbs of light pulsing tiny beams along the ocean's edge...from docks, garages, homes....

Jane saw Storm trudging up the wooden pier. He was a big man, always moving with ease as though he were walking on water. Not that he was Christ. More like Noah or Moses with the flowing beard...approaching the world with a calm, level bearing. But tonight his head was down and he seemed tired.

"Hey there, Mr. Nosmot! I'm dying to know what's dragged you out here in the middle of the night."

"Jane...good to see you. Sorry about this unexpected visit." Storm opened his arms wide for a hug.

"I gather you're not here simply for a social call...no midnight charmer routine? After all, we know you're a happily married man."

"It's a lot worse than that, Jane. There's been a murder apparently. In a cabin at the end of Orion's Spit. Can you drive us there?"

"What? Who? How come you know about this and I don't?" Jane complained as they both got into her truck.

"An anonymous call came into MCU-Central about two and a half hours ago."

"Figures. I never get enough respect out here."

"Don't take it personally. The caller dialed 911 to report a dead body, so it got routed to me. No reflection on your abilities."

"Well then, I'm glad you're here. If it's a murder, I can always use the company." Jane gave him a bleak smile.

Storm said nothing. He could not bring himself to tell her. If he didn't say anything, she would hate him for it later. And if he tried to act as if he hadn't known, she would see right through it. Still, he sat there wordless.

Jane drove towards Orion's Spit. It was odd that Storm was unusually quiet, but she followed suit.

She thought back to the buzz now and then that would circulate about the cabin down on the point. The place belonged to the middle brother of the Tunny family, ne'er-do-wells who were known to throw game jacks and gash point screws on the road in front of their house. Flat tires for day trippers motoring by were the Tunny idea of fun. So was chaining young family members inside closets. But again, it was all just now and then...just rumblings.

Jane drove past the Tunnys' worn-out, multi-gabled heap that must have been a solid residence once upon a time, when adults were adults and worked hard to earn an island living. Nowadays, however, the Tunny offspring tended to let even simple, seasonal jobs at the island boatyard escape from their grasp. The sagging structural lines and worn, naked clapboards of their home and the spilled guts of rusted machinery and dead household appliances flung about the starving grass in the yard reflected the hearts and souls of the people who dwelled within, who clearly didn't give a damn.

The cabin was another building altogether. The cabin was special...notorious. A hangout where the middle brother and his buddies would gather and drink, especially during hunting season, or so Jane had heard.

She drove slowly down the narrow way, her truck jolting cock-eyed as she swerved to dodge potholes as wide as half the road. Then they saw the log structure in her headlights. She couldn't remember how she knew the way. She must have been down here at some point, but she had never been inside.

It was completely dark out...beyond dark. Black in the way rural Maine was on a moonless night. Too dark to tell if one's eyes were open or shut. Too dark even to feel the air or to take the next step with any confidence.

Jane turned off the engine. "So what do you say, Storm? Spooky enough for you?"

"If we use our flashlights, we'll manage." He felt helpless. He should say something...get it over with. But he couldn't.

They stepped out of the truck and started walking towards the cabin's front porch.

．．．．．．．．．．．．．．．．

Storm swept his flashlight like a wand around the cabin's main room...tracing wide circles of light over the log pole walls, looking for the reason the anonymous caller had dialed 911. Jane did the same. She could feel a night breeze blowing freely through the cabin.

Jesus Christ.

Perhaps the fresh circulation was helping to flush out the stench to some degree, but Jane wouldn't be surprised if she passed out within seconds.

Jesus Christ.

If not from collapsed lungs, then from the extreme effect of pair upon pair of dumbfounded eyes staring down at her from the cabin wall in the thin roaming beam of her flashlight. Eyes set in time...set by death...so many haunted, grieving gems. And the incisors, all the little fangs, jutting out like ivory punctuation marks in the gruesome, withered smiles.

Jane's sanity was urging her to leave immediately. But curiosity made her hold her flashlight steady to take inventory of the cruel spectacle before her...to identify what kind of animal head, in each instance, was nailed to the wall....

"Oh God, Storm. Raccoon, skunk, squirrel...."

No discriminating between wild and domesticated...*a cat!*, turkey, deer, fisher, mink, chipmunk. Head after head, walls of wildlife voodoo.

"What is all this?" Jane grimaced as she spoke. "Trophies? Shockers? Conversation starters?"

Storm hacked hard to clear his throat. "I'd say it's a hunter's decapitated harem."

"What are you thinking?" Jane looked to Storm for some kind of anchor, some kind of sanity.

"I'm relieved to see it's only animal heads. We're OK, Jane. Just take a deep breath."

"Are you kidding? My nose hairs are falling out. I'd spray them with bleach right now if I didn't plan on using my nostrils again."

"I hear you. Let's just take a look in the rest of the cabin, and then we can leave. Maybe this has all been a prank...at least on the part of our anonymous caller."

"OK. I'll look to the right. You check out the left. Does this goddamn hut have any electric lights anywhere?" Jane griped as she walked towards a small alcove off to the side.

She stepped into the alcove and automatically felt on the wall for a light switch, while aiming her flashlight into the interior. Her left hand slapped something that felt like fabric...damp fabric? Something solid and long and slick. And she was vaguely aware of a tackiness under her left sneaker.

She swung her flashlight to the left. A leg in pants? "Storm! It's a body!"

Jane heard the sticky sound of both her shoes, the tug of something gummy as she shifted and aimed her light higher. Storm had reached her side. They both looked upward.

They felt the shock slam into their hearts, and slam again. They felt the rush of cold panic in their limbs, cold panic they had been steadfastly taught to ignore in training seminars. Textbooks and lectures proved useless as Jane and Storm looked up at the human being they knew well, who was now slaughtered beyond comprehension.

28

AUGUST 2022
Slab

Three weeks after Storm and Jane investigated the anonymous tip about the murder in the Tunny cabin at Orion's Spit, Jane drove herself up to Augusta. She hated the drive to Augusta, and now she hated herself as well.

Alone in the car on Route 17 West meant too much silence and more psychic pain. More time to obsess on what she and Storm had experienced that night in the Tunny cabin...the stinging stench of the place...the initial shock of all those decapitated animals gaping down at them. And then the unthinkable—truly the worst night and nightmare of Jane Roberts' very ordinary life down to her foot on the gas pedal in this very moment.

But why repeat the torture? I should shut down my brain immediately and not go near the "replay" button. What was the perverse, sick point of "replay"? Really, what was the point?

Maybe the point was that it was impossible to refuse entry to the unimaginable, once it had landed in front of you.

....

Jane leaned over to embrace him gently and kiss the purified face of the dead. She gave him a kiss as if she were his sister, the kind of kiss she would have given him at Christmastime, to say I love you without any strings or expectations attached. And then she squeezed him tight, because she had to. Because it was forever.

She watched herself doing this, thinking how could it matter now that he was gone? But saying goodbye to your dead always mattered. It had to.

Christmas.

Oh, Christmas.

There would be no more for them together. There would be...but no. She could not dwell on the impossible now. She had lectured herself all the way up to Augusta. She was not going to cry, not in front of the State Medical Examiner, Dr. Andreas Kerner. He had been very kind when she called to let him know she needed to see the decedent one last time.

She wasn't going to cry. She would remember him as he was in the photograph someone gave her of the famous rescue mission she had missed on that beautiful day in July. There he is—smiling into the sun, covered in kittens, kayaking them all home to safe, dry ground.

"All I want to know..." Jane said to Dr. Kerner as she turned from the corpse, but she stopped and looked away from the doctor.

"All I want to know is," she lifted her head and tried again. "Did he suffer?"

"Jane, I'm very sorry. And I appreciate how important your question is to you. So...as reported on the crime scene paperwork, and as you and Storm observed that night when the team lowered the body off the wall hook, the victim's hands were unharmed, no defense wounds or signs of fighting off an attack. Nothing unusual there, yes?

"Yes, that's true. But all the blood...he was drenched in it. My shoes were drenched in it. The cabin floor...."

"As I reported to Storm Nosmot during our post-mortem review...." Dr. Kerner paused to silently question Jane with an inquiring glance.

"I know. I know. I'm sorry Dr. Kerner. I just couldn't attend. I know I should have been at the post mortem, but I just couldn't." Jane took a deep breath.

"As I was saying, we found evidence of a puncture wound on the arm where the victim was injected by needle, presumably before bodily violence occurred. I say 'presumably,' because we also found postmortem traces of the animal tranquilizer xylazine in the victim's system. It would not be logical to cut into a person so thoroughly and then administer such a drug afterward to induce sedation or coma, correct?" Dr. Kerner asked.

Jane looked up at him under the weight of her tears.

"That would be a waste of time and product. So concerning all the blood you encountered, Jane, I am quite certain our victim was in an altered and unaware state, all for the better, when the numerous stabbings occurred."

"Wait. Did you just say 'cut into a person so thoroughly'?" Jane asked. "I thought he was stabbed. His clothing was on him when we found him. I don't know what you mean."

"Maybe we should let it rest, Jane. You can read my report later when it's done."

Dr. Kerner brought his hands together and looked calmly at Jane. She stood there, trying to convince herself not to bend in the way that she knew she would. She was a Public Safety Officer. Knowing all the facts helped to solve a case. This, however, was not her case. It had not been assigned to Jane. Others had been tapped to collect and analyze the data of the homicide.

And that is why Jane intended to punish herself...to succumb to that perverse inclination in humans to thrash themselves with guilt and remorse by digging for information best left untold, best left to others to resolve.

"Could you elaborate, Dr. Kerner? Were the stabbings meant to kill him? Or did they seem intentionally brutal for the sake of brutality? I mean, I don't really want technical details or gruesome details. Maybe you could describe it in metaphors?"

"Jane, are you trying to torment yourself? If so, why?"

"Just use some metaphors, Dr. Kerner. I need to know."

"Yes. I understand. The need to know. All right. I suppose...I suppose one might say gutting a deer is what comes to mind. Do you know how that is done? Do you want me to keep going?"

"No, no. You're right. Let's stop there. I am punishing myself. I need to stop."

"I think that's a wise decision, Jane. I'm sorry to sound trite, but what is done is done. At this point, we have no control over the fact that this specific death occurred."

"But, Doctor, what you said means that whoever did this went to the trouble of putting the clothing back together again, so he looked, well, I guess you'd say, he looked whole when we found him. He was dressed."

"That would seem logical, Jane."

"Oh, God. It makes it all the worse...." Jane crossed her arms and held herself tightly. Then she let go.

"OK. Well...thank you for your time, Dr. Kerner. I should let you get back to work, and I really have to go...stuff to do at the office...."

Jane's awkward exit faltered. The crying melted her face. She said a quick goodbye and began walking towards the exit door, her shoulders shaking now and her head bowed.

She suddenly looked back at Dr. Kerner. "You know, it was all my fault. All mine." And she broke down in grief.

....

Later that day, as the pathology assistant pushed the mortuary trolley towards the refrigerated storage unit, the ID toe tag slipped off the cart. The orderly bent down to retrieve the fallen label. He thought about the body's name in life—Israel Tenner. It was an interesting name...or had been.

29

AUGUST 2022
Need to Know

Helen knocked on the door, opened it, and put the freshly made cup of tea on Jane's desk. She stood there without a word and looked at her PSO.

Jane's head was down on her folded arms on top of her desk. She didn't move. She didn't look up. But after three days, she was finally ready to speak. She raised her face, all red and puffy, like strawberry jam smeared across a white popover.

"Helen, when I find out who did this, I am going to kill."

"Jane...." Helen couldn't think what more to say. She knew better than to say anything.

"I am going to kill. And you're not going to try and talk me out of it or stop me," Jane added. She got up out of her seat and left the office.

....

The final homicide report from Maine Crimes Unit-Central on the matter of Israel Tenner came out in late August. Storm Nosmot felt he owed it to Jane to bring it to her in person.

"Storm, this is an insult to human intelligence," Jane said, flicking at the report in her hand. "How did Harriet get away with manipulating the facts to such a pathetic, absurd conclusion? Because, believe me, this report stinks of her input."

They sat at the Public Safety Office table, while Jane turned each page as if she were slapping someone's face. The homicide report pinned Israel Tenner's murder on one of the Tunny men, Fredly Tunny, based on his confession.

Apparently the Tunny brothers had heard all about Israel helping their niece Monica rescue some kittens out in the ocean earlier in the summer. The Tunnys obsessed and fantasized about the innocent event until they twisted it into Israel somehow trying to go after the girls in unsavory ways. And when the Tunnys got drunk, they berated their young niece Monica until she crumpled and told them what she knew they wanted to hear (false though it was, Jane was certain): Israel had tried to come after the girls several days later, though nothing ever happened.

So, the brothers anointed themselves their own posse anyway, went after Israel Tenner, and the middle brother, Fredly Tunny, killed him...according to Maine Crimes Unit-Central...and Harriet Buxton, Jane was sure.

"This is a mountain of shit, Storm. And I'm going to disprove it, all of it. I promise you."

"I'm on your side, Jane. If it's of any help," Storm said. She looked at him, her Viking colleague, solid as the granite that anchored St. Frewin's Island to the earth. She thought of the hours and hours they had spent together looking for Truth. Did any of that still matter? She wanted to believe him. But could she trust him?

....

Jane thought one phone call to Dr. Kerner would suffice for her inquiry. One simple, confidential phone call to ask about the blood samples taken from the crime scene where Israel was found...i.e., the Tunny blood versus Israel's blood...were both samples truly contemporaneous?

Dr. Kerner convinced Jane it would take a lunch meeting in Augusta to navigate through all the details...his treat. He didn't have to twist her arm. She was hesitant, but also vaguely curious about Kerner the person. What kind of individual chose autopsies as a career path?

....

"So, ya, ya, you ask if there was any time difference in the Tunny blood samples versus Israel Tenner's blood samples. And I will treat your question most confidentially. Unfortunately, I do not have a definitive answer for you, Jane," Dr. Kerner said as he aimed his fork into the pickled beets on his plate.

"The science in this area is broad, but not yet clinically or legally sound. Laboratories run tests on the hemoglobin in the blood or apply various chemicals or enzymes to the blood to detect differences in blood characteristics over time.

"They can analyze the molecular breakdown of various molecules and do studies in spectroscopy. And some researchers have focused on color changes in blood over time, and so forth. But truthfully, our profession does not yet have reliable instruments or methods to determine how long a blood sample has been in place."

Jane felt frustrated by the limits of forensic science coming up against island realities. "Dr. Kerner, did anyone fill you in about that cabin where Israel was found? It's not surprising Tunny's blood was present.

Apparently he's been cutting the fucking heads off of all kinds of poor animals and tacking them up on the wall like cruel keepsakes for quite some time. He's a very sick fuck, please pardon my language."

"Your word choice reflects your internal emotions, Jane. It is all very natural. No need to apologize."

"But if we assume any blood of Tunny found at the scene was the result of his hobby of decapitating animals, then trying to tie his blood to Israel's death is such an apples and oranges façade, it could be malpractice, no? I mean I'm not threatening you professionally or your findings, but how else are you and Homicide proving Tunny is responsible for Israel's death?" Jane watched Kerner cut into his runny rare steak and pour more ketchup on top.

"Jane, you are ignoring the obvious. Fredly Tunny confessed to the murder," Kerner said.

She watched him take a sip of his cranberry cocktail and shook her head. "In all confidence, Dr. Kerner, it's all…all…I'll use the word malarkey. Tunny was put up to it somehow…he's a scapegoat. Or, OK, maybe he assisted, but he was not alone. And that's what I've got to prove. But you can't tell anyone."

Jane leaned in towards Kerner. "I also don't believe the initial premise…that the Tunnys sat around stewing about Israel bothering their sister until the middle brother jumped up and decided to stab Israel to death. That's a sordid fairy tale!"

"Well, Jane, as they say in your business, you and your criminal investigators and homicide colleagues must prove the truth…marshal the evidence and facts of the case. My focus is the victim's medical history, the flesh and blood, and anything they can tell us under scrutiny."

30

AUGUST, LATER IN THE DAY
Till Drugs Do Us Part

On her drive back to the ferry, Jane drew up a list in her head of the next steps she would tackle...call Todd Chisolm, the lead crime scene investigator, and beg him to have his team look again for prints at the cabin...especially any prints that didn't match Jane, Storm, Israel, or the Tunny family and their close acquaintances. And Jane would make sure to have all those Tunny cronies fingerprinted for comparison.

Jane also called State Police headquarters in Augusta to request more information about the anonymous call to MCU-Central the night of Israel's murder. She was impressed when the office staffer faxed Jane a transcript of the anonymous phone tip some ten minutes after their call. Helen Orbeton brought it in to Jane's office.

Oh my God. Jane read the transcript twice. The caller knew. And Storm had said nothing that night...never said a word then or later.

The unknown caller (male) actually stated he thought it was Israel Tenner's body.

Jane got up from her desk and rushed outside. Her head was filling up with cotton and her cheeks, with blood. Her ears felt as if someone had slapped pounding mufflers on them. She knew this was anger and shock in a way she had never felt before. She had to keep moving.

She stomped two full circles around the building, expelling her rage with every step as Helen watched from the door. Jane returned to her office phone to dial Storm Nosmot. "Even keel, Jane. Even keel," Helen cautioned.

....

"You knew, Storm, and you didn't say a word!"

Storm remained silent, except to say "Jane, please...."

"Why didn't you tell me right off the bat?"

"Jane, I couldn't. I was shocked. I felt so awful, I didn't know what to do."

"So you said nothing."

"Right."

There was a long pause. "And you knew I would forgive you, didn't you? That ultimately, what else could I do, but forgive you. You were counting on that." Jane's heart sank. She hung up.

She bent her head and felt her tears falling from her cheeks onto a DEA bulletin cluttering her desk. What was the point of yet another fucking DEA dispatch about drugs? Her world was swimming in drugs and what they had done to Israel Tenner. The whole world was swimming in drugs.

Would it help to point fingers or assign blame in this global miasma? Would that make anyone feel better?

People could read all the bulletins officialdom wanted to issue...about drugs, the drug wars, the players, the money, the borders, the politics, the deaths. If anyone was asking Jane, all she could surmise was that profit trumped lives...in any century.

On the supply end of the pipeline, no one cared about the lives of drug users; on the receiving end, addicts were often incapable of caring enough about their own lives. And there wasn't much to be done about this intense, driven coupling, despite all the law enforcement, all the intervention, all the family efforts, all those bulletins.

Whether or not it was consciously deliberate, China today in the twenty-first century was managing brilliantly to boomerang the impact of the infamous Opium Wars back on the West. During the 1800s, Great Britain and others had flooded China with opium and all its destructive consequences...endless balls of opium made in India from rolling the dried sap of poppies into globes—like white globes of an all-white earth—countless bleached, dead earths—stored on endless rows of shelves reaching up to cathedral-ceilinged warehouses. An infinity of false bliss....

Wars and sweeping historical changes resulted. Whether all the chaos sprang from opium profits or free trade or the balance of trade or whatever economic struggle, Chinese addiction to opium bloomed.

Now it was China's turn for revenge—cosmically if not intentionally—with special thanks to its handmaiden, Mexico, the neighbor of the United States, the abutter, importing raw ingredients from China, and cooking up the illicit brews south of the border.

China and Mexico were power-washing the American population with addictive drugs. If this was crushing America, Americans were rushing in with mouths and veins wide open...to the point of no return every time someone dropped dead.

Jane Roberts had to have her own means to absorb the relentless pace of all these ruined lives. She had to digest the very idea of humans killing themselves with drugs by filtering the problem through a horticultural lens. She had to shield herself with vegetation.

Otherwise, she wouldn't have the chops to handle the deadly statistics.

Each person born was like a plant, and each plant was unique. Some plants flourished when coddled season after season. Some plants, though nurtured, grew thin and slumped. Other plants were simply plopped into the dirt and left to fend for themselves. And they thrived!

At times, plants refused to thrive or seemed to die off for reasons Jane, the gardener, could not always keep on top of...nutrient imbalance in the soil, microscopic worms in the roots, invisible fungi, too much water, not enough light, poor drainage, too many tortoise beetles.

So many variables. Even the most attentive, enthusiastic gardeners lost plants each year. Even the most loving, conscientious people lost a child or a spouse or a relative to drugs. Not everyone or everything on the planet would live to 100 years old, with low cholesterol and blood pressure, great bone density, money in the bank, love and laughter, and winning three Nobel Prizes.

Life wasn't like that. Each person, each plant, was unique. Variety. Jane had to accept that each person's own sheer existence encompassed that person's own knife edge—with some part of the edge inherently beyond the total reach of parents and society and the law. Otherwise the daily tragedies would be too hard for Jane to bear.

She would be the first to admit she had to rationalize drugs through gardening because she really could not bring herself to approach the problem up close. She thought of her compassion towards fellow humans as good enough, but not effectively compassionate enough to minister to drug addicts. Jane did not have the nerves and big heart to be a caregiver for the addicted. She was not a healer or a shoulder to lean on. She didn't have the patience. She did not want to have to pay attention.

It was easier for PSO Jane Roberts to look an underaged clam in the eye than an overdosed accountant slipping away on a park bench. Easier to chase a hound on the loose than to track down parents when their teenager was gone forever, thanks to a speck of fentanyl.

As for Storm and the here and now, Jane still didn't feel like she could trust him implicitly. She wanted to open up to him totally about Harriet and Finn, but she couldn't. She had voiced aloud her fury towards Harriet over the homicide report pinning Israel's death on Fredly Tunny. But that was all Storm had heard. So for now, maybe he and Jane were even on the score card of withholding truths from each other.

Maybe, though, just maybe Storm had enough remorse for Jane to muscle him into helping her with something specific. Something she wouldn't be able to accomplish on her own. She called him back.

....

"Sam, can you talk?" Jane said after she hung up with Storm and dialed Samantha Lloyd. "I'm really in a funk and need you to listen a few minutes. Can you?"

"Sure, what's up, Jane?" Sam, like everyone else on St. Frewin's Island, had heard about Israel's murder. Jane knew Sam would make the time to spare.

"Thanks. You know, I still can't reach Konstantin because he's swimming around in the Pacific. And everything about Israel is torturing me, Sam. You were there the night he blurted out knowing the Ferguson Mountain guys. Well, you walked in right after he spoke.

If only he had kept his mouth shut...." Jane felt as though she might break down again.

"Jane, I'm so sorry about Israel. We all liked him. And there's something I haven't told you about that day." Sam began slowly. "It may tie into the big picture, but I don't know."

"What?"

"Well, ah...Oxford and I cooked up a plan to destroy all this electronic gear those guys set up at the mountain house."

"Destroy it?! You were the ones? Whatever for? Are you crazy?"

"No, wait...just listen. See...Oxford figured out that those guys were tapping into our phones somehow and eavesdropping on our conversations. I mean that's not legal, Jane. Right? Oxford was absolutely furious."

"So you took it into your own hands to wreck the place? Millions of dollars of equipment?! That's insane, Sam! Why not call the police?"

"Well, Oxford figured they were the police, more or less. So what good would that do?"

"Shit. All of this citizen DIY activism is getting out of hand," Jane said.

"And to my surprise, Jane, I also had to lock some turkey of an FBI guy in the bathroom while I was at the mountain house. We had no idea he would be there. We knew the four guys would be visiting Oxford at the guest cottage she's been renting from Konstantin, and we thought that was everybody."

"An FBI guy?" Jane flushed. "Did he have a name?"

"Yes, something like Alec or Alex Champion...Champ something?"

"Alex Champus?!" Jane let out a wild laugh.

"You're laughing, Jane?" Sam said.

"I didn't think it would be possible right now. But yes, I guess I am laughing. Though it's a bitter laugh, Sam. I mean, you single-handedly butchered some very important, but illegal spyware. And in so doing, you inadvertently thwarted certain corrupt people from grabbing it for themselves. So that's a victory. But however the spyware fit into Israel's life...and death, nothing can bring him back now."

"I don't think I understand everything you're saying, Jane. Can we start with who this Alex Champus is?"

"Alex Champus is an FBI pain in the butt whose path has crossed mine in the past, always in a highly charged situation, it seems. I can't stand him, and I'm fairly certain the feeling's mutual."

"Well I left him hopping mad, and I left him a pie saturated with salt...so he's probably still on the warpath."

31

LATE AUGUST
Fredly

Why were prison interview rooms so uninviting? Jane knew it was a useless question. Doom and gloom were intentionally and strategically orchestrated to bear down on anyone being questioned in prison about a crime.

The walls and floor in this cubbyhole, the table and chairs, they were all the same muddy, swampish, rotted pickle color—with surfaces scarred and embedded with guilt that had seeped out of nerve endings for centuries.

Jane wished she had not had the brilliant idea to convince Storm to clear the red tape and snag her this face to face with Fredly Tunny. Next time, whenever that might be, for whatever reason, Jane would bring one of those tiny Maine balsam pillows to barricade her nose. As an antidote against whatever institutional ingredients were blowing out of the jailhouse air ducts...bleach? Barf? Bipolar BO? Lunchtime shit on a shingle?

The shuffling was the first sound Jane heard from her fake felon. Fredly Tunny tottered in slowly, with chains dragging from all his moving body parts, even his neck. The guard sat him down across from Jane.

"Ma'am?"

"Yes, Officer Crane."

"If there's any trouble, you just holler. I'll be right outside."

"OK, thank you."

The guard walked out the door and Jane was left alone with Fredly.

How she hated him. If he had anything to do with Israel's death, that was one strike against Tunny. For those poor dead animal heads adorning his cabin walls, that was another reason. And for harassing young Monica until she had to lie to avoid further emotional abuse from her older male relatives, that was the third reason.

Jane looked at Fredly's face. Such an agitated face...yellow, gray, scabbed...and slumped where drugs had gnawed into his facial muscles. Nearly gone for good were the attractive features of who he had once been. He was living proof of the simple truth: Drugs Are Weapons.

Jane also felt bad for Fredly. No matter how often she quit asking the questions, she would again ask the questions: Why did people chase drugs? What happened to them from the day they were born until turning five years old? Weren't those the first vital years when brains and abilities blossomed or not? Had their parents loved them and fed them and swooped them into the air to make them giggle? Did Mom and Dad keep them safe and warm and blow bubbles for them? Were there songs and dancing, books, playing hide and seek and cards and wiffle ball? Cookies for Santa?

Maybe a lot of nos for answers in Fredly's case? And as the rehab counselor at Jane's panel, "Drugs Are Us," had explained to the audience, scientists think a person's genes account for forty to sixty percent of the person's risk for becoming addicted. That's what Fredly was up against. On top of that forty to sixty percent range,

Fredly's gender and ethnic background might have also shaped his tendency towards drug abuse and addiction.

So there could have been half a deck of genie cards possibly stacked against Fredly's little embryo when he was only a tiny squirt floating around in his mother's womb. It was as though death itself—Fredly's own death—was already chasing him down in there, and he had no way out.

Once he was born, all the environmental factors and nurturing or lack thereof kicked in, so Fredly may have never had a chance to be anyone but the opioid-vein-packed individual he turned out to be. Jane was nearly ready to forgive him.

"So, you got a name?" Tunny was the first to speak. Jane resurfaced from her ruminations.

"I'm sorry, Mr. Tunny. I'm Jane Roberts, the Public Safety Officer on St. Frewin's Island. Thank you for meeting with me today," Jane said.

"You going to ask me questions?"

Jane looked away from Fredly and thought again this was a stupid mistake on her part. What did she expect to accomplish?

She looked back at him. *Go for the jugular.*

"Did you kill Israel Tenner?"

"That's why I'm in this joint, isn't it?"

"I mean really kill him."

"I don't answer twice."

"Well, then, why did you kill Israel Tenner?"

"Private business between him and me."

"What business?"

"Private."

"OK. What did he look like?"

"What's it to you? He's gone."

"What color hair did he have?"

"I heard blond."

"Heard? So you never saw him?"

"It was dark."

"Were there other people at the cabin with you the night Israel was killed?"

"I don't squeal."

"Come on, Fredly. I'm almost certain you're not guilty, or at least not entirely guilty. If you cooperate and tell me the truth, I can help get you out of here."

"And then what? You going to babysit me until the day I die? Keep me safe so the boogeymen out there don't deep fry me? You must be high."

"What do you mean by the boogeymen out there?"

"No comment."

"Are you saying someone might kill you if you get out of here?

"No comment."

Why was Jane wasting her time and his? This was futile. Tunny knew better than to say anything that mattered.

"OK. I guess you really have nothing to say, do you?"

"You know, Israel talked about you that night."

Jane's heart jumped and shrank back just as quickly.

"What did he say?"

"What's it worth to you? Maybe you can come see me again. Bring something with you to make it worth my while to tell you about Israel Tenner."

"Bring something for you?" Jane sat back quickly.

"Yah. What? Were you born yesterday?"

"Wait a minute. You don't mean, like drugs? I can't do that!"

"Course you can." Fredly gave her a big, obscene smile of encouragement.

"Forget it. Can't you please just tell me about Israel? And then I'll never bother you again."

"You really are as naïve as she said."

"She? Who is she? Are you talking about Harriet Buxton?"

"I didn't say that."

"Oh, but I'm guessing that's who you mean, and I'm going to run with that comment, Mr. Tunny."

But where to would Jane run?

32

LATE AUGUST
Fear of Death

Jane felt like a tiny, minor planet flung out of its orbit by evil gods. She had no one on her work force to turn to. No one to trust. Certainly not Harriet, not Finn, not Alex Champus, probably not Lieutenant Adderley, and Storm was on probation in Jane's book. So she sat by herself and culled through what she knew.

Obviously, Israel hadn't planted himself as a betraying mole into the State Police system on his own. It had been orchestrated by powerful people in the know. Harriet had to be involved. And she was so high up the food chain that if Jane took one misstep, she'd be demoted to clerical sausage. And if the corruption was that far up the ranks, Jane might even get herself killed, like Israel. So everything she now had in mind had to be done with stealth under fear of death. Nice. What kind of job description was that? What kind of life? She wasn't getting paid enough.

....

"I can't believe we can finally talk, Konstantin!" Jane was so relieved. She needed someone to help her focus, and not just a lover. Konstantin barely even qualified for that role these days...he was a million miles away in an ocean full of pirates and short on fish. What Jane wanted right now was his advice, his insights, his solutions to the scrambled shit and eggs her life as a Public Safety Officer had become.

180

"We don't have much time, Jane. The ship is heading into another dead zone. Better say what you can quickly," said Konstantin.

He didn't say "I love you." Neither did I....

"Oh, great. OK. Well...Israel Tenner is dead."

"Dead?!"

"Yes, and I'm sure it's because Harriet Buxton and Finn Gallinen and other cops on the force are bent. They've sold out to the drug lords. And somehow Israel got swept up in their mess. I think these corrupt people killed him to prevent him from revealing their secrets." Jane gave Konstantin a quick recap of Israel's slip-up at the charades party, the Feds' decision to take him away to protect him, and Lieutenant Adderley's follow-up assurances.

"So what happened to get him killed?"

"Well, Finn says he found Israel walking on the camp road leading to the Fed team's mountain house. He supposedly convinced Israel to get into Finn's car, they drove back towards the coast, had a few drinks, and then Finn dropped Israel off at the St. Frewin's ferry terminal. They hung out until Israel got his ticket back to the island. Finn says he left and that was it. The ferry terminal people backed up most of the story."

"But did the ferry terminal staff actually see Finn drive away? Did they see Israel board the ferry?"

"They could not say for sure on either of those points."

"Then you don't know, right?"

"Right. And no matter what Finn or the ferry staff say, I'm sure Finn and Harriet had everything to do with Israel's murder. I'll spare you my supporting details for another day."

"Well, you've been uncomfortable about Harriet and Finn for a long time, and I never quite understood it. But if they're guilty of murder now, that's devastating."

"No kidding," Jane said. "Recognizing their guilt has just about blown up my work reality and it's going to skewer the whole police force in the end. I keep saying I blame Israel's death on Harriet and Finn entirely, but I can barely come to grips with it."

"Look, Jane. It's time for me to sign off. But before I go, here's what I think. You have to be ultra-cautious. Don't declare your position until you have all the hard evidence you need to lock someone up."

"Right. I get it."

"And you should go back to the beginning. Check Israel's HR file...especially his application. That's where his story begins. What was in his application that gave someone control over him? Or what else can you find in his file that would explain why Israel became a candidate for corruption? Someone was holding something over him. You need to find out what that was."

"That's an interesting point," Jane said. "And Konstantin, I love...wait, are you there?"

Nothing. Gone.

Jane closed her eyes. And sat still for a moment. She was tired of bearing this hunger.

....

Gail was a sweetie all right. She was the girlfriend of Jane's buddy Sean Peters in the State Medical Examiner's Office. More importantly, Gail worked in the Bureau of Human Resources.

DEEP FRIED FATE

Sean had assured Jane that Gail would be helpful. Sean had assured Gail that Jane had every good intention in her role as PSO.

Whatever that meant, it worked. Gail agreed to make certain the door to the Bureau of Human Resources file room remained unlocked, once the work day was done. But Gail refused to wait for Jane and stick around for the action. She wasn't comfortable joining Jane's SWAT team. Gail could tell there was nothing special about Jane's weapons; there were no weapons; and Jane had zero tactics.

It would be up to Jane to find, pull, and make a copy of what she needed without Gail's assistance. Gail did not want to get fired. But Gail did give Jane her cell phone number...just in case.

....

At 5:30 PM, Jane crept out of the bathroom in the central area of the third floor of the Maine Bureau of Human Resources. All employees had piled out promptly at 5:00 PM, and the hallway lighting was now reduced to 24-7 emergency lights and EXIT lights.

No external, natural light reached this inner realm. And this evening, no external, natural air freshened the halls. The atmosphere was heavy with the scents of everything six floors of human beings brought in with them in the morning and left behind them at the end of the day.

But tonight, the hermetic ambience of the government building did nothing to deter PSO Jane Roberts. With a 00# (something between 6 and 8) bounce in her stride, Jane prowled across the hall into the main file room and found herself in a vast and deep space, windowless with low ceilings that continued into semi-darkness, with minimal, after-hours low lighting. She took a hike, limbs tingling, following directions Gail had texted to her. Eventually she reached the employee "T" file cabinets for the Maine State Police. She paused to breathe deeply.

OK. The T files. Here I go again. Peeking into files. Is this going to work? Am I trying to act like I know what I'm doing? Am I a crackpot and a fake PSO? Why am I about to laugh at all of this? How could anything about this be funny? Am I or am I not a jerk?

Jane took another deep breath. Training her flashlight at the file names, she moved through all the Ts before and after the location where Israel Tenner should have been. She did not find his file. She checked a second time. Nothing.

What does this mean? Has someone deliberately removed Israel's file? Was it misfiled? Has it been pulled because he's dead? Dead. Maybe that's it. Maybe deceased employees' files are kept elsewhere. Since dead employees, and hell, while we're at it, let's throw in murdered employees, are no longer active, their files might logically be deemed no longer active...maybe.

Jane dialed Gail, who apologized she hadn't thought about Israel's changed circumstances. She told Jane where to find the archived files in another, distant part of the file room.

Jane moved towards the archive section, with Gail coaching her over the phone on where to walk, then turn, then go straight, then a right turn...then the sound of voices....

What?!

Voices?

Strands of conversation started filtering into the room. Jane whipped her head around. She halted, whispered bye to Gail, and turned off her phone. She sunk down behind a flank of cabinets and waited, alternately terrified, tired, and stiff. She thought of the night time prayer and the line repeating in her head...*If I should die....*

Several people eventually parked their discussion in a different section of the file room cave. They were speaking in quiet voices. Jane strained to hear the number of voices and their genders, and to recognize who they were.

She smiled at her apprehension that she might know the voices. Because she had been on high alert all evening for something exactly like this...that at any moment, Harriet & Co. might swoop in, grab Jane by her skinny arms, and stuff her head first into a file cabinet forever; no obit intended. Fear had turbo charged batteries.

Jane began crawling towards an aisle near the voices. She crawled hoping she made no sound, no sound that might compel Harriet to launch a fentanyl blow dart straight at Jane Roberts' puny butt. And what if the carpet under her was polyester? Better pull her sleeves over her hands. Avoid all contact. No sneezing, please! Out, out damn polyester...God damn allergies.

When Jane was close enough to discern an occasional word, she peeked around a cabinet and listened. She recognized Harriet's domineering cadence weaving through Finn's flat monotone. *Listen to the two of them. Pure evil having an office conference...the buzzing architects of Israel's murder.*

But who was the third speaker? Jane let his voice sink into her mind, again, and again. Until the words fell into place.

To her utter shock, she knew this voice. Jerome Williams...from the Calderwood Boatyard...he was standing in the near dark, conversing intently with Harriet and Finn.

Jerome Williams! Jane felt faint. She reached in her pocket for two chocolate-covered almonds and shoved them into her mouth. Combat rations.

She could not hear entirely what the three were saying. She knew Tom Clancy's Jack Ryan would have taken a picture, but Jane didn't dare. She did not want to chance her cell phone camera flash going off.

What Jane did hear inside her head was the memory of casual comments about drugs that Calderwood Boatyard employees had made in the past...and then backed off from admitting any of it was true. She had been interviewing them about the beating of a boatyard employee.

But Jerome Williams! Good old Jerry. Mr. Goodbar, lover of the candy bar Jane had seen on his desk at the boatyard. He was the odd-shaped piece of the conundrum Jane had not imagined. Somehow Harriet & Co. had notched him into place in their evil puzzle. Payback perhaps for a drug debt owed? For some dumb fuck-up? Jane would have to figure out how Harriet had bagged Jerry, but it would surface...like greasy fat always did.

A slow-motion video of Israel's final hours began running through Jane's mind, frame by harrowing frame...Israel gets off the ferry, might be a bit tipsy, Jerry offers him a ride home, overwhelms him, injects him with a pet sedative. Jerry and whatever brutes are helping him (a Tunny? a Harriet? a Finn?) then haul the spaced-out Israel to Orion's Spit. They slice him to death, they hoist him onto the wall in the cabin, they admire their murderous swag....

The Gang of Three finished talking and left the file room. Jane waited another half hour before she stood up. She finally found Israel's file in the archive section and concentrated on taking cell phone pictures of his application and any other documents. No reading now. She would save that for later.

Jane left the file room and made sure she had no company as she exited the building—genuinely shaken and convinced more now than ever to trust her gut.

....

Before boarding the last ferry back to St. Frewin's Island, Jane stopped at the internet cafe in the terminal. She brought up the Abenaki County Registry of Deeds and searched the real property records for Calderwood Boatyard and Jerome Williams. Both boatyard and man were mortgaged through the nose and weighed down by liens. No surprises there. Jane cleared her search terms and returned to her truck to drive aboard the ferry.

33

LATE AUGUST
Three Leaf Clover

Jane was on her office phone the next morning, trying to herd her evidence into the fold. "Hey, Todd. It's Jane Roberts. How's it going?"

"Ahh...Jane of the deadly island. Good to hear from you. What can we do for you today? Need to add to your list of dabs?" Todd Chisolm asked from his office at the Evidence Response Team in Augusta.

"Right you are. I'd like to name one more fiend concerning possible finger prints at the cabin on Orion's Spit."

"Whoa, Jane. Hold on there. Innocent until proven guilty...remember? You don't want to get a bad reputation."

"Come on, Todd. Pamper my cynicism a little," Jane said. "But seriously, please be on the lookout for the prints of one Jerome Williams when you re-sweep the crime scene. He runs our local boatyard. He's now a potential suspect in the death of Israel Tenner."

"Will do. Keep the faith, Jane."

"Wait! One more thing, Todd. This would be another enormous favor for me...you can say no if you absolutely have to. But could you also check for Harriet Buxton and Finn Gallinen? They're both employees of our police force."

"Wow, Jane. No kidding. That is going out on a tricky limb. Are you going to owe me one, if I tack on those two?"

"Sure, I'll owe you one. In the next life."

Jane hung up the phone and dug her cell phone out of her bag. She tapped into her camera, and scrolled to the first page of Israel's application to join the Maine State Police. She had resisted looking at it last night, afraid of what she might find.

Where the form asked about history of criminal convictions, Israel had actually answered yes. Three times for OUI, operating under the influence—which was cruising towards felony territory under Maine law. And yet he had been hired! And plunked down in Jane's office! Stunning!

Jane leaned back in her chair and threw her arms over her head. She stretched out long and asked the simple-minded question. Who could actually hire a triple-OUI offender to become an assistant to the Public Safety Officer on an island in Maine?

It just wasn't allowed. So who could do that? Who else, but Harriet Buxton. And she would hold Israel's three-leaf OUI clover over his head to make him behave. Lucky him...Harriet had given Israel a generous break— she had hired him. In return, he gave her his life. What a cruel equation.

Jane decided to ring up loan officer Ryan Young at Abenaki County Bank. She asked him if he could ethically tell her about the boatyard's financial picture. He could not. But he asked if she had heard about the newer, bigger, better boatyard on the mainland that was sucking up lots of customers and business. At least he had fed Jane a clue.

All right. We've got a potentially failing boatyard where drugs might be an issue, and the manager of that boatyard appears to be in cahoots with Harriet Buxton about XYZ, let's say. Now how is Junior Jane going to bring these people down with scant evidence? What does she have for evidence?

That led Jane to zero in on her next call...to the Capitol Police Office.

"Yes, this is PSO Jane Roberts out on St. Frewin's Island. We're working on a case and I've been asked to obtain a copy of the security camera footage at the Maine Bureau of Human Resources from last night, August 23, 2022, say from 5:30 PM through 7 PM. Is that possible?"

"No, Ma'am. First off, we don't hand out copies without a special request form submitted to our Head Supervisor. Secondly, we prefer you come see what we've got so you can be sure it's what you want. Thirdly, you better get up here before the week is through, because they usually only keep the footage for one week."

So efficient. OK. Play ball.

Jane checked her work schedule, saw nothing was pressing, jumped in her car, and drove to the ferry. She arrived on the mainland with enough time to scoot up to Augusta and view the security footage in question.

Ta-da. At approximately 6:15 PM on August 23, 2022, Harriet, Finn, and Jerry could be seen entering the Maine Bureau of Human Resources. Jane thought they looked as guilty as murderers ever had, but that was her biased opinion.

She again asked for a copy and was told no. So she politely asked the staff not to erase the tape, to hold on to it for at least another week. That it was seriously a matter of life and death. Jane would have the Boston

DEA or FBI call the Maine Capitol Police Office to confirm this before the week was over.

The staff seemed convinced enough to say OK. Jane didn't let on that the death was already cold.

34

LATER IN AUGUST
Gone Viral

Dr. Andreas Kerner triple-checked his latest test results while he sipped red hibiscus tea at his desk. He had acted quickly to collect what blood he could when the corpse first arrived at his office.

And then, given the violent, messy nature of Israel Tenner's death, Kerner decided to run additional tests on samples of Israel's blood that had been stored since the autopsy. The murderers might have exposed themselves to something dangerous in Israel's blood—perhaps a transmissible disease such as HIV or hepatitis.

And indeed, Israel Tenner's blood test came back positive for hepatitis B. Jane Roberts must be told. But only Jane. Kerner understood the importance of not reporting his findings through official channels quite yet, thus leaving Jane's suspects in the dark for now. Perhaps his news would help her expose the truth she so desperately sought to force out of an intolerable reality.

....

"Jane, you missed Dr. Kerner's call, but I think I took good notes and he's faxing his latest update shortly." Helen Orbeton sat down with Jane at the PSO long-plank table for an info session.

"An update?" Jane said. "This better be helpful. I had to sit through Dr. Kerner eating everything red on the menu the last time I saw him. It was kind of kinky. He owes me...sort of."

"Well, it turns out Israel Tenner had hepatitis B. I had no idea. Did you?"

"What?" Jane sat up straighter. "That's news, Helen!"

Helen continued reading from her notepad. "Dr. Kerner says people can carry it and not show signs of the disease. Or they can manage their hepatitis B and lead an otherwise healthy life."

"Wow. I didn't know," Jane said.

"Most important, Dr. Kerner said to tell you whoever was present when Israel was stabbed could have been exposed to the hepatitis. He said infected blood droplets can splash into someone's eyes or get into someone's system through a small cut. If there's any blood residue on the hands, gloved or not, the hepatitis could enter through someone's mouth."

"Hepatitis could enter through your mouth? Uuck...this is getting kind of technical, Helen. Maybe I should speak to Dr. Kerner directly. I'll go ring him up in my office." As Jane walked towards her door, she turned back and looked at her receptionist. "Remember, Helen. All of this is confidential. Not a word to anyone."

....

"Dr. Kerner, thank you for this amazing news about Israel. Do you have time to fill me in more and answer some questions?" Jane was mouthing silent victory shrieks at her walls and waving her fist in the air.

"Certainly, Jane. Grill me, as you people like to say," Dr. Kerner was chuckling.

"So you're thinking people at Israel's stabbing could have contracted hepatitis from his blood?"

"Yes, that's highly possible, unless these people were masked, wore eye goggles, double gloved, and were very cautious in their activity around the body," said Dr. Kerner.

Jane looked up to the heavens and shook her head. There was no way Harriet, Finn, and Jerry would have been prepared with all that protective gear the night they became murderers. No way.

"So how can you tell if someone has contracted hepatitis B?" Jane asked.

"It may take some time for someone to come down with hep B and shows signs of the illness. Eight weeks to five months is not uncommon. We look for a yellowing of the eyes or skin, maybe fatigue, vomiting, some nausea. Or, like Israel Tenner, the person might not show he is carrying hep B."

"Eight weeks to five months? I can't wait that long."

"Nature must take its course, Jane."

"OK. I know. So here's my next question. If it's not always obvious, how do people even know they have hepatitis?" Jane said.

"If the subject donates blood, it is routinely tested for problems such as hep B, hep C, HIV, and so on."

"A blood test...right. Well, if you are exposed, but don't yet have signs of hepatitis, how soon would your blood test positive for the disease?

"Oh, let us say on average, a blood test would come back positive within one month...maybe a range of one to nine weeks," said Dr. Kerner.

"Well, those numbers are looking a little more helpful. So what happens if you do have tainted blood?"

"Usually, your doctor would notify you. Or if it was a blood collection agency, the agency would notify the donor." Dr. Kerner cleared his throat while the implications of the late Israel Tenner's health hit home.

"This is all very interesting, Dr. Kerner. Very useful. And remember. Not a word to anyone else yet. I can't thank you enough!" Jane said.

The minute they hung up, Jane called Storm to ask if he had ever given blood at a work-sponsored blood drive. He said politically it was a good idea to give unless you couldn't for some health reason. Supervisors stressed that message to all the Maine State employees. *Good news!*

Jane next dialed the Maine State Police general switchboard and asked when they were holding their next blood drive. Not until next April? Not good!

Jane wondered how she was going to tackle the strategy coming together in her head. Her goal was clear. To find out—surreptitiously—if Harriet, Finn, or Jerome Williams were coming down with hepatitis. But Jane couldn't wait until the cruelest month to pin down whether the Gang of Three had poisoned blood.

So what to do? What to do? Yes! That's what she would do. Jane dialed Sean's girlfriend at work. "Gail, it's me again, Jane Roberts. Thank you so much for all your help the other day with the file room. Really made a big difference in my research project.

"And uh, now, do you think you could help me with one more tiny thing? It's kind of strange, I'll admit right up front. But if I could call you say, three times a week, starting in late October and continuing until say mid-December, and just ask you one or two questions where all you'd have to do is look at Harriet Buxton's face and answer yes or no...do you think you could do that for me? And here's the question, just in case you're wondering...."

**

Bernie Pushaw stepped into the Public Safety Office. It had been a while since he last talked to Jane Roberts and Helen Orbeton.

"Bernie, come right in," Helen stood up and swept him along with her arm and hand. "Jane says she may have a very special request for you, if you have the time."

"The shirt off my back, Helen, if that's what Jane Roberts needs. She's special. We haven't had such a lively PSO out here for ages, what with all the dead bodies pilin' up one smack after the other. Keeps the blood pumpin', I say." Bernie stood next to the PSO long-plank table to wait for his possible assignment. His khakis and pale blue shirt were a far cry from the stinking, filthy work outfit he had traipsed around in for the past decade.

Jane came out of her office after hanging up with Gail, who had sounded vaguely annoyed and possibly harassed when she reluctantly agreed to Jane's plan.

"So, Bernie. What's new with you? I've been hearing all kinds of happy rumors," Jane said.

"That's right, Jane. Environmental Fields is history. This young man no longer plows the mud to bury everyone's crap. State DEP finally shut us down. Everything now goes to a treatment plant. Amen to that."

"I'm glad to hear that chapter's behind you, Bernie. And what's with this other news of yours?"

"I'm gonna give you some of these here brochures, Jane, so you can catch up on my latest venture and spread the word. Me and Hansen Moody, that'd be

Noreen's father's cousin, any way you look at it. We call ourselves 'Old Farts Analytics.' "

"Way to go, Bernie! And?"

"Well, we're kind of intellectual trouble-shooters. You need a thoughtful problem solved, that's our game."

Jane looked at Bernie. She had braced herself and was prepared to count on the old maxim: You fight the war with the army you have.

"Very impressive, Bernie. Might be exactly what I need. Are you expensive?" Jane said.

"For you, our PSO, I'm gonna say you get a 30-day free trial. We're at your service, Jane."

"That's just great, Bernie! So, please, have a seat at the table. Here's how you might be able to help me...."

....

If the blood drive would not come to Mohammed, Mohammed would go to the blood drive. Jane began searching on the computer at the internet cafe how to organize an American Red Cross blood drive. Holy Moly. One website went on for pages and pages, with sixteen dizzying pointers per page.

All Jane wanted was to prick her main pricks and be done with it. Now she gathered she was going to have to pull together granola bars and orange juice and red balloons and crisp lettuce and donor stickers like "I gave at the elbow!" plus a spacious location with cubicle curtains? WTF?!

Jane got up from the computer, crossed her arms, and began slapping her hands on her shoulders. She was on the brink of needing a transfusion. She heaved big breaths. And then it came to her.

Sam!...that's who would be good at knocking a blood drive into shape. She had years of prep under her belt from catering and organizing St. Frewin's Island's annual Solstice Spree celebration. And Torrance Balankoff came in a close second...both women oozed endless dexterity and charm when it came to yanking men and other types off the sofa and pumping them up for their civic duties. That settled it.

<h1 style="text-align:center">35</h1>

<h1 style="text-align:center">STILL LATE AUGUST</h1>
<h2 style="text-align:center">Dabs</h2>

"Your timing was impeccable, Jane. I think I've got something for you." Todd Chisolm was calling Jane to inform her about finger prints his team had collected on a subsequent trip to St. Frewin's Island.

"You don't say, Todd," Jane sat back slightly flabbergasted but delighted to think the pursuit of justice was something she might actually accomplish in honor of Israel Tenner.

"It didn't come from the cabin, though. Once Fredly Tunny confessed to Israel's murder, we automatically widened the evidence search to include his home and also Israel's home."

"Right. Of course. Standard procedure. Too bad I'm not officially included in all this hubbub in my own backyard. Which is all the more why I appreciate your quietly keeping me informed, Todd."

"Sure, Jane. Any time. So this is where the plot thickens."

"How so?"

"The second trip out to collect evidence did not produce any prints on Harriet or Finn or this Jerome Williams. Lots of prints at the cabin for the Tunnys and the friends you singled out, but nothing on your colleagues."

"Well, maybe Harriet & Co. used their heads and wore gloves thick enough to shield their prints," Jane said.

"Could be, Jane. As it turns out, one of our techs forgot his camera at Israel's apartment. So a few days later, before we had lifted the crime scene order from the site, the tech ferried back out to St. Frewin's and went looking for his camera at Israel's. And guess what?"

"He found something obviously," Jane said.

"Yes, something we did not expect, but which you anticipated. The tech thought things looked different at Israel's from when the team last left. Possessions shifted just a bit. As though someone had searched, but was trying not to leave a trail. So the tech took photos with the camera he retrieved, and he got out his fingerprinting gear and dusted again for prints."

"Oh, for God's sake, Todd, just tell me!" Jane said, gritting her teeth.

"Your wish come true, Jane. The prints have since been inspected and we have not only Harriet and Finn on site at Israel's place after the initial search, but also this Jerome Williams on your list."

"Even Jerry?" Jane said. "I mean Harriet and Finn might have an official line about following up to see for themselves if there was anything in Israel's home that might be connected to his murder." *Or rushing in to scour illegally for incriminating evidence in Israel's home that would cook Harriet's or Finn's goose if it got into the proper hands. Otherwise, why would the Director of Human Resources be there at all? And what about Jerry?*

"I can almost read your mind, Jane. You're probably thinking, of those three people, why on earth would Jerome Williams be there at all?"

"Exactly," Jane said, her nerve endings sizzling all over. Jerome Williams poking around in the victim's home.... Jane felt like she had won the lottery. "This is really valuable, Todd. Could you fax me a copy of your report on this additional evidence? And tell me, if you can...who else will see this addendum to your initial findings?"

"Funny you should ask. You know, strange as this may sound, there wasn't a specific homicide detective assigned to this case. It seems like Lieutenant Adderley's office generally managed steps along the way, though without his direct input."

Jane could picture it...no designated homicide detective to dissect Israel's murder...just Harriet picking up Fredly Tunny by the scruff of his neck and plopping him on one of the scales of justice and then Harriet, Finn, and Jerry racing over to hop on the other scale for the tipsy seesaw ride of what? Fall Guy versus Bent Law Enforcement? Despicable, horrifying...Jane's HR superior, her PSO colleague, and the boatyard manager...all guilty until proven guilty.

Why, oh why, had Israel's murder happened? Was there a message for any of them in this? Jane thought back to Superman Christopher Reeve's response when TV reporter Barbara Walters probed if he thought there was a lesson or a reason for his horse-jumping accident, for his becoming paralyzed from the shoulders down for life. Reeves answered Walters a bit annoyed, Jane sensed, and rightly so...he said there was no lesson or message. What happened in the Universe was random. There was no message.

There was no comfort to be had. So Jane would improvise. She would keep the fact of Jerry's poking into

Israel's possessions like an ace up her sleeve. She didn't know when or where the card game might occur, but she would have her ace.

36

LATE SEPTEMBER
Little Shop of Horrors

Muffled in a brain fog, her heart numbed by the death of her assistant, Jane groped her way for weeks from one task to the other...roaring crepes suzette flames that nearly incinerated a knitting circle's Sunday brunch, bored male retirees blasting guns at each other, a stranded harbor seal that somehow got as far as the island post office and then needed rescuing....

Jane felt as if her life force had gone dormant until sufficient time would pass for certain evil viruses to incubate and go hog wild in three certain human hosts. *Go forth and multiply, Sweet Hepatitis!*

Helen Orbeton had no baked goods that could pump Jane up, no old-fashioned homilies to soothe the wound. All the more reason Helen cringed over alerting her PSO about the latest municipal news.

"Jane, keep your cool while I update you here. The Town Office called earlier this morning to let us know Abe Jenkins has filed an application...for an adult use marijuana retail store."

Jane's eyeballs locked onto Helen's...the sheer mention of Abe's business plan torched the propane core of Jane's internal torpor.

"What?! The guy who runs the water taxi? Out here?!"

Helen shrank back. "That's what the application says. The Town faxed over a copy. They'd like your PSO review and comments."

"They'd like my PSO review? Oh Sodom and Gomorrah, they would!" Jane was up on her feet, plugged back into her life force, ready to aim her torpedoes.

"You know, Helen, some people don't have an ounce of decency in them. Here Israel Tenner is barely dead. Injected with xylazine. His whole torso sliced open! Not even two months ago. Thanks to the American War on Drugs. And that oceanic Uber imbecile, Abe Jenkins, wants to sully our island with a seedy little pot shop? No way! It's not going to happen. Over my dead body."

Helen ducked as she handed over the application. Jane stared at it, imagining she could turn it into hot ash with her 20/20 vision.

"So what's this toxic paper say? Jenkins and his wife, one Dahlia Jenkins, will own the business, and she will run the store day-to-day."

Jane looked up abruptly. "Who is this Dahlia woman, Helen? Do you know anything about her? Or anyone who knows her well? We have got to kill this idea before it sprouts."

"Let me think a minute, Jane. Dahlia Jenkins....she's good friends with Grace Cleveland who has the Apple π bakery. And I think Dahlia is the daughter-in-law of Beatrice Jenkins."

"Beatrice Jenkins. How do I know that name?" Jane wondered.

"Beatrice has done pretty well for herself all these years. She became a beta-tester for video games early on, and made some good money along the way," Helen noted.

"Oh, that Beatrice. OK. She's in Oxford Monteith's book...that's where I've heard the name. But you say Dahlia knows Grace Cleveland, the baker? So is Dahlia going to con Grace into creating like what? All kinds of ganja brownies for Dahlia to sell to sweet-toothed, gonzo housewives who believe chewy, chocolatey edibles are morally superior to taking a hit on a fat doobie in front of their preschoolers?"

"God knows, Jane."

"And Helen," Jane added, "I seem to recall that in *Methamatics*, Oxford wrote that Beatrice's daughter-in-law is really jealous of Beatrice's beta-testing career. If that's our Dahlia, maybe she's all hot and bucking to run a shabby joint shop to try and catch up with Beatrice's entrepreneurial success."

"God knows, Jane. Have you...by chance, ever thought of moving to Singapore?"

"What's all this 'God knows' business, Helen? And Singapore? Are you trying to say something without saying something?"

Helen scrunched a smiling face at Jane and strolled back to her desk, adding with a backward glance, "I do know one way you can lay an eye on Dahlia and maybe get a chance to talk with her, or at least observe her."

"What's that?" Jane asked.

"The annual Baked Bean Supper is coming right up...the first Wednesday in October...at the Town Hall. Dahlia's one of the bean captains."

"Now that's an excellent idea, Helen. I'll get a ticket right away. No. Wait. I'll get two tickets and invite Sonny Mannix. He's the State ferry captain and Abe's out there with his water taxi dodging Sonny's ferry all day, so I bet Sonny can bring me up to speed on Abe's plans to flood St. Frewin's with dope."

37

EARLY OCTOBER, 7 PM
Hide and Seek

"OK...Remember, we've got one hour to stuff these turkeys, and then we're out of here." The three men grabbed their backpacks and exited the car. They hurried towards the *Synchronicity*, a monohull racing yacht that had gone through recent repairs. She was now cribbed in the remote lot of the Calderwood Boatyard on St. Frewin's Island. Her crew planned to sail her back down to the Caribbean in November for the winter racing season in the new year.

Walking quickly towards the boat lot, one of the men asked, "Did either of you take a look at that book Turk and Chummy sent us...something about *Methamatics?*"

"Oh, yah," said one of the other two men. "I started it last night. I got it right here in my vest. Talk about pulp. That crazy author's description of Turk will make you choke. In the book, he's tall and lean, and he graduated from Yale. He even plays polo in the book! Ha ha!! Can you picture Turk on a horse? And the author's got him playing oboe, too. Shit on shit! He couldn't sing 'Happy Birthday' if you held a gun to his head."

"So in the book, he's everything he's not. Is that what you're saying?" the second man chuckled.

"Exactly," said the reader as he pulled out *Methamatics.* "Here, let me show you this page where she describes Turk getting his degree in the Classics...."

"Hey, back to reality, you guys. We got to focus," snapped the leader of the three.

"How are we getting up onto the boat?"

"They've got ladders stored nearby. Don't worry. And get your gloves on now. I don't want any prints left behind."

....

"OK...up we all go and let's find those life jackets, PDQ. Step quiet and steady. We don't want to pitch the boat off its supports."

"Where should we look for the jackets?"

"They should be stored in the chests—both sides of the deck. About 20 vests in all."

The men split up to search.

"If we're stuffing these babies with shit, what happens if the crew needs to wear them?"

"The guys who race this boat? Are you kidding? They wouldn't be caught dead in life jackets. They hate life jackets."

"Macho men, hey?" smirked one of the men, striking a wimpy front double bicep pose.

"They'd rather be caught dead if they drown without a life jacket. I say what the fuck?"

"So here's ten jackets in this locker. What'd you find in that one?"

"Yah, another ten."

"OK, let's start an assembly line...you slice open the tops of two pouches on each jacket. And take the foam out of the pouches. Then hand the jacket to your buddy."

"And you there, dump a couple handfuls of a-bombs and b-bombs into each empty pouch."

"Wait a minute. Do these guys even use dope?"

"Not that anybody's told me. Probably get their buzz from booze. Probably all alcoholics. But back to our job, OK? You hand the jacket to me, and I'll seal the slits with the glue gun. We've got forty minutes left. Let's go. One-Two-Three. Less talk.

"But Boss, you got to tell us how this is supposed to work. 'Cause if these fellows don't go near their life jackets, who's ever going to find the drugs?"

"That's not for us to worry about. Turk and Chummy will figure out the logistics. They know how to stage a raid if anyone does."

"That's right. Turk can pull off a raid all right. But I just can't see him on top of a stallion in a pair of those skinny, tight britches the polo nuts wear...."

"And why are we picking on these sailor boys when the real drug traffickers are out there thick as cockroaches?

"Who the hell knows? Turk and Chummy personally gave us this assignment. If they've got some bone to chew with these *Synchronicity* dudes, that's none of our business. What do we care? This is just a job. Not a question-and-answer session. Let's get the fucking job done, all right? Keep the jackets coming to me so I can glue them closed."

The man ripping open the pouch tops started up again. "So back to that whacky book, *Methamatics*. Clearly the author chick has no idea her hot flame, Jamie, has a loving wife and two kids back at the ranch."

"You mean Jamie who works with Turk and Chummy? He's married?"

"Yah...and happily, I heard."

"Huh...well, nothing lasts forever."

"What about Turk? Any wife and kids?"

"Turk? He's kind of slippery, that one. I don't know. Maybe he deep-sixed any wives he had in the past. But he might be a good specimen for a commanding, dominatrix type. You know, a dame with some frenzy in her, who can kind of whip around and throw daggers. And a good cook, too. If that combo even exists."

"Where are you getting all this from, Boss?"

"Oh, just bits and pieces you hear around the office."

....

"Guys...four more life jackets to go and then we vamoose. We take all the foam with us. And we tuck the jackets back into the lockers like we found them, and close those locker lids so it looks like no one was ever here.

"Uh oh, Boss...I think we got a guilty jacket here."

"Meaning?"

"The back pocket on this one has no foam. But it does have a surprise." The man pulled out a plastic-wrapped brick of what looked like flour. "I'm betting this ain't baby powder."

"No shit. That is a surprise. Maybe these guys are more interesting than Turk and Chummy know. All right. Let me think a minute."

"Should we take it? Or leave it? There aren't many other choices, are there, Boss?"

"Right. But both choices raise a lot of questions. I'm under oath to report something like this, but we shouldn't be here in the first place. So I'm thinking we're going to leave it as is."

One of the other men had a question. "Who owns this boat anyway?"

"Some son of some kind of mucky-muck...like a CEO or a bank president. I don't know for sure."

The two men looked at one another and then at the Boss. One of them spoke up. "OK. We say we take the brick. No need to turn it in. We could sell it, make a little killing on the side. No one's gonna know we were ever here."

"Look, we're running out of time," said the Boss. "I wash my hands of it. You do what you want."

Ten minutes later, they climbed down from the *Synchronicity*, put the ladder back where it had been resting, and walked away into the night to drive back to the welcoming ambience of the Grand Harbor Inn. They checked out the next day and returned to the mainland.

Whoever dropped the copy of *Methamatics* into one of the lockers didn't realize it. What happened to the book, no one could remember later.

38

OCTOBER, FIRST WEDNESDAY
Baked Bean Suppah

Jane parked her truck and jammed her fretting about plaque and high triglycerides into her glove compartment and slammed it shut. She didn't have to be health-conscious every single damn day, especially when her beeswax was slumping on both ends over trying to round up Israel Tenner's Murderers of the Year and save St. Frewin's Island from grass. Yes, Jane was going to enjoy herself tonight, Last Supper or not.

She could see eager eaters streaming through the front doors from a line that continued at least the length of ten thirty-foot whaleboats down the walkway and along the road in front of Town Hall. Proof of the satisfying, comforting food the Baked Bean Supper put forth year after year when St. Frewin's Island was glowing in the copper bowl of fall colors. People even ferried over from the mainland for the good old down-home evening of classic Maine fare.

Jane found Helen, Dr. Leckman, and Sonny Mannix near the front of the buffet line. Thank God! Jane was hungry as usual—like a prisoner of war—and she could practically feel her hand thrusting the big serving spoons into the casserole dishes and piling the bounty onto her plate. She was also anticipating squeezing Sonny Mannix for all he was worth about what made toking Abe and Dahlia tick.

DEEP FRIED FATE

Spread out on two long rows of five long tables each, graced with white paper table cloths, were platters and platters of food...puffy dinner rolls, slices of steamed brown bread, green and orange Jell-O salads, pickled beets, potato salads, coleslaws, macaroni and cheese, crispy frankfurters, rosy slices of roasted ham with little clove nibs quilting the rind, and a fleet of apple pies, chocolate cream pies, and Indian puddings for dessert. And the beans! Huge, hot, black iron pots of smoky, sweet-smelling baked beans with condensed steam bubbles crowding the undersides of the glass lids.

"So, Helen, what does it mean to be a bean captain?" Jane asked as she ploughed a culvert through the potato salad and plunked it on her plate.

"You mean like Dahlia? Well, she's one of the organizers and she's in charge of making sure the best beans in the world show up at this buffet...with enough of those beans to go around."

Sonny put in his two cents right away. "Dahlia really knows her beans. They've got just the right sweet but tangy, salty flavor. I don't know how she does it."

As the quartet shoveled all the fixings onto their plates, Jane's brain was already in her own bean pot, simmering away. Maybe in the end, after her invisible campaign to annihilate Abe and Dahlia's Empire of Weed, Jane would miraculously suggest to Dahlia a consolation prize...that she do something with her beans on a larger scale. Try and deflect Dahlia's lust for mercantile Mary Jane into commercial baked bean capitalism...something sane and beneficial along those lines.

But for the immediate future, how should Jane approach Sonny at this supper about Abe Jenkins' nefarious venture without Sonny feeling like he was in front of a firing squad? Had to be a subtle persuasion.

Jane reviewed the classic interrogation techniques in her head. Prolonged wall-standing? Probably wouldn't work. There were more than enough seats for everyone.

Hooding? Well, that would cause a scene. And Sonny wouldn't get to eat his bean supper.

Subjection to noise? Probably not. Dahlia and her fellow bean captains had already hired Pub-owner Connor Mulroy and his Donegal Boys band to subject the innocent diners to noise. That's why the Pub was closed tonight, and that's why there was more than enough subjection to noise for everyone right here and now...nearly appropriate for interrogation, but not quite.

Binding in contorted stress positions? No way. Too many people watching.

Sleep deprivation? Who could sleep around all these beans?

So where did that leave Jane Roberts? Maybe a classic non-confrontational technique would work, with a "neutral control question" thrown in up front...all woven into conversational gibberish.

A "neutral control question" being some bland, non-confrontational inquiry Jane already knew the answer to.

"So tell me, Sonny. Did you vote for legalizing the sale of marijuana in the State of Maine, which God knows could transform every man, woman, and child on this island into powder zombies."

"Here we go again, Jane. I can see you're about to lambaste me from a nautical mile away. You know damn well how I voted, so I'm not going to say out loud in polite company here. And I'm not going to let you grill me about Abe and Dahlia Jenkins' application for a pot shop. OK?"

"Well," Jane hesitated in surprise. *How the hell does Sonny Mannix know my secret agenda?* She had to do some quick recalculations about her entire dinner conversation and why she had bought the god damn baked bean supper tickets in the first place. Especially since in reality, Jane Roberts had so very, very little time to waste on Mr. and Mrs. Jenkins' cannabis canapés smeared with clam jerky on top of the devil's lettuce, when Jane was the only responsible human being in all of New England determined to get to the bottom of Israel Tenner's slaughter. But she could be flexible. It was OK. It was OK.

"I have no idea what you're talking about, Sonny. I was just casually shooting the breeze…trying to talk politics while avoiding talking politics. Let it fly…."

"Happy to talk about Desdemona Spode's newest release," Sonny said with a leer. Desdemona Spode being Jane's sister, and yes, a hot porn star, and Jane was not going down that path, even if Sonny Mannix was the proud owner of a boxed set of Desdemona's bestsellers.

Jane leaped to throw gasoline on the conversation's fire. "You're right on top of cultural trends, aren't you, Sonny? And how is the State ferry these days? Do you have any wild anecdotes for Helen and Dr. Leckman and me?"

Jane could not believe the absolutely insipid direction her subtle interrogation of Sonny Mannix was taking. He was a pretty shifty fellow when it came right down to it. "It" being the possibility that Jane's beloved island was about to become the premier junkie destination in Vacationland, which might make Dahlia more money than her mother-in-law had ever pulled in from beta-testing *Candy Crush.*

Jane switched tactics. Deliberate small talk ensued....

Thirty minutes later, after jubilantly scarfing down the four-inch-high burial mound of sweet and salty cholesterol nodules on her plate, Jane now sensed her arteries were coursing with four-inch wads of lipids. Time for the ladies' room. She excused herself and made way for the hallway facilities.

Naturally, there were twenty women clutching their stomachs and crowding the approach to the two bathrooms for femmes, so Jane kept walking around the corner and quickly turned into the men's room. Zero occupants. Crafty Jane.

When she was all but done in her stall, she heard people hustling into the rest room. Jane quickly stepped up onto her toilet seat to hide her womanly ankles. She struck a silent pose with her ears on high volume.

Two intruders were stifling all kinds of giggling as they shoved something like the giant trash can (?) against the door to wedge it closed? Their whispers and laughter caught Jane by surprise...a man *and a woman* were in the men's room...together!

Lo and behold...it was Sonny Mannix...with an u..n..k..n..o..w..n female. Unknown that is, until Sonny started moaning, not speaking, her name with what Jane knew could definitely qualify as raging hot Trinidad Scorpion Chili Pepper passion....Dahlia! Dahlia!

Holy Shit! Am I holed up in the middle of a sweet and tangy BAKED BEAN TRYST?! But this is a very interesting development, Jane Roberts. So wise up. Precious manna (Intelligence!) from heaven has just landed on your toilet! Yes, SELF, I can see that now. ("Dahlia! Dahlia!") And I am going to flip this to my advantage if it kills me, but saves St. Frewin's Island from Abe and Dahlia Jenkins' master plan to turn our sacred turf into a bunch of hash heads on granite.

39

LATE OCTOBER
I Am Curious Yellow

Oxford Monteith drove down the camp road to the Fed team's mountain house. Turk, Chummy, Random, and Jamie were breaking down their makeshift quarters and packing up for good.

Oxford found Jamie hoisting boxes of equipment into the back of a work van. They talked about the weather, about this and that, about nothing.

"Well, we managed to escape actually sleeping together," Oxford said laughingly.

"It wasn't something I wanted to avoid, Oxford," Jamie answered without looking at her.

"Oh really? You definitely mean that?" Oxford felt a euphoric wave flushing through her blood again...that wave where Jamie was looking up at her from down in a bowl full of cheesy linguini.

"I definitely mean that." Jamie was staring at her. Then he walked over and gave her a very long hug. "Don't go anywhere in December. I'll be in touch. Maybe we can rendezvous somewhere warm and tropical."

"Oh my goodness," Oxford thought she heard herself whisper into his ear.

....

The huge banner stretching across the Yacht Club's magnificent main hall read "We're here to honor Israel Tenner, where blood is red and donors mellow." Jane and Torrance had cooked up the jingle, based on a traditional fall melody, to move the community blood drive forward towards a total success.

No one but Jane knew her one and only reason for the blood drive, no, make that her two and only reasons for the blood drive were (1) to honor the memory of Israel Tenner, taken from them all too soon, and (2) to identify anyone whose donated blood might test positive for hepatitis B. Like maybe Mr. Goodbar!...Jerry Williams, that is.

Sam and Torrance had waved their unique wands, each a different length, style, and temperament. The end result was an orderly assembly of fifty-six donors all efficiently scheduled, with three cubicle curtains to shield people as they lay on their gurneys waiting for the Red Cross Draculas to stick it to them.

Jane could not be prouder or more pleased. Everything was coagulating remarkably well. Even Joe Miller, Jane's friendly carpenter at Calderwood Boatyard, was ninety-nine percent certain Jerry Williams intended to make an appearance and push up his sleeve.

Jane felt a tap on her shoulder. She turned. "Dr. Kerner! What are you doing here? Such a surprise...."

"Yes, well Johanna, I decided to ferry out here to show my support for your heartfelt efforts in memory of Israel Tenner. A truly wonderful tribute to the dead and the living.

"Johanna? Who's Johanna?" Jane said.

"Oh, my apologies, Jane. My mistake! I am translating your name into a German version for no reason at all. I am sorry to startle you."

She was ready to blurt out, "Well, then, move along; move along." It just didn't seem kosher that Dr. Kerner would be hanging around a community blood drive, given his propensity for the stuff.

But Jane tried to relax and act civil. After all, the State Medical Examiner had done her the service of detecting that her alleged butchers were poised to contract hepatitis B from their hapless corpse. And the State Medical Examiner had done her the kindness of informing her confidentially. So of course she was expected to let flawless manners rule the hour. Right. So....

"Well, now that you're here, Dr. Kerner, why don't I treat you to a strawberry milkshake at the pub after we call it quits for the day. How's that sound?"

Just then, another minor commotion began taking place at the blood drive registration booth, and Jane had to excuse herself to investigate the issue.

"Oh, God, what are those four doing here?" Jane wondered in crushing dismay. She could see the Red Cross Rep questioning Turk, Chummy, Random, and Jamie about donating blood. They wanted nothing to do with the cause, and the Rep was suggesting that in that case, they should leave. To which they vociferously objected.

Enter Jane Stage Right. "Look who's here! How are you gents doing? What brings you to St. Frewin's?" Jane asked as she shook hands with Turk and the boys. She could not believe she was even acknowledging these blowhards after they goofed and let Israel slip through their stubby fingers and into the murderers' claws. She had to keep her bitterness to herself...and get a grip on her nerves.

"Oh, we thought we'd take a day trip out here for the scenery. This is quite the set-up you've organized, Jane. Collecting blood and guts," Turk said. "Impressive."

"Well, why don't you donate and help our blood drive?" Jane asked.

"No way!" the men yelled at once.

"We've all had hepatitis C in the past...from too many tattoo parlors all over the East Coast. Sorry, Darlin'," said Chummy.

"Hepatitis C? Oh dear." Jane rushed to add, "Please don't go anywhere near our vials."

"By the way, Jane, any chance Samantha Lloyd is coming by today?" Turk asked.

"Why, do you want to arrest her?" Jane asked.

"Hah! Now that's almost funny." Turk's comment hung in the air between them, like hydrogen just waiting for oxygen to cozy up and explode....

"Except for the price tag, right?" Jane threw back.

"Hey, I'm the kind of guy who's all 'Let bygones be bye-bye.' No, I just thought it'd be fun to look her up. Maybe get to know her a little better. Maybe lure her away for some fun in the sun in Barbados."

"After she demolished your multi-million-dollar Phantom surveillance system in one afternoon with her garden clippers?!" Jane was astonished.

Chummy pushed towards Jane's face. "We have no idea what you're talking about. Got that, Jane Roberts?"

"Got it." Jane was catching on to these guys.

"Besides...that Sam...I like a woman with balls," Turk said with an almost dreamy vision on his grizzly box turtle face. Jane tried not to laugh.

"I find that kind of hard to picture, Turk. And I'm sorry to disappoint you, but Sam's already spoken for...more or less."

"I'd say 'less,' Jane. Way I see it, Nathan Herinton is always running off to play hooky on his buddy's yacht.

He doesn't make enough time for someone as special as Sam. Kind of makes you wonder what's going on with his pal's boat, *Synchronicity*...."

"How would you know anything about the *Synchronicity*, Turk? Don't go trying to make trouble. Nathan and Sam are an item," Jane insisted.

Chummy nudged Turk and spoke into his ear.

"Ah, Chummy here reminds me we can probably sweep up enough dirt on this Nathan guy to get him out of the way, if you keep trying to close the door on us."

Get Nathan out of the way?!? What the hell does Turk have in mind? Did he just say what I just heard him say? Jane wanted to slug all four of them, right there, right then.

"Look, enough. I'll let Sam know you were looking for her. Give me your number again on this donor info sheet and I'll pass it on to her. You hear from her, then you hear from her. You don't hear from her, then you better bark up another tree."

Turk handed the donor form back to Jane. "Here you go, Miss PSO. And let Sam know she won't want to end up regretting she did not get back to me."

Such presumptuous jerks! I am turning my back and walking away. There, I am walking a...w...a...y.... I have more important things to do, like checking up on the health of Harriet, Finn, and Jerry Baby. Where is he anyway, Jerry Baby? I thought Joe Miller said Jerry would get down here to get jabbed. Hmm....

....

Back in the PSO Office, Jane rang up Gail for the third of her thrice weekly calls about Harriet's face. "So, Gail, am I Curious Yellow?"

This was Jane's nifty code to Gail to disguise Jane's spiffy scheme where Gail would pop into Harriet's office

CASUALLY and take a good look at her. But Gail would NOT ask Harriet pointed questions about sallowness or vomit. She would simply observe: Were Harriet's eyeballs turning yellow? What about her skin? Was she fatigued or running to the ladies room to barf? Yes or no?

"Jane...this is growing tiresome. What if Harriet starts to suspect something? What if I get into trouble? I don't even dare tell you about the *Sinaloa Cartel Approved Escuchar y Aprender Narco Killer's Living Language Guide* I noticed under some papers on her desk the other day. Are you going to find me a new job when I'm booted out of here?" Gail wanted to know. She always asked the sensible questions.

"Relax, Gail. What's the worst that could happen? So what if Harriet barks at you to stay out of her office? Or to quit gawking at her sclera. Send someone else in to take a sharp look and report back to you. It's not like you're exchanging critical mass with Harriet about anything."

"OK. OK. I'm just uptight, you know?"

"Wait a minute. What did you just say? *Narco Killer's Living Language Guide?* Jesus Christ, Gail. What is that?"

"Oh, you didn't hear this from me, Jane. I'm not the one telling you about the violent language drills in this Guide. Stuff like "Shall I kill him? Shall you kill him? Shall he kill him?" With all the words in Spanish so you can practice. "Debo matarlo? Debes matarlo? Debe matarlo?" And it gets worse, Jane."

"Oh my God, Gail." Jane's jaw had dropped. "You've gone above and beyond. This is an incredible finding. Listen, don't say a word to anyone else. Let's just sit tight on this for now. And Gail, in my book, you are the Queen of Sleuths!"

....

At the close of the blood drive, the Red Cross Rep scanned the list of scheduled donors. Remarkably, all potential donors but one had shown up to do their part. Only Jerome Williams was unaccounted for. The Rep had instructions to update PSO Jane Roberts on that particular individual as soon as they were done.

40

EARLY NOVEMBER
Evidence

Bernie Pushaw met Jane at the Public Safety Office after dinner. They entered the dark building, she turned on one interior office light, and hurried Bernie in to have a seat at the PSO long-plank table.

"You're actin' kind of covert, Jane. Are you in trouble? Am I gonna be in trouble?"

"No, Bernie. Not at all. I'm just trying to keep a low profile about this leg of our mission."

"Well, sure. OK. Whatever you say."

"So, let's review our strategy." Jane gave Bernie a reassuring smile. "You've got two subjects. Two destinations. Two observations. Remember: Take all the pictures you can...surreptitiously. But don't attract attention. Don't raise any suspicions. Don't dilly dally. Stay out of trouble, please. But if not, you cut out of there FAST. Got that?"

"Yes, Ma'am. And don't worry, Jane. Can't be all that hard. I'm gonna pop over to the boatyard and look in on Jerome Williams first thing tomorrow mornin'. Just a casual drop-in, tell 'im I'm thinkin' of gettin' a thirty-foot day cruiser, ask his advice. Shoot the breeze. Then I'm gonna drive to the ferry to Catunk Isle in the afternoon and zip over to the new PSO out there and look in on Finn Gallinen. Just another meet 'n greet, tell 'im it's a day trip to get away from the missus for a few hours. Then I'm gonna head home to debrief with you after dinner here. You can count on Old Farts Analytics to deliver, Jane—guaranteed."

"Old Farts Analytics? Does that mean Hansen Moody is tagging along?"

"Maybe, maybe not. We'll see."

"OK. I have your cell phone number. You better give me Hansen's number, too. So, what are you on the lookout for in both cases?"

"I'm gonna check on their peepers and their pigment."

"And what specifically are you looking for?"
"Yeller."

"You mean 'yellow'?"

"Yes, Ma'am."

"OK. And...ah...there's one last thing, Bernie."
"What's that?"

"Zip your lips, mind you. This is not for public consumption. Do you know anyone who's got the goods on Sonny Mannix's love life?"

"That's sure outta left field, Jane. Like you take me for some gossip or somethin'?"

"It's for the greater good, Bernie. I can't go into the meat and potatoes, but it's to save St. Frewin's way of life."

"Oh, you must be talkin' about that marijuana shop. Everybody's worried about that shop and St. Frewin's way of life."

"Let's just stick to the question...anything on Sonny Mannix's love life?"

"OK. So you wanna know who's he pluggin' with his polliwogs these days? Well, Jane, you know Maggie Banner's sister was married to Sonny not so long ago.

Maybe them gals have the scoop you need. I really am empty-handed myself at the moment."

"Maggie's sister. That's right. Perfect. I'll check with Maggie. And I think we're all set on your assignment for tomorrow. I'm counting on you, Bernie. You're the man!"

....

"So, Maggie, you're saying your sister, Waikiki, never ended up using her snooping video because her divorce settlement with Sonny Mannix worked out all right?"

"That's right, Jane. At first, Waikiki felt she needed some proof of raw infidelity, some kind of punch, to advocate for herself in her divorce. But in the end, she didn't. I even think she made more than one copy of the video...just because. You know how divorce is...such a strange journey."

"And no one's seen this video, as far as you know?" Jane had to ask. Such priceless sabotage material if it were totally fresh!

"To my knowledge, Jane, my sister shelved it all once her divorce was wrapped up. In fact, Sonny, and for sure Dahlia, know nothing about the video."

"And are you at liberty to tell me how this video was made, Maggie?"

"Well, it was actually quite funny. My sister had her suspicions about Sonny, but she was so into discretion, she didn't dare ask around or let on that she was worried...and hurt. She couldn't bear to talk about it. At some point, Sonny announced he was flying out to San Diego for a national ferry captains' conference, but he didn't suggest Waikiki accompany him. Of course, the hair on her back was already up at that point...she knew something fishy was going on."

"OK, Maggie. I think I can picture it...Waikiki snuck down to the airport with her video camera and discovered Sonny Mannix and Dahlia Jenkins piling on the PDA in the airport terminal. Am I right?"

"You're right," nodded Maggie. "So Waikiki, who of course had worn a pretty heavy disguise, started shooting her video from a safe distance."

"And that's what she has more than one copy of," Jane said.

"Right. And Jane, I know you well enough by now to know you're going to ask me for the copy of that video. You're going to say 'St. Frewin's way of life is at stake.' Right?"

How the hell is everyone I'm dealing with lately getting so amazingly clairvoyant about my motives?!

"Look, Maggie. I'm not going to jump into a genteel boxing match with you. I'll lay it on the line. I have got to plunder Abe and Dahlia's joint account. Get it? Anyway, I need to drive a big, fat wedge between the two of them...and hope to God they never plaster St. Frewin's with Godfather OG, Gorilla Glue 4, Chemdawg, Strawberry Banana, or whatever other godawful strains are coming down the pike. You know I'm all for gardening...peonies, phlox, day lilies, rhubarb. But not this other green thumb explosion. We don't need it. We don't need Jacks and Hazes, Tropical and Floral, Original Gangstas and Gas, Sweets and Dreams. Do you get my drift?"

Maggie expelled a dramatic sigh. "Ease up, Jane. I'm on your side. I don't want a pot shop on St. Frewin's Island either. There are already five of them within ten miles of the ferry parking lot on the mainland. Enough is enough."

"OK, Maggie. OK. Sorry. I've been going 100 miles per hour since Helen Orbeton first breathed a word about the Jenkins' trying to take the Saint out of St. Frewin's Island. Just one next to last question for you. People seem to think Abe Jenkins has no idea he's married to an adulteress. How can that be?"

"Jane, I don't know. Though my guess is that Abe is simply working all the time and brooding the rest of the time. So he's not keeping track of his marriage or his wife. What's your last question?"

"Um, Waikiki? The name?"

"Jane, don't be dense."

....

"Listen, India, I know you feel a little weird about this favor I'm asking of you, but no one has to know that you are definitely 100% implicated—that you're guilty as sin for helping me." Jane gave a supportive smile to India Barton, the assistant manager of Grand Harbor Inn. India moonlighted as the secretary to the local Select Board of St. Frewin's Island. And the Select Board were about to hold their public hearing on the Jenkins pot shop application.

"Love your technique of persuasion, Jane."

"Hah. Just trying to lighten things up a bit. I mean, India, we'll all be dead before we know it, so what's a little bold, obstructive black mail right now to preserve St. Frewin's way of life for centuries to come? I mean, you help Maggie run the Inn. And you need civilized standards to keep running that Inn, don't you?"

"I get it, Jane. It's just that the Select Board and the folks who want a pot shop may crucify me when I turn on Abe and Dahlia's promotional, explanatory video about their new adult use marijuana retail store and up pops a covert video of Dahlia Jenkins and Sonny Mannix groping each other at the American Airlines ticket counter."

"That'll be perfect, India! Just do it! Anyway," Jane rambled on, "I've got to run. There's so much moral high ground on my plate right now, it's about to topple over. And it's driving me bonkers. But you are all set, and it sounds like you know exactly what to do. And remember. There's a public break right before Abe and Dahlia's presentation is scheduled for the public hearing. So who knows what asshole might switch the video tapes while you're on your break as well? It could be *anybody*. You're there to assist the Select Board; you're not an armed guard. And be sure to wipe your fingerprints off the airport video before you substitute it for the presentation video in the Jenkins' package that they submitted to the Select Board."

"OK, Jane. I figure the lights will be dimmed while I prepare the video player, and I'm sitting way off in the corner, so everything should be fine. I'll quit worrying."

"You've got it, India. Chicka Chicka Boom Boom!"

"You've read that children's book, Jane?"

"Nah. But I love the title. It's my new war cry."

41

EARLY NOVEMBER
More Evidence

The Calderwood Boatyard probe went very well the next day, in Bernie's humble opinion. Jerry Williams was real friendly to Bernie, thanks to the Pushaw Methodology. And Bernie got some smokin' hot shots without Jerry catching on. Plus Bernie could now offer his own personal testimony that Jerry was tossing his cookies in the restroom all right. Jane was gonna be pleased as punch.

The ferry ride to Catunk Isle was Bernie's first trip out there. As an island guy, he didn't have much need to go island hopping. You seen one island, you don't need to go see the next. 'Cause either you're gonna see stuff you could see back home, or you're gonna see stuff that'll make you wish you were back home. Or you're gonna see stuff that would turn you green with envy, and that ain't healthy unless you can do somethin' about it.

And besides, even though Bernie was now a man of substance thanks to a mysterious windfall he didn't want to talk about, he realized he had been sittin' in the middle of the universe on St. Frewin's Island all along, dough in the bank or no dough.

As Bernie drove his new truck towards the Catunk Isle PSO, it struck him he wasn't seeing many houses or trailers or traffic. Not that anything was hoppin' much anywhere on Maine islands in November. The light switch turned off just like that when the tourists and the summer folks went home. But this was different. This was like a ghost island without faces or places.

The PSO had one car in the parking lot. Bernie hoped that would be Finn Gallinen, or Bernie might have to abort his mission. He knocked on the door and looked through the door's window into the building. He knocked again. And stood there.

After seven minutes—Bernie was clocking it to report back to Jane—Finn Gallinen appeared from a small room at the back and walked towards the door. His stride looked weak and uneven. Bernie felt in his pocket for his cell phone. Got to be ready to gather evidence.

Finn opened the PSO door, and Bernie walked in like he was sunshine itself. "Hey there, Officer Gallinen! Remember me, Bernie Pushaw, from over on St. Frewin's Island? How ya been?"

"I'm afraid I don't...Mr. Pushaw, did you say? From St. Frewin's...are you a friend of Jane Roberts?" His slightly startled gaze took in Bernie from head to toe.

"She's our PSO. But I don't know if I'd go so far as to say we're friends," Bernie said with a snicker. "She can be kind of a Miss-Know-It-All...if you know what I mean."

"Hah! That's one way to put it," Finn said. "So what brings you to Catunk Isle?" Finn continued to eye Bernie with a quizzical, humorous look.

"Just wastin' the day away to get a break from home life. Thought I'd come out here and say hi, since Jane said you were new and all alone out here. And I wanted to give you some info about my latest venture, Old Farts Analytics. You never know when you might need a seasoned think-tank to help you solve some kinda PSO work obstacle."

Finn began looking over the leaflet Bernie handed him.

"So how's life treatin' you on this island, Officer Gallinen? You gettin' bored yet? I'm only askin' 'cause I seen how quiet it is out there on your roads...not many folks, not much action."

"Not the metropolis St. Frewin's Island is, right Mr. Pushaw? It is a quieter scene here. But everything will explode in June when the summer residents return and the tourists come pouring in. Same as much of the state."

"Well now, any chance you could maybe give me a tour of this place," Bernie asked.

The office telephone rang. Finn excused himself and hobbled to the desk to get the call. Bernie took a quick video of Finn's unsteady gait from behind and then put away his phone. Evidence.

While Finn talked on the phone, Bernie stood up and motioned to him that he was going to the bathroom. Finn shook his head OK. Bernie went into the bathroom and closed the door.

"No kidding," Finn was saying after a few moments on the phone. "Yep. You're right. OK. I'll call you back."

Finn stood up and knocked on the bathroom door.

"Hold on, Officer Gallinen. Be done in a jiffy."

Finn leaned close to the door and started talking.

"So, Bernie," Finn began.

"Yes, Sir," Bernie said from inside.

"That was Jerry Williams over at the Calderwood Boatyard. You know him, right?"

"Sure," Bernie said, wondering if he might be on the hook somehow. He spoke a little louder through the door.

"I just got through visitin' with Jerry about Old Farts Analytics before I jumped on the ferry to see you. Today's my turn to do in-person promo for our venture along the coast, while my other business half, Hansen Moody, stays home to do research."

Finn again spoke to the door. "Well, Jerry says he thought it was kind of weird how you took about a hundred photos of him in five minutes, after staring at his face all bug-eyed. His staff also saw you with your ear to the door of the men's room when Jerry had to excuse himself."

Finn could hear Bernie washing his hands. With that, Finn opened the bathroom door.

Bernie looked at Finn confused. "No kiddin'."

"Now in my line of work," said Finn, "we call that suspicious behavior. And since you told Jerry you were heading to Catunk Isle, Jerry thought he'd better check in with me."

Bernie grinned at Finn until his face hurt.

"So, if you don't mind my restraining you," Finn said, as he whipped out some white plastic flex cuffs from his pocket and lunged at Bernie to tie his hands...but Finn was unable to finish his sentence. He buckled at the knees and began swaying.

Bernie knew in this instance he had the upper hand because Finn had the wobblies. Bernie pulled out his cell phone and aimed it at Finn in burst mode, repeatedly. Evidence.

But Finn re-gained his composure. He shoved Bernie down on the toilet and whipped his hands together to cuff them. Finn then looked around on the floor and grabbed a bottle of Rid-X with one hand and yanked Bernie's head back with the other hand.

"What the heck you tryin' now, Officer Gallinen? Is that Rid-X I see? Don't you know that stuff's supposed to blow through your toilet clogs all the way to China?"

"That's why I'm pouring it down your throat, you moron," Finn said as he attempted to untwist the Rid-X cap, using one hand and the other hand, with Bernie's head in between.

No way in hell! Bernie jerked to the side, causing Finn to spill Rid-X all over his front. At which point Bernie kicked Finn in the shins hard and jumped up to push past him and run out of the bathroom.

Then Bernie ran for the main door, managed to twist the knob open, and rushed out of the PSO. He looked back as he ran towards his truck. Finn had regained his balance and was at the door, attempting to aim a gun at Bernie. Bernie darted right and scrambled to the side of the PSO building. When he looked back, he could see Finn shooting at Bernie's truck tires.

No time to stick around. But Bernie absolutely could not leave his beloved truck behind. His beautiful baby! And how would he get home?

Probably wasn't a good idea that he had decided to drive his shiny, new, red Jeep Gladiator to Catunk Isle. Look where showin' off got him...a crippled Jeep Gladiator. But maybe Finn's aim was havin' a bad day...maybe he would fuck up and Bernie could sneak all the way around the building and get back to his jeep and take off somehow, even though his hands were still cinched tight.

Bernie ran towards the back of the PSO building. He was going to circle around, while keeping away from Finn's unsteady aim. Then he saw the dumpster. Should he hide in there? Was that a dumb ass idea? Probably. But he shoved his bound hands under the lid and lifted it to check if there was room for one dumb-ass Jeep owner.

Then again, Finn was a cop. So that was probably his HK45 semi-automatic pistol he was wavin' around. God knows—if that's what Finn was packin', it might shoot clean through this dumpster any day.

Holy shit! What was this? Bernie didn't want to stick around and get too caught up in the contents of this dumpster, but it wasn't every day a common man like him ran head into whatever the hell was these gazillion plastic-wrapped bricks of some kind of white junk? He looked around him; he looked at the building windows. No Finn yet.

Bernie crept along the side of the office closest to the front door and peeked around the corner. Finn had fallen to the ground, eyes closed, not moving.

Bernie crept towards the downed Finn. He looked like a sleeping public safety officer soaked in Rid-X. Bernie wanted to leave while no lopsided PSO was tryin' to blow Bernie's brains out, but he decided he better investigate inside the office. Better that than Jane yelling at him why didn't he poke around when he had the chance. And he might find something sharp to free his hands.

He entered the office and ran to Finn's desk. He managed to pull open some desk drawers. *Yes, M'am! There's the ticket!*

He was able to pick up the box cutter and move the blade open with his fingers and lock it. Then he pulled a chair close to the wall, sat down on the chair, and positioned the cutter horizontally between his knees with the sharp side of the blade facing up and the tip stuck into the wall deep enough to hold the blade still.

He then carefully rubbed the flex cuff against the box cutter blade, in one direction and then the other, slowly back and forth, slowly carving into the thick plastic...until it gave way.

He closed the box cutter and pocketed it. He looked around the main room but found nothing of interest. He walked towards the door of the room Finn had appeared from when Bernie arrived earlier. It was a small storage space with shelves. He yanked out his camera again...time for another video and lots of photos.

Jane was going to have guinea pigs for sure. Bags and more bags—plastic bags—full of pills and little plastic packages of more white stuff filled the shelves. Bernie used his shirt tail to hoist a few bags up for a closer look. Awfully colorful stuff in them bags...like an Easter basket of Sweet Tarts to choose from...like an addict would be fussy. Sure looked like Officer Gallinen was runnin' his own DIY super pharmacy. But Bernie wasn't pointin' no fingers...yet.

When he was satisfied he'd seen enough and videoed enough, Bernie walked out to his truck. Finn looked like he might wake up soon, as he moaned and turned his head back and forth, still lying on the ground. One more brilliant idea struck Bernie, and he ran back to the dumpster.

Then Bernie loped back around to the front of the PSO building and got into his Jeep Gladiator. He kissed the steering wheel and told the truck he was sorry, turned it on, and drove cautiously out of the parking lot, not daring to aggravate the tires with speed.

When those tires touched the road, Bernie looked back. Finn remained flat on the ground...a little more arm waving now and some movement. Bernie thought it best not to stop and say goodbye. He stepped on the gas just a hair and motored on delicately towards the ferry, nursing the wobbly tires along.

Once he was at the dock, he rang up Hansen Moody.

"Hansen!"

"Yo."

"Hansen! I need an extraction! Quick!"

"What's that you're sayin'?"

"I need an extraction!"

"An extraction?"

"Yes, Hansen! An extraction, now!"

"Well, what are you callin' me for, Bernie? If you need an extraction, you call your dentist."

"God dang it, Hansen. Just come pick me up on the mainland at the Catunk Isle ferry terminal. I'm headin' back from Catunk towards you on the ferry...should take me about thirty-five minutes. So you got enough time to jump in your car and get over to the damn ferry dock and come pick me up. That's the extraction I need! You got it?"

"Oh, sure. OK. Lemme find my drivin' glasses and I'll see you in a pinch. But, Bernie, what happened to your truck?"

"She's OK, Hansen. But my truck and I need an extraction. I'll explain everything when I see you."

42

EARLY NOVEMBER, SAME DAY
The Pushaw Methodology

Jane was sitting at the PSO table when Bernie rolled on in two hours later...a radiating mass of dandelion yellow in his shrill yellow baseball cap, lemon yellow pants, and an over-sized Hawaiian shirt swarming with huge bananas—worn over a bright yellow flannel shirt.

There he is, my sunny hemorrhoid....

"For God's sake, Bernie. Look at you! What the hell did you think you were going to accomplish dressed like a giant ear of corn stuck in a banana tree?"

"Now, Jane...."

"Don't 'now Jane' me, Mr. Chiquita! You were supposed to concentrate on 'yellow' in your surveillance. Not go broadcasting it to the whole world." Jane threw her head down on her arms on the table. A muffled "Heaven help me" rose from her person.

"Jane, there you go again. All day long I been up the Yangtze and down the Wazoo for you, and all you can do is grouse at me. You're lettin' your stress triggers run wild. You're all upset about Israel. And I understand. We're all sad. But you got to move on, Jane. He ain't comin' back," said Bernie.

"How would you know anything about stress triggers? What makes you the expert?"

"I'm gettin' to be well read, Jane. I done a lot of research on unsympathetic nervous systems and all that.

And this here yeller outfit of mine you're all umbrageous about? It's a vital part of the Pushaw Methodology."

"Are you serious?" Jane groaned.

"Look, Jane. I been thinkin' about the art o' persuasion since me and Hansen started Old Farts Analytics. An' I come to conclude that if I get all decked out to look like a nutty good old boy, people will think that's what I am. And that's when they let their guard down and relax, maybe loosen their tongue a little. 'Cause they think I'm the village idiot. They want to get down and be friends with a local dude like me...get into the coastal groove."

"Fine, the Pushaw Methodology. Ground-breaking," Jane fumed. "But I'm in charge here, and I emphasized the need to proceed low-key. Now word is out that you apparently left Jerry at the boatyard steaming with suspicion. Plus someone on Catunk Isle called the State Police about Finn lying on the cold ground in a questionable state of health, drenched in some kind of cleaning fluid. That sure doesn't sound like they let their guard down and started grooving with you."

"Hold on there. You ain't heard the whole story yet," Bernie blurted.

"And a neighbor near the PSO office reported a human-sized lemon diving into the office dumpster repeatedly. Now who could that be? Were you scouting for treasures to bring to *Antiques Road Show?*" Jane dragged her hands down her face in frustration.

"Jane, you ever heard how inventor Alexander Grayham Bell wanted the whole world to say 'Ahoy' as the official telephone greeting? But Thomas Edison came up with 'Hello.' And here we are today."

"Meaning what?"

"All I'm sayin' is when you work hard for a certain result, you don't always get your say. But everything works out in the end, one way or the other. So don't fuss."

"You know, just.... Oh...God damn it, Bernie. Sit down and show me the evidence you collected."

Bernie handed Jane his phone and she skimmed through the pictures. Bernie had endless shots of Jerry Williams and quite a few of Finn Gallinen. Jane peered at all the photos of both men. And twice she watched the videos Bernie had recorded—of Finn's erratic walking, his dumpster cache, and his office "supplies."

"If you ask me, Jane, both these fellas look like they been swimmin' in lemon meringue pie," said Bernie.

Jane wanted to point out to him that it might be the reflection from his outfit that colored both men's faces in his photos, but she let it go. He really had delivered.

"Jesus, Bernie. Well done! This is bona fide evidence. I knew the hepatitis would finally kick in. But I did not know Finn was babysitting a mountain of illegal booty on Catunk Isle. Wonder how he plans to squirm out of this incriminating news. I've got to report everything to the head honchos in Boston right away."

"You be sure to give this to your head honchos, too," Bernie added as he yanked a plastic-wrapped brick out of his pants pocket and plunked it down in front of PSO Jane Roberts.

43

STILL EARLY NOVEMBER
Select Board Public Hearing

Intermission was over at the Select Board Hearing. The raw, chilly evening slithered into the public meeting room as the overflow crowd hurried back in to their seats or to huddle upright along the walls. Everyone was eager to see how Abe and Dahlia Jenkins would present their new adult use marijuana retail store.

While the Select Board Chair made his introductory remarks, the body heat grew palpable...from marijuana aficionados all gung-ho for the pot shop...and from non-users and conservatives and old-fashioned residents hotly against the very idea. India Barton stood up and cracked the door open to bring down the temperature.

As the Select Board's secretary and also Jane Robert's ally, India had her mission and she had her trepidations. She was no dummy. She knew that her finger on the video machine "play" button, even her entire body, might be the target of violent physical reactions once she launched Abe and Dahlia's "alleged" video. So she had an exit plan.

Waikiki Banner was no dummy. She knew better than to go anywhere near the public hearing that night.

Maggie Banner and Jane Roberts made sure to sit far apart from each other. Emotional popcorn was bursting through their bodies in anticipation.

With Dahlia at his side, Abe Jenkins stood up very tall and spoke about their plans. Jane thought what a striking

242

likeness Abe had to a young Clint Eastwood and Thomas Jefferson combined. Too bad, but very important, that he was about to be crushed.

Abe signaled India to start the video. She pressed PLAY, turned off the lights, and immediately got up and left the room.

A long, sweeping view of the Portland Jet Port filled the screen. Abe Jenkins jumped forward a few inches at the podium, his head still, his eyes strained forward like a super-sized hawk zeroing in on its prey. He looked around the crowded room and spoke.

"I'm sorry, folks. We may have gotten some family clip mixed up in what we meant to show you tonight. India, are you back there? Can you pause it?"

The image and audio of the airport suddenly burst alive with the laughing and hooting of Dahlia Jenkins. She could be seen racing towards Sonny Mannix and leaping onto his body with a big, fat, sexy hug. Then they began tickling and giggling, both bodies twirling in circles.

People in the audience gasped.

"What the hell! Is she braless?"

"Look at her...all dolled up in that sheer organza thing...not exactly a blouse, is it?"

In the relative dark, Dahlia froze. No one could quite see the look on her face. Nothing came out of her mouth.

People continued to gasp and whisper. Some noticed Sonny scrape back his chair and stand up to leave.

Abe called out to him, "Hang on there, Sonny. You're not going anywhere." Abe strode towards him and shoved him back into his seat.

"Dahlia, don't you move an inch. I want to see what's going on here."

"So do we!" someone shouted from the audience.

The Chair of the Select Board stood up and tried to take command, but Abe Jenkins wouldn't hear it. India Barton was nowhere near the video player to stop it, and no one else offered.

The scenes kept spilling forth...a tight, tidy record of high infidelity.

Abe watched, mesmerized by this spectacular end to whatever love he thought he felt for his wife. He ate up the pain, standing there with Dahlia at his side, and Sonny Mannix nearby—the wife thief. The three of them were surrounded by their fellow islanders, everyone more or less aghast or possibly amused as they stared at the screen. A family meltdown in living color.

The camera zoomed in for a close up of Dahlia as she waited for an American Airlines ticket agent to search something on the computer. Sonny's hand slipped down into the back of Dahlia's pants and everyone saw her bounce in place. She let out a cooey shriek and then turned to hold Sonny tight while he plunged his tongue down her throat.

"Looks like he's aimin' for her intestines!"

"That's what Abe gets for marrying a girl from New Jersey...."

India was amazed at the comments. People would say anything in the dark. She peeked around the corner at the spectacle as the Board Chair rose abruptly, reached for the light switch, and violently signaled India to get back to her post and turn off the video machine.

He then announced the public hearing had come to an end and that they would reconvene at another time, which would be posted at the Town Office.

People were bent forward, mouths open, quietly swearing their heads off, and in a few cases, rubbing their partners' backs affectionately.

Jane knew she should act as thunderstruck as everyone else. She looked at her pal Rajiv Basrak, the Indian restauranteur, sitting next to her. "What just happened?"

"The truth, maybe? I guess?" he said.

<h1 style="text-align:center">44</h1>

<h1 style="text-align:center">LATER IN NOVEMBER</h1>

Hot Potato

New England's DEA Chief Maxwell Dunham had been in this business long enough to know he had a hot potato on his hands. Whether the hot potato was PSO Jane Roberts, or her determination, or her hypothesis, or her hunches, or her photos and videos and brick of heroin, or the suspect parties, or Jane's request for all kinds of dodgy court orders and warrants to obtain all kinds of information, or some of the above, or all of the above, was the stinker.

Dunham had suggested to the FBI's Alex Champus in passing that Champus might be ideal to help Dunham tackle this roaring wasp nest up in the Pine Tree State. But Champus hurriedly bowed out due to what Dunham was convinced was a fictitious assignment on a fictitious case. Champus acted as if he never wanted to go north of Sturbridge Village again for the rest of his life.

Dunham knew Jane was on the right track, but he had his overall priorities to adhere to. He had concluded he had to start looking like he was reining in cowgirl Jane Roberts and her stampede over the professional reputation of her colleagues.

He picked up the phone and dialed St. Frewin's Island. Helen Orbeton took the call and put him through to her boss.

"Jane, it's Chief Dunham. Any more suspects gallop up to your front door?"

"Oh, Chief Dunham, so glad to hear from you! I hope you've had a chance to read my report. And I hope it didn't bowl you over with all my conjectures and evidentiary requests. I'm really determined to bring Harriet and Finn and that Jerome Williams to justice if you can find ways to obtain those warrants and court orders for the info I need." This was Dunham's hot potato speaking.

"So let me walk through all of this with you, Jane, to be sure I understand your reasoning. OK?"

"All set, Chief."

"First off, you believe the arrest of Fredly Tunny for the murder of Israel Tenner is total bull, that the homicide report was deliberately misleading, and either the wrong person was arrested or Fredly wasn't working alone.

"That's right, Chief," Jane said.

"You know, call me Max, Jane. Just Max. No Chief necessary."

"OK...Max. As I was saying, those Tunny men are a bunch of big bacteria balls. They hunt, shoot, drink, and kill animals, all of which they probably think entitles them to collect social security. But no one or more of them is solely guilty for Israel Tenner's death. I'm sure of that."

"Your basis for that certainty?"

"Before Israel was killed, he misspoke. He revealed something that suggested he had knowledge of an ongoing, top-secret mission on Ferguson Mountain to round up drug dealers and corrupt members of Maine's law force. Knowledge that he shouldn't have had. And he told me that blunder made him fear for his life. That his corrupt fellow force members might want to kill him for spilling the beans. Out of fear that he would give up their names—the names of the guilty, their plans, what have you."

"Who heard what Israel said?" Dunham asked.

"Ah, well, I need to confess, Chief. I mean Max. There were several guests at a private party who may have understood the implications of what Israel said, but no corrupt State employees heard anything at that point." *Should I just bite the bullet? Swallow the whole gun for Christ's sake? Yes!*

Jane elaborated, "In all honesty, Max, it was my big mistake that probably led to Israel's death. My fault...."

"And what was that, Jane?"

"I reported the incident to Finn Gallinen, and he reported it to Harriet Buxton. But then, as I started to look at the big picture, I began to sense they both might be crooked. And suddenly Israel was dead. And all these suspicions and misgivings I had about Harriet and Finn fell right into place. So I think we can forget Fredly Tunny for now."

"Go ahead. Continue."

"Well, look at Israel's fear," Jane said. "If Israel was correct—that people would want to kill him—then there's a lot at stake here, Max—high stakes. And I don't just mean the destroyed Phantom spyware."

"You didn't say that last point, Jane. And I didn't hear it."

"Yes, sir."

Dunham continued to discuss with Jane the basis of her belief that Harriet and Finn were complicit in Israel's death, along with Jerome Williams. To Jane's perplexity, Dunham took in stride her report of a hidden tomb's worth of drugs in Finn's office and dumpster on Catunk

Isle...and the *Sinaloa Cartel Approved Narco Killer's Living Language Guide,* which Harriet might be using to really get into the swing of things to learn how to kill people in Spanish.

"And don't forget, Max," Jane said, hoping to pile on some kind of sweet and gooey evidence that would finally entice him. "The Maine Capitol Police are holding a security camera video for you that shows my three suspects entering the HR building after hours. That establishes they know one another. And if you can provide the warrants, we could get our hands on Israel's application for work, on all the suspects' cell phones, on all their blood tests for hepatitis. We could get down to the nasty truth."

"Those are a lot of hunches, Jane. Why is Israel's work application so important to your hypothesis?"

Jane had to keep her mouth shut on that one. No blithely admitting she had snooped around in the HR file room after hours. She owed it to Gail in HR not to get her fired. Jane owed it to herself as well.

"Max, that is exactly why we need those warrants ASAP. To see what information exists to fill in the gaps in my thinking."

"Jane, if this turns out to be a fishing expedition, are you going to regret pointing the dagger and taking the first plunge at your colleagues?"

"Well, with all due respect, Max, they already got their hands on that dagger where Israel was concerned."

"You're absolutely convinced, Jane?"

"Yes, sir."

"Even about the hepatitis B?"

"Sir...Max, how could it be a coincidence that out of the blue, Harriet, Finn, and Jerry are all turning yellow? What else could it mean?"

"All right. I'm going to speak to Harriet and Finn next to see what they have to say for themselves. And I'll get started on a probable cause affidavit to obtain an arrest warrant for Jerome Williams. But I'll hold off on filing that for the moment. Believe me, Jane, I would love to take down whoever is stirring this cesspool."

....

One week after her conversation with Maxwell Dunham, Jane was glowering at the flow chart she had kept to build her case against Harriet & Co. She traced through for the hundredth time her spidery yet tensile, methodical leaps of faith that were meant to wad Harriet, Finn, and Jerry into a criminal ball that Jane could lob into prison for a very long time.

So, why was Jane feeling utterly crestfallen today? Why was she ready to quit and go bury herself alive in the potato fields of Fort Kent? Had she been gravely mistaken in her zeal and spirit of vendetta? According to Chief Maxwell Dunham, yes.

He called Jane to give her the bad news. To wit, Harriet explained their hepatitis came from eating at the Lonely Owl, a restaurant they all went to the night they were seen on the Capitol Police security tape. However, they came down with hepatitis A, not hep B.

Furthermore, the trio met that night at the state office to discuss how the local drug trade might stash drugs on boats around Catunk Isle. Jerry came along to provide schematics and insights about boat design.

All of this was purely innocent and necessary if Finn was going to learn how to pierce the drug traffickers' schemes. In fact, Finn had caught some drug traffickers just last week, which explained the contraband duly seized and temporarily stored at the Catunk Isle PSO. Maine State Police were withholding news of the bust until the apprehended parties could be questioned further.

Obviously, Harriet reasoned, Jane Roberts had gotten carried away on a flight of fantasy and was trying to force an alternative conclusion on innocent events, saddened as she was by the death of her assistant, Israel Tenner.

Jane wasn't buying any of it. "Max, did anyone in your office hear any news about Finn's miraculous arrest of drug traffickers? And why would the State allow such hot product to sit around in a PSO storage room and a dumpster with no locks whatsoever?

"Then there's the three of them, Harriet, Finn, and Jerry, meeting about boat blueprints in the dark of night in the State office file room. Does that make any sense? And if I'm part of the anti-corruption team located on an island, why wasn't I included in the blueprint discussion? Are we going to sit back and not ask for official hepatitis blood test results? And what about this contagious restaurant serving up hep A on a week night? We need to ask all those questions, Max."

"Jane, I do have two questions...how did you know to check the Capitol Police security camera for that specific night? And what makes you say the three specifically met in the State office file room?"

"Me? Well...*this had better be good, Roberts...it's got to make sense! Sweet Jesus, please airdrop me some bull shit—NOW!*

"You see, in the late afternoon, I met with Dr. Kerner at the Medical Examiner's building to ask him more questions about Israel Tenner's death. And then I was hungry, so I grabbed a piece of pizza from the Capitol Cafeteria and ate it in my car in the Human Resources parking lot. That's when I saw Harriet and the others enter the building. It struck me as fundamentally odd, especially when I recognized Jerry Williams with them."

That's it, Jane...keep deflecting from "see Jane fib" to "see Harriet and Finn fib." Put the spotlight on the killers!

She took a deep breath and gave Max another false crumb. "Did I say file room? How silly. I have no idea where that came from. And, Max, it continues to strike me as odd that Harriet, the Director of Human Resources at the Maine State Police, would not delegate to our official DEA squad the task of spoon-feeding drug training information to Officer Finn Gallinen."

Jane heaved back in her office chair and made all kinds of faces into the phone mouthpiece.

"I'm sorry, Jane," Dunham said. He had to keep playing the game a little longer...just a little longer.

"I've gone over your points with my team down here in Boston and none of us is convinced you have a case. So we think it's now time to repair the creative damage you've done to your colleagues' efforts to fight crime."

"What does that mean, Max?"

"I'd like you to meet with me individually in Augusta next Monday to look over your future options. Then we'll join Harriet and Finn, and you're going to apologize to them officially."

45

NOVEMBER, THURSDAY
Born Detectives

Next Monday? My future options?? Apologize to Harriet and Finn? Next Monday! The motherfuckers. OK...I have until next Monday to set the world straight....

"So what do you say, Joe? Want to drive up to Augusta tomorrow to help me with my investigation? It could be a PSO treat," Jane said to Joe Miller as they sat munching on macho nachos at the St. Frewin's Island Pub on Thursday evening.

"Are you permitted to have a civilian tag along as you're suggesting, Jane? Especially when that civilian happens to work for one of your key suspects?"

Jane frowned. Why was Joe being such a thoughtful and cautious American?

"Don't be a wet blanket, Joe! Look, I admit this is possibly about Jerry Williams. I've been very up front with you about that. And I realize you have a built-in conflict of interest here, given that you are a boat carpenter at Calderwood Boatyard. But I hate to drive up to Augusta all by myself. And this research may involve eating lunch at a restaurant...and I hate eating alone in restaurants. So, come on...be a good sport. Come along with me."

"What about Konstantin? What's he going to think?"

"Konstantin? Why would he have a say about our doing epidemiological research at a restaurant in Augusta?"

"You know what I mean. You're his woman, right?"

"God, you are too old-fashioned, Joe. I'm his modern woman. And besides, Konstantin is thousands of miles away at sea. And I suspect he could care less if you and I have lunch together while I'm hunting down some contagious virus in a greasy dive."

"This is really sounding appealing, Jane. I think you better tell me what's involved in your trek to Augusta, or I'm walking out of here in a minute."

"OK...relax, relax. I hate having to say this again. But everything I'm about to tell you is confidential. I'm already in hot water with my superiors in at least four different divisions of State and Federal government."

"Understood."

"Good. Because I'll kill you if you slip up, Joe. So, here it is. Your boss, Jerry Williams, and certain unnamed parties claim they got hepatitis this past August at the Lonely Owl, a restaurant in the Augusta area. So I want to see this Lonely Owl with my own eyes, and I want to investigate the hepatitis incident."

"The Lonely Owl? You don't say." Joe closed his eyes momentarily as if concentrating. "I think that's where Jerry mentioned he was going to meet some folks from the Maine State Police for dinner. And in August you said. That sounds right."

"What? Jerry mentioned his little outing out loud? I wonder if that was deliberate."

Jane reached for another macho nacho. "I know. I bet he was sauteing his alibi, even at that point. Sprinkling details of his activities to anyone listening, to enhance the seeming innocence of his dinner plans. And remember Joe. This is all confidential."

"Cross my heart, Jane."

"So are you with me? Or are you out?"

"Jane, I like you. I think we've got a simpatico thing going on whenever we're around each other. So, sure, count me in. It's quiet enough at work, so I'll take a personal day off. And I'll go with you to Augusta and hold your hand while you eat infected French fries. Satisfied?"

"Joe—I've always loved you! From the moment you first walked into my office and declared me a swirl baby. Ha ha!!"

"That's right. You'll have to tell me more about where those crescent eyes of yours came from...and those high cheek bones that look like little docked lambs' tails. Over lunch, that is."

"Deal."

....

Todd Chisolm leaned forward, chin on his hand, and studied the photos on his desk at the Evidence Response Team Office in Augusta. Before and After evidence photos. What had changed? What had someone— Harriet and her crew, or whoever—been looking for?

The photos had taken forever to reach Todd's desk, and Todd had taken forever to pay them any attention. But on Thursday evening, Todd stayed late to review the two sets of pictures supplied by the evidence tech who had forgotten his camera at Israel's apartment.

Many objects had been "gently" pushed around in the apartment, and Todd hoped to God he could discern what, if anything, had been taken.

On the fifteenth photo, he found his answer. The Before photo showed a cell phone beneath a magazine on a bureau...hardly visible, but visible all the same.

The After photo showed the same magazine on top of the bureau. But where was the cell phone?

Todd scoured all of the After photos a second time. None of them contained a cell phone. He would put in a call tomorrow to the St. Frewin's Island PSO.

46

NOVEMBER, FRIDAY
The Lonely Owl

It wasn't hard to dissect the menu at the Lonely Owl. They offered everything every other "Home-Cooked! Never Fast Food!" outfit in the State of Maine offered...cup o' chowder, house green salad, ranch or Italian dressing, fried clams, burger, French fries, sweet potato fries as an add-on, grilled cheese sandwich, club sandwich, ham steak with pineapple, and grape nut pudding.

Hot damn! Jane loved exotic gourmet junkets at exclusive enclaves frequented by the rich and famous. No time like the present!

She and Joe were soon seated in a booth by their hostess, who looked like she was on the loose from the nearest assisted-living complex. Jane asked if the manager or owner was on duty, and the ancient maître d' pointed to a giant standing behind the bar. He had rump roasts for cheeks and an intensely black pile of hair swirled in a nest of styling gel.

"Joe, I'll be right back. Don't order quite yet," Jane said.

She walked past fellow diners ripping into their ham steaks and approached the manager? owner? at the counter. "Hi there! I'm sorry to bother you with a crazy question, but did I hear your place had an incident with hepatitis this past summer?"

Rump Face picked up a large knife with his huge hands and started wiping down the blade. "Now young lady, do you want me to call the cops before or after you eat your contaminated lunch? It's up to you. That's what I ask all my guests who come in here with questions so full of bull shit, they're liable to choke to death before they decide what beverage they want."

"Ah, is that a yes or a no, sir?"

The giant turned away from Jane and busied himself with pouring endless ingredients into a blender. Jane Roberts recognized a frosty shoulder when she saw one. She returned to the booth and started pelting Joe with her indignations.

"Wouldn't it be simpler," Joe said quietly, "to call the State CDC office and ask if there's been a public complaint or official investigation into hepatitis at this joint? Isn't that how such situations are usually handled?"

"That would be too easy, Joe. Boring. This is more fun, don't you think?"

"Not if we're going to get hepatitis ourselves."

"OK...you're right. Wait a minute. I'll step outside and call the CDC on my cell phone and see if they can answer my question quickly. Be right back," said Jane.

As she slithered into the booth a few minutes later, Jane had a conspiratorial look on her face. "Just as I suspected. The CDC hasn't heard a word about any contamination tied to the Lonely Owl...never, ever."

"So how does that fit into your big picture? Or maybe you can't tell me?"

"What I can say, Joe, is it's time to order our lunch!"

....

"Here, Jane. Open your mouth." Joe aimed a sweet potato fry at her lips. She was hungry.

"Open again," Joe said, as he carefully forked part of his burger into her mouth.

"Are you trying to avoid eating, Joe? Just in case the CDC hasn't caught up yet with all the microbes feasting on the Lonely Owl?"

"I'm not that unchivalrous, Jane. I'm trying to nourish you...."

"How kind of you to care."

"I do care. Come closer."

She leaned in towards the Michael Corleone sitting across from her...his flowing hair like thick, soft ropes of licorice. That's how he struck her, every time she saw him. In another time, in another place...this could be her Sicilian lover...except....

"What about Konstantin?" Jane whispered with Joe only inches away.

"What about him?" Joe asked, as he hesitated for a moment and wiped his hands on his napkin. Then he slowly touched her lamby-pie cheekbones and gently slipped his middle finger between her lips.

Jane didn't know how to respond. Though she didn't jump back or bite him. With Joe's finger quite at home on her warm tongue in her warm mouth, she sat there, hoping Rump Roast was looking at them. And she sat there, wondering if she should order the grape nut pudding for dessert. With or without whipped cream?

....

The tiny sounds of the song "Count on Me" were pinging in the air when Jane focused and realized it was her own cell phone. She smiled at Joe, politely released his single finger, and settled back in her seat to take the call.

"Jane, it's Helen. Where are you?"

"Still in Augusta. Why? What's up?"

"Well, I guess you don't have to rush right back. But I wanted to let you know out of the blue I got a little hand-written letter in my mail box from Monica Tunny. Remember Israel and I told you about her? She's Fredly Tunny's niece. Monica who rescued the kittens with Israel this past summer?"

Jane perked up. "What does it say?"

"I'd rather we don't do all this on the phone, Jane. I also have an update from the Town Office about the Jenkins' pot shop application. And Todd Chisolm from Augusta wants you to call him. So let's talk when you get back."

"OK, right. I'll jump in my truck in a minute. I'll meet you at the office about 4 pm." Jane hung up.

"Joe, we've got to go. New developments back home."

"Sure...I'll go pay and we can get out of here."

"But this was my treat, Joe."

"No, I'll pay. And Jane, I was wrong to try that finger move on you in this place of all places. You're coming to my house for dinner soon...a far better setting for getting to know each other better."

....

"So this is what showed up in my mail box at home today, Jane," Helen said, handing Jane a small card with a kitten on the front of it. They were seated at the PSO table.

Jane opened the note and read its short contents. "Dear Mrs. Orbeton, It's not true. What I told my uncle is not true. Israel was a nice man. He saved the kittens. That's all he did. —Monica"

"Helen...we knew this all along. You knew it, right?"

"Yes, Jane. Israel wouldn't think to bother any kids. Those Tunny men are warped. Always have been."

"I guess this won't officially be very useful as acceptable evidence, but it makes me feel a whole lot better. On the other hand, I have to think this through about who to show this to, if at all. I don't want to get Monica in any kind of trouble with her insane relatives."

"I won't tell a soul, Jane. But I knew you'd want to see the note."

"And what about the Jenkins matter, Helen?"

"It shouldn't come as any surprise. The Town Office reported that Abe and Dahlia pulled their application. I don't know much more, though some people say he's had a huge jump in bookings for his water taxi. I guess that says something."

"I bet it's a show of support for Abe's real business," Jane said as she pondered the news. So, Abe and Dahlia were off the agenda...for the moment anyway. Almost kind of a let-down. And if they wouldn't be back at some point, someone else probably would. But for now? Well, Waikiki's hot adultery tape had worked its magic. For now. Jane let the warm glow flow through her.

Next she settled in at her desk to focus on the ammo she had clawed together since Max Dunham had informed her that the figurative axe would be figuratively ready to chop off her accusatory head on Monday.

First of all, the Lonely Owl restaurant had no outbreak of hepatitis. Therefore, Harriet & Co. did not contract hepatitis of any alphabet at this particular outfit.

Second, apparently the Tunny menfolk had squeezed a sort of false positive out of their young niece, Monica, no matter what their link to Israel's murder. Jane wasn't sure she could wave this fact in front of anyone's nose, but it stoked her bravado.

Finally, Jane would continue to hold her Prying Jerry ace close to her chest. Though its impact as evidence was quickly fading. What was the point of reporting to Max Dunham the fact that Jerome Williams had snooped around in the late Israel Tenner's apartment while it was still a crime scene? Max wasn't in the mood for Jane's pleas and posits. And she assumed Lieutenant Adderley's office had negligently buried this juicy piece of the picture for the rest of time.

"Jane," Helen called out to her PSO. "I'm going home now. Don't forget to call Todd Chisolm. He said it was important."

"Oh, that's right. Thanks, Helen."

....

"Holy cow. Could you repeat that, Todd? I'm trying to take notes here while my hair is on fire." Jane tried not to hyperventilate while she grabbed paper and pen.

"Sure, Jane. I've got two sets of photos...the photos our team took in Israel's apartment the first time they visited, and the photos our tech took the second time he returned to get the camera he left behind. I finally had a chance to compare both sets of pictures last night. And you need to know that apparently someone took a cell phone from the apartment after Israel's death."

"Unbelievable," Jane said.

"Based on the fingerprints the tech dusted on his return trip over, I'm guessing Harriet Buxton, or Finn Gallinen, or Jerome Williams had something to do with the phone's disappearance."

"Hold on, Todd. There's one problem I see," Jane said. "Why didn't the evidence team take the cell phone during their first sweep through Israel's apartment? Why leave it behind? It's valuable evidence."

"Maybe you need to ask whoever is really in charge of this investigation."

Right, Jane mused. Like talking to a wall...a heartless stone wall.

47

NOVEMBER, MONDAY
Shark Tank

Monday!

Jane took a long look in the mirror. Anne Boleyn stood to her left; Marie Antoinette, to her right. Mary Queen of Scots phoned in to say she couldn't make it that morning.

AB & MA were smiling at Jane, and they told her what she needed to do. First of all, out with the wild and crazy hair. She brushed it smooth and wound it into a fat French twist. Like lifting the veil to reveal the profile of a Down East Nefertiti.

Out with the stark, unembellished eyes! Smokey grey blue Lancôme eyeliner, lower lids only. L'Oreal Plum Wine for the lips. Parfait...stick with the French cosmetics Marie Antoinette advised.

And by the way, on top of the fact that her PSO job was heading for the Trash Master, Jane was irked about The Lipstick Problem. L'Oreal had discontinued Plum Wine! Her favorite shade! She was nearly at the end of her stick of this beloved cosmetic and it didn't exist anywhere anymore on the planet.

Oh sure, L'Oreal had waited ten years after retiring Jane's Plum Wine, and then the company reissued a new Plum Wine. But it looked nothing like Jane's Plum Wine. Jane wanted to know why? Did hazardous chemicals produce the first perfect shade of Plum Wine? Who cared nowadays?! What would one more daily layer of gorgeous toxic matter on Jane's lips matter? Jane certainly wasn't planning on getting pregnant.

Poisons were everywhere anyway. Everyone was infused with plastic microchips from just walking around the house. Apples, broccoli, and kale were loaded with crap. Chemical tanks exploded daily. Fatal fentanyl dust was ubiquitous in certain neighborhoods, like Harriet Buxton's desk—possibly—for instance. So why not reissue Plum Wine lipstick? Jane needed to write somebody at L'Oreal a letter.

She turned in the mirror. Black military-tailored dress jacket with the striking double row of muted gold buttons, paired with deep grey, silky wide-legged pants and slim, black Dolce Vita day boots.

Forget the ermine, Anne Boleyn said. She didn't bother to wear it either, no matter what the Tower of London registers of beheadings claimed.

Jane was more than satisfied with her armor. She had her pride after all. If the blade should fall, it would fall on the slender neck of a fashion icon...well, as much of a fashion icon as was going to show up in Augusta, Maine, in late November.

Meanwhile, Joe Miller had remained attentive over the past forty-eight hours, which surprised Jane, despite the incident of the bold digit at the Lonely Owl. He called her twice to remind her their dinner was in the stars. Jane kept dismissing him with "Oh, Joe!" but she had agreed to let him drive her to Augusta on Monday.

....

Joe parked his truck in front of the Maine Bureau of Human Resources office. He watched Jane jump out on her side. She took long, confident strides as if her upswept hair and swanky outfit infused her with the energy of a rock star leaping onto the stage.

Joe hurried to reach her side to walk with her. "You look like you stepped out of *Town and Country*, Jane."

"Yah, right. My thumbnail pic squashed on the bottom of the society page with full spreads above of Camilla and Kate towering over me. No thank you," Jane demurred.

"Listen, I'll take a hike around the Capitol while you're in your meeting." Joe stopped them both then and took Jane's hands. "I've got your back. You need to know that."

"You're so corny, Joe. What are you trying to say?"

He left her to wonder as he walked away.

....

God, here goes nothing. Here goes Jane Roberts. I really don't like being inside government administrative offices...painted concrete block walls, dull posters about germs and terrorists, people pacing the halls trying to look meaningful, the permanent microwave popcorn plume, the desk-bound lethargy. And what is wrong with Max anyway? Why doesn't he get my points? I bet he had a blast picking his tie for today's decapitation of PSO Jane Roberts...maybe rainbow fentanyl chewies on light blue silk?

Chief Maxwell Dunham came up to Jane as she passed through the entry. "Good morning, Jane. Let's take the elevator. We're heading to the executive suite on the top floor."

Whoopy ding. I get to see the executive suite before I crash and burn. At least he didn't open up with a chokehold.

Jane was impressed when she and Max stepped out of the elevator. The executive suite proved to be tastefully designed in bleached pine and granite...clean lines, no curlicues. Impossible to believe, but there were no moose, lobsters, chickadees, or State o' Maine cutouts to remind her that she was, in fact, in Maine.

Simple sofas and armchairs upholstered in pale greys were arranged in clusters about the large room. An expansive glass wall with a glass door separated the main room from a smaller side room, which was empty at the moment.

"Jane, have a seat." Max directed her to a chair facing the glass wall. He cleared his throat.

"Now I know how committed you are to your job. And the unique outlook you bring, plus your energy, are all working in your favor at this point."

"Thanks, Max."

"What I'm about to say won't make you happy. I realize you've put a lot of effort into trying to make sense of Israel Tenner's death. But it's time you take a break from that, Jane. Take a break from your duties, your post, all of it. In other words, we've decided you are going on a mandatory leave of absence for three months."

Jane wondered if she should object. Start jumping up and down snarling, or race out of the room and pound the elevator buttons dramatically. She did none of that.

Instead, she began thinking deep thoughts about Israel, about cell phones, about the Before and After photos of Israel's apartment that Todd Chisolm had recently analyzed. And her thoughts wandered into fancy and that "funny feeling" territory. Maybe she had a hunch...maybe....

"Consider it a cooling off period—time for you to reflect and relax," Max continued. "Instead of leave without pay, you will receive half your regular salary plus health benefits, which fortunately, I was able to negotiate for you."

What a motherchucker. What a canned speech off a can of tuna. He sounds like he's giving Last Rites. He's so smooth, he must be popping something...Xanax, Valium...some kind of Benzodiazepine prodigy.

Jane noticed movement through the glass wall. She looked up and saw Harriet and Finn AND Jerome Williams walking into the adjacent room.

The sharks have entered their tank. They've even dragged in Jerry Baby. What pathetic aquarium mates. And I'm supposed to apologize to these felonious schmucks?! How long can I put off the torture?

"Max, everything you say is fine. Acceptable. I can live with it all. But now I have a demand if I can call it that. It's something I never got around to doing, and I don't know why not. But with you here to chime in, it will be all the more fitting. Your presence will bring added dignity and official acknowledgment to the gesture."

"What is it, Jane?" Max said.

"I'd like you and me, together, to call Israel's parents right now and tell them how very sorry we are for what happened to their son. I have their Vermont number here in my phone...OK for me to call them?"

"Sure. That's fine. I'm quite willing to thank them for their son's service and give my sympathies."

Jane dialed the out-of-state number. Her call began to ring. Two seconds later, the sound of another ringing phone sang through the glass wall where Harriet and the two men were standing.

Jane and Max watched Harriet open her bag to fish out a phone and look at the call. The phone kept ringing.

Harriet raised her eyes towards Jane and Max. A ribbon of fear or some indecipherable emotion slipped across her face. And the "here and now" were as though they were happening in ever so slow motion...Jane and Max both suspended in a vat of psychological molasses, unable to stir themselves to respond. They were witnessing the unimaginable, even after all of Jane's persistent finger-pointing. Even after Todd Chisolm's latest finding about the missing cell phone.

Then, like a rogue wave, the weight of the truth crashed through the glass wall.

Jane leaped up. "Max, I've had it! This can't be yet another coincidence!" She yanked the glass door open and half-stormed, half-tumbled into the shark tank in her military buttons and spindly boots.

"I have to ask the obvious question, Harriet," Jane roared. "What the hell are you doing with Israel's parents' phone?!"

Jane wrestled the phone out of Harriet's hand...almost. Harriet yelped and clenched the Android to her chest.

Jane chopped sharply at Harriet's wrist. The phone flew to the floor and Jane flew after it. As she reached for the device, Finn aimed his boot to kick the phone away from Jane, and he threw his arm out to grab her hair.

"Get the fuck out of my French twist, you homicidal robot!" Jane screamed. She lowered her head and rammed her whole self into Finn's groin. He yelled and fell backwards. Jane could see Jerry Baby trying to duck out the exit door on tip toes, as if he had entered the room by mistake.

Jane scooped up the phone and stood up straight, glaring at the Director of Human Resources. "There is no way on earth I'm apologizing to you murderers!"

A rush of bodies slammed into Jerry and filled the small room before Jane had finished her sentence. She turned towards the stampede. Joe Miller—JOE MILLER?!—and four men, who looked like giant pine trees, were charging at Harriet and Finn. A fifth giant yoked Jerry Williams into a headlock.

Joe Miller...Jane was ready to faint. What was he doing here?

Harriet started up again, squawking rubbish, asking why Jane was so misguided and jumping down Harriet's throat.

Jane knew she would die if Harriet managed to slither out of one more tight spot. But that wasn't going to happen today. Thirty-six limbs were twirling like weather vanes blown off in a hurricane. Five times as many expletives collided with all the flailing. Shiny metal handcuffs flashed in the air and snapped tight.

Joe and the hulks finally strong-armed Harriet & Co. into submission. But what just happened? How did Joe miraculously appear? Would someone please tell Jane Roberts what was going on?

....

"Jane, I brought you a glass of water. Are you all right?"

A glass of water?! Listen to this guy! A glass of water? How about a trough of gin and tonic, Jefe??

Max Dunham had finally dropped the unctuous tack. He and Jane were seated alone once again in the executive suite. "It's been an explosive afternoon, so if you don't want to talk or stick around any longer, I can understand. We can catch up tomorrow by phone."

"True, Max. Very true...explosive. Hah." Jane let out an elephant shudder. How was she going to get home?

"Is Joe Miller around, or did he head over to the police station to book his prime suspects?"

"He's gone to help with all the paperwork, Jane. He might be at it half the night. But he did tell me to let you know the keys to his truck are on top of the right rear tire. You can take his truck. He'll borrow one of the state cars to get home later."

"You know, Max. I will be going now. We can talk tomorrow. But one last question. My post on the island, my PSO job–all intact, right? Like none of this ever happened?"

"Yes, Jane."

"Then I want a raise."

48

EARLY DECEMBER
A Tale of Two Islands: First Island

Helen Orbeton tossed around several baking ideas and narrowed it down to snowy, ground almond Greek wedding cookies...Jane and her visitors would have that perfect something to nibble on during the homicide wrap-up on Israel Tenner's death.

Jane welcomed Storm Nosmot and Mr. FBI—Alex Champus, of all people—into the PSO office. What a contrast of characters, she mused, as they trooped past her...the warm, kind, honest giant versus the scrawny, deceitful Federal Broomstick of Immorality. Was that going too far? No, it wasn't.

The two men sat down at the PSO long-plank table. Helen brought out a pot of tea and her cookies rolled in confectioner's sugar.

"Not too much salt in these cookies, is there?" Alex Champus winked at Helen and Jane.

"It's so unlike you to make a joke, Alex. That's an encouraging sign," Jane said.

"You know, Roberts, I'm going to admit something. But don't let it get to your head." Champus reached for a cookie.

"And what's that," Jane said.

"I honestly admire your work on this case. You almost single-handedly brought down a vast, deadly cabal, and it didn't cost the State a whole lot."

"Not so fast, Champus. It cost us Israel Tenner's life. Don't forget that. Remember him in your prayers, please."

"OK, you two," Storm jumped in. "In Israel's memory, let's get professional and focus on the evidence that's sending his murderers to prison. As you, Jane, suspected, Harriet, Finn, and Jerome Williams tested positive for Hepatitis B, not A."

Alex Champus continued. "We sent all their cell phones and computers off to technical forensics. They found texts and emails tied to the killing of Israel. Plus the coordination of the corrupt police force mob and efforts to abort legitimate drug busts. They even had drug trafficking plans of their own in the works."

"But wait a minute. I want to know why it took so long to close in on these guys?" Jane said. "I was chasing down evidence for more than three months. What were the DEA and the FBI doing all that time? Don't tell me they swallowed Harriet's mythic arrest of Fredly Tunny? And why did Max Dunham string me along and pooh-pooh my analysis? What do you know, Storm?"

"Jane, after you alerted Turk about your concerns for Israel's life and before he wandered away from the mountain house, Turk and Chummy talked to Israel long enough to confirm your suspicions about Harriet and Finn were on the right track. The DEA and the FBI had your suspects in their sites, but the government wanted to time their arrests...they wanted the facts to pile up so they had enough to cut down Harriet and all her cronies for good," said Storm.

"And Jane," Champus said, "obviously no one intended for Israel to take off and land in the clutches of Harriet and Finn and Jerome Williams. After Israel's murder, the landscape changed. Maxwell Dunham was no longer chasing down simply rogue law enforcement doing dirty deals. Now the scoundrels had real blood on their hands. And your tenacity in pulling the strings tighter and tighter helped bring it all home."

"But Max didn't know I would want to call Israel's parents. And neither Max nor I knew for sure that Harriet would be carrying that certain cell phone," Jane said.

"No, he did not. As it turned out, what you did was pure gold, Jane. But like I said, Max did have a handle of sorts on what Harriet was up to by that point. The DEA and the FBI obtained wiretap orders on various people's cell phones to track them after Israel's death."

"Wiretap orders?" Jane was surprised. "What about all that Phantom equipment at the mountain house? I thought Turk and his buds had the power to control the phones of anyone that mattered. Didn't that surveillance help before Israel's death?"

Champus paused in his answer. "Look, I can't say anything. But I will say this. The use of the Phantom on U.S. soil was a temporary experiment...it didn't go far and it's over."

"Hah...didn't go far. No, it didn't. Samantha Lloyd castrated it."

"Let's just leave it at that, Jane."

She could see Champus was tired of her questions and probably wished she'd shut the hell up. But she couldn't.

"So why on earth did Harriet still have the phone that I thought belonged to Israel's parents?"

Champus looked at Storm. "I've got this. OK. The tech guys were finally able to crack the phone. They discovered it was loaded with technical data about using drones for illegal drug drops...something Israel had been researching for the corrupt cops. So Harriet really wanted the contents of that phone."

"Drones for drug drops? Oh, good. So instead of 'Hellooo, Federal!' it's now 'Hellooo, Fentanyl!'?"

"Jane, it's no longer 'Hellooo, Federal.' That's an old commercial," Storm said.

"Yes, but cocaine drone deliveries? To whom? Shut-ins?" Jane said.

"No. Well, yes, sort of, come to think of it," said Champus. "To prisoners in prison—it's the latest trend."

"Good God." Jane shook her head.

And then she continued with her questions. "What about Jerome Williams and Fredly Tunny? Why were they involved?"

"Again, as you suspected," Storm explained, "Jerome Williams is a man deeply in debt for all kinds of legitimate and illegal reasons. And when he tried to skim off the profits of drug sales at the Calderwood Boatyard, Harriet heard about it from her narc buddies and turned the screws on Williams for her own purposes. As for Mr. Tunny, he's an unlucky addict who was in the wrong place at the wrong time, and he got dragged in to take the fall."

"And the officials handling all this...are they going to bring in everyone involved, do you think?" Jane asked.

"The cell phone logs are helping us track down a large network, and if people open up enough, we'll pin down everyone we can," said Storm.

"What about Lieutenant Adderley?" Jane wondered. "Guilty or not?"

"He really knew nothing, if you can believe it. Harriet made sure of that. She knew he would never go along with her schemes, and this way if she ever fell from grace, he would remain a free man."

"Wasn't that loving of her...." Jane looked disgusted as she said it.

"Harriet admitted she was the one who got Adderley to call you that night to assure you Israel would stay safe with the mountain guys. Adderley had no reason not to believe her," said Storm.

"Did you hear Adderley's about to retire?" asked Champus.

Neither Storm or Jane had heard. So now they had something else to hold their breath about. Who would replace Lieutenant Adderley?

Everyone got up from the table, to stretch, to bring their meeting to a close.

"Storm, why did Harriet ever start down this path?" Jane needed to hear it from him.

"Money? Power? Money, the thrill, money. It's always the same, isn't it?"

"Is it that simple? Is that what people want out of life?" she said.

"Well, Jane, look at Harriet's best friends. People like Winnifred Billings and Diane Savoy, both wealthy women who have never had to work. Meanwhile, Harriet's reporting to Human Resources five days a week all these years, with nothing glittery to show for it. She may have finally decided to try and catch up to them."

"And that meant Israel had to die? That's pure evil."

"I'm afraid so. That's our tragedy...Harriet's own version of the Law of the Jungle," said Storm.

"OK. I have one final question. Just one. Promise." Jane looked hopefully at Storm and Champus. They both took a cookie and nodded their assent.

"What about Joe Miller?"

49

EARLY DECEMBER
A Tale of Two Islands: Second Island

Oxford Monteith was strolling down the flagstone path of her home in Lincolnville, Maine. She held the day's mail in her arms and was opening envelopes as she made her way back to the kitchen door.

A medium-sized manila packet was in the mix, in handwriting Oxford did not recognize. Postmarked from Barbados...?

She raised the wings on the metal clasp and thumbed open the sealed edge. Then pulled out the contents: one round-trip ticket?...in her name?...to the Caribbean! and a post card of a luxury hotel. On the back of the post card was printed the name of a plantation estate located on the west coast of Barbados. Oxford looked at the handwriting...a room number, the dates of her hotel reservation...and the words "Come hither...."

Oxford Monteith was no longer a teenager. Female adults in Lincolnville, Waldo County, Maine, did not ordinarily commence leaping in joy and shrieking with ecstasy over the United States mail. A stable, well-heeled woman tempered the urge to display such physical jubilation, to feel her head blowing off like a mega-mondo firework. But Oxford wasn't one to let convention stop her. And she wasn't going to breathe a word of this to Sam.

....

DEEP FRIED FATE

Where did I put those binoculars? Don't tell me they got buried in the sand. Oxford raised her head above Jamie's tattooed arm to look around her. Oh, there they were, behind the cooler...her 60 X 60 field glasses...for allegedly watching the exotically plumed birds on Barbados...for actually scanning the walking, bouncing implants and enthusiastic adulterers populating this wealthy plantation hotel.

A half hour ago, she had opened her eyes to a couple arriving with their blanket, much further down the beach away from all the designer beach furniture and umbrellas. Oxford could hardly make them out, but something stuck with her.

She dozed on it for a while and then turned away from Jamie's arms. She rolled the magnifier on her binoculars to see what she could see. Just a little more to the right, then to the left. And there...she had it...perfecto.

She stared at the two tiny heads in her binoculars. Two tiny heads connected to two fused bodies.

She leaned further towards the edge of her lounge chair to bring the image into sharper focus, and that's when her body hit the sand, and her brain misfired and spat out a question in answer to her silent question....
Sam and Turk?? Sam and Turk?!!

"Hey, Oxy! Over here!"

"Who the hell could be calling you, Oxford?" Jamie mumbled from under his Panama.

Oxford jumped up out of the sand and brushed her hands all over to get rid of the grit on her swim suit and limbs. "I have no idea. Let me check."

She raised the binoculars in the direction of the main plantation complex and focused towards the voice calling her.

Nathan Herinton!!

Oh my God! Oh my God! Ummm....Ahhhhh, "Hey there, Nathan!"

Oxford ran to meet him and turned him right back around. "Son of a gun. So good to see you, Nathan! You know I was just heading to the gift shop to buy more sunscreen. Come with me and tell me what you're doing here."

As they walked further and further away from the two-headed creature on the far side of the beach, Oxford caught her breath and her senses. Nathan was explaining he had noticed Oxford and Jamie earlier in the day and finally had time to track them down.

Oxford looked up at her sister's golden god, so strapping, well-muscled, confident...entirely in his element...sun, sand, waves to conquer...and so oblivious to the absurd reality on the far beach.

Nathan flashed his white lightning smile at Oxford. "It just so happens my yacht crew has been down here practicing in the waters off Barbados. We're eyeing Barbados Sailing Week in mid-January...may aim for the Mount Gay Round Barbados Race this year."

"What do you know, Nathan? What do you know!" Oxford exclaimed. *You don't know anything, you idiot! How am I going to get rid of you? And how are we not going to bump into Sam and her primate playmate?! God damn it! Whose big idea was this getaway anyway?*

50

MID-DECEMBER, ONE WEEK LATER
Wreck the Halls

"Well, Sam and Oxford, it's been so long since we've all been together. This is great! We can catch up!" Jane was fizzing like a human Alka-Seltzer as a tired-looking Samantha Lloyd and her equally frazzled sister, Oxford Monteith, made their way into the PSO office. They collapsed into chairs at the long-plank table.

"Did you drop by to hear all about how we miraculously put Israel's murderers behind bars?"

Sam and Oxford did not return Jane's fizzy bubbles. No hugs for her, no questions about murderers. Sam got straight to the point.

"Jane, Nathan's in prison in Barbados. Drug charges of all things! We have to get him out."

"How in the world did this happen?" Jane tried to look shocked. Maybe it would do Nathan some good to be stuck in a tropical clanker for a spell. Yank him down a peg or two.

"We have some ideas," Oxford said, "and that's why we need to talk."

Oxford put a copy of her book *Methamatics* in front of Jane. It was enclosed in a large, sealed plastic bag. "Don't open it. We'll explain."

"Wait. Before we dive into Nathan, what's this I hear about you on Barbados...with some other man?" Jane asked Sam with a wily Cheshire smile.

Sam shot Jane a "No Trespassing" kind of glare. "I don't want to talk about it."

Oxford looked at both of them. "So I guess we can get started on the fate of Nathan Herinton?"

"And what were you doing down in Barbados, Oxford?" Jane and Sam asked at the same time.

"No comment."

Jane grumped a sigh. "So it's all about Nathan Herinton. Fine. Not my favorite person in the world, but he's from St. Frewin's, so he's part of my flock."

"I just don't understand you, Jane. You've never liked him." Sam's iron focus was dissolving into emotions. "He's been so sweet to me from Day One. Mixing all those drinks for my catering events. Paying for scores of port-o-potties for my gatherings and making sure they actually arrived on site. Which, mind you, is no small feat when 200,000 brides are getting married in Maine in the summer on septic-tank-system-less solid rock."

Jane almost thought she could see tears brimming in Sam's eyes. How could she be such a sap for the guy?

"Anyway, none of it makes sense. If there's anything you can think of, suggest, whatever we have to do....." Sam wasn't her usual self.

"Wait. Let's start at the beginning," Jane said. "Can you at least describe the charge or the probable cause for the arrest? And how you think it happened? Then we'll get to solutions. You do know what he was charged with, don't you?"

"Oh, let me look at my notes...we're just so on edge about everything," Oxford said, a little diary in her one hand, her other hand running through her hair over and over.

Sam waved a tourist flyer at Jane about "8 Things Not to Do in Barbados."

DON'T Disturb Turtle Nests
DON'T Wear Camouflage
DON'T Do Drugs
DON'T Drive on the Right
DON'T Sunbathe Topless
DON'T Touch Machineels
DON'T Light a Beach Fire
DON'T Overdo the Rum

"So what is it?" Jane asked. "Did Nathan sunbathe topless?"

"No, that was Sam." Oxford pointed her finger straight at her sister. Then wiggled it.

"Shut your face," Sam warned.

Jane studied the flyer. "OK, I get it. Nathan was in camouflage briefs, at a campfire on the beach, and stirring his sorrows in a mug of Mt. Gay, when he jumped up and grabbed some sea turtle eggs. Guilty!"

"Jane, quit joking."

"OK. Here we go," Oxford said, looking up from her diary. "Nathan reports they've thrown him in jail for possession of controlled drugs. And those controlled drugs are a-bombs; i.e., marijuana cigarettes with heroin or opium...and b-bombs; i.e., methamphetamine."

"Which, as you know, Jane, makes no sense whatsoever," Sam insisted. "Nathan doesn't go near drugs! He's ignorant about drugs."

"Right. He is ignorant. And this is serious. What about your book, *Methamatics,* Oxford? How is it tied to Nathan's plight?"

Oxford pointed to the bagged book. "That is the copy Nathan was surprised to find inside one of the life jacket lockers on board his friend's yacht. That was during their sail down to the Caribbean."

"Just curious, Sam. Why is Oxford telling me all this instead of you?" asked Jane.

"Well, Oxford ran into Nathan in Barbados. She actually talked with him down there. I only spoke to him by phone last night, right after I got back home."

"See, the guys had recently delivered the yacht to Barbados in advance of the winter races." Oxford kept referring to her little diary. "Nathan's friend, whose father owns the boat, and the rest of the crew flew back to the States. Nathan stayed to clean up the *Synchronicity* after their long trek down there."

"So how did you get the book, Oxford?"

"When I went to say goodbye to Nathan, he handed it to me. Said he and his mates had no idea how it got on his friend's yacht, but since I wrote it, I might as well take it."

"And you really do believe him?" Jane asked.

Oxford fended off Jane's question with a dismissive toss of her chin. "Of course we believe him. Then, later that night, Nathan called me to say he had been arrested. He was on board the boat when Barbadian police appeared. They flashed a warrant, told him they wanted to see his life jackets. He opened the lockers, and the police took one life jacket and cut into it. Nathan says the police found all twenty jackets stuffed with laced joints and meth."

"Unbelievable, right, Jane? Not the Nathan we know, right?" Sam looked miserable.

"So, schemer that I am," Oxford was saying, "I started to wonder why would a copy of *Methamatics* mysteriously appear in the chest with life jackets that were apparently doctored with illegal drugs? What kind of bullshit coincidence is that?"

Jane picked up the bagged book and was able to open the book part way without opening the bag. "So I take it you bagged the book to avoid more fingerprints until we get this tested?" Jane looked at Oxford.

"That's right. But as you can see, you can read inside the book."

"So what am I looking for? I mean, I read the whole book when it came out. So now what?"

Oxford shook her head with a sour smile. "Take a look at page 39...the description of Chummy? Suddenly he's suave and truly handsome?"

"I don't remember that at all in your book, or in real life. He's bow-legged and has salt and pepper facial stubble," Jane recalled.

"Exactly," said Oxford. "So now I have a confession to make. Those bozos pressured me so hard about changing the book to suit them...you know, blanket them with tattoos, and recast them to look like a Copper-toned Ronald Reagan or Pierce Brosnan. And then they would buy 1,000 copies! Well, I had planned to fool them into thinking I was making the revisions, but in the end, I finally caved. I assure you, though, it's only those 1,000 copies that went out all bastardized. No more than that."

Jane looked at the author for a moment. "So, Oxford, what you're saying is that Turk and his gang are the only ones who bought the altered version of the book. Which means they may be somehow connected to the book Nathan found in the life jacket locker. Which further means whoever turned those life jackets into illegal commodities may be linked to the book...and to Turk and his tribe. Fascinating. Very good, Oxford!"

"This whole thing has been so idiotic. I may never write again." Oxford slouched in her seat.

"She's just jittery and crestfallen about dream boy," Sam explained.

Oxford hissed at her.

"What do you mean?" Jane asked.

Sam made a show of aiming a dramatic stage whisper at Jane. "Turns out there's a Mrs. Jamie...and bambini."

"Uh oh," Jane said.

Oxford dug in her nails. "And what was our canned Spam doing in Barbados? Canned Spam was cavorting with George of the Jungle's tiny twin."

Jane watched the sisters glaring at one another as she thought back to the blood drive and Turk swooning over Sam. "Ahh...the yin and the yang came together...."

"But what does this mean, Jane? That it's all Turk's doing that Nathan is in prison in Barbados?" Sam began wilting. "You have to go down there, Jane. You have to go to Barbados to help Nathan."

The three women looked at one another, gritting their teeth. This was going to get ugly.

51

DECEMBER, ONE WEEK LATER
Guess Who's Coming to Dinner?

Helen Orbeton walked into Jane's office towards the end of the work day and sat down as if she were balancing a thirty-pound head dress. She looked at Jane with a sort of homey divination and said, "Anything you need to discuss with me? Any kind of confession, something to get off your chest?"

"What on earth are you talking about, Helen?"

"Well, Joe Miller keeps calling to remind me he wants to cook the dinner of the century for you...tonight. And I keep taking his messages. Here are eight of them. That's a lucky number, isn't it?"

Jane turned her blushing face towards her paperwork. "This is crazy. What am I going to do about him? And no that wasn't a question. And no, we don't need to talk about it."

"OK. No problem. And you'll notice I'm not asking about Konstantin," Helen said as she rose, like her eyebrows, and walked out of Jane's office.

I have got to call Joe. I don't want this dinner business getting out of hand. Will turn him down gently. Low-keyed, diplomatic. Good game plan.

. . . .

"You know as well as I do, Joe...you probably shouldn't be here," Jane said to him an hour later. He was hauling an armload of groceries through her hallway to cook her the dinner of the century, all upbeat and cheery as if they loved cooking together and did it all the time.

Longish swaths of his dark hair wandered over his eyes while he hustled his foodstuffs into the kitchen. Jane looked away and gripped her hands together. She must not come under his spell, must not imagine her fingers tucking those rogue locks of his hair back in place...behind his ears...half way down his neck....

She had phoned him from work and told him to forget the whole idea. No dinner. No way. One of his fingers in her mouth at lunch did not grant him carte blanche.

But he had shown up at her office like he never heard a word she said. "We'll drive to your house in your truck. I'll leave my truck here at the PSO. No need to raise suspicions." A man with a plan.

And now he stood before her in her kitchen with his hands out wide. "Jane, Jane...relax. I haven't been officially appointed yet." Then he tucked back his own stray strands of dark hair.

"But what about the Maine State Police Manual of Conduct?" she frowned. "Me knowingly fraternizing with you, my soon-to-be new superior officer? That must violate some kind of standard operating procedure," she insisted.

"What's gotten into you, woman? I'm only making you the dinner of the century. Does that qualify as a mortal sin?"

Wipe that impish grin off your face, Joe Miller.

"You know exactly what I mean, Joe Miller."

"Like you ever follow any SOP, Jane Roberts." Joe laughed and began pulling groceries out of the bag.

"So, I'm just curious." Jane picked up a lemon and started tossing it in her hands. "At what point did you decide to entirely forget to tell me you were operating as a Federal undercover agent at Calderwood Boatyard?"

"Oh, that's ancient history," Joe said.

"And this new State position of yours? Created to manage high crime cases on the Midcoast island communities, including St. Frewin's Island? Is that stale news too? And I'm the only person on the planet who didn't know?"

"Did you hear how Harriet Buxton will probably get shipped down to FCI Tallahassee?"

"You're avoiding my topic, Joe. And yes, Storm said that's where they plan to send her to prison."

"Well, apparently Harriet's in heaven, because she's sure she's going to meet Ghislaine Maxwell behind bars!"

"And about your new position managing high crimes on Maine islands? Do you seriously think it makes sense for us to be socializing like this?"

"You're going to love this main course, Jane. I've been experimenting all week, and I think...just maybe...I'm going to crush it tonight."

"Ah, circling back to your new position, maybe you can tell me if you've heard anything about Nathan Herinton and those fake drug charges down in Barbados?"

"Now why would I be privy to the buzz that his wealthy parents are considering a mega contribution to the Barbados Cancer Society to secure their son's release? The more important detail for us here, tonight, is the dessert I made for you."

So much for Jane's diplomacy and her game plan to finesse her way out of this entire evening. She tossed the lemon on the counter and stretched her arms. "I give up. What's the main course?"

"Lightly fried chicken with a citrusy crushed tomato, basil sauce, served over linguini fini." Joe kissed the tips of the fingers on his right hand.

"Oooo...that does sound good." Jane reached into her pantry for an apron and handed it to Joe. "Tell me more."

"Well, I'm going to sauté some broccoli in olive oil and whole garlic cloves with a dash of hot pepper flakes, and I'll toss us a simple salad of curly leaf lettuce, pine nuts, and a white wine vinaigrette."

"Hah...cook me three more dinners like this, and I just may forgive you for freezing me out of your professional loop," Jane said with reluctant approval.

"You do know you're going to report to me directly, once they give my new post the green light."

"That's been my whole point, Joe." Jane looked at him with a perturbed face, trying not to imagine his arms wrapped around her skimpy rib cage. "You'll be my boss in a matter of what, 120 hours? Please don't try any funny stuff tonight."

"When have I ever been anything except honorable, Jane? You need to unwind. Here, I'm opening a Pinot Blanc...tell me what you think," Joe said as he pulled the cork and poured Jane a cold glass of pale, straw-colored wine...the first of many that night. Plus the grappa.

And the sambuca....

....

They talked about their families; they talked about the worst things they had ever done. They talked about books and Billy Collins' poetry; they talked about their first big loves and dogs they had adopted from shelters. They laughed about the funniest things that ever happened to them, and they compared notes on the bird and mineral collections in London's Natural History Museum, ice skating, cheeses, and how to make bread. They talked about Israel.

Jane forked in her final mouthful of linguini and fried chicken with lemony tomato sauce. "To be honest, I feel totally guilty enjoying your company and your wonderful dinner after everything that happened to Israel."

Joe put down his silverware. "It's only been five months, Jane. It takes time...to absorb the loss into your life, to accept how life has unfolded. It's natural to still be feeling sadness and grief...but why guilt?"

"Well, I don't know if I ever told you this, but it was my fault that Harriet and Finn tracked Israel down that night. I was the one who told Finn about Israel's slip-up concerning the undercover Feds at the mountain house. I thought Finn had been vetted like me...a safe member of the force, not corrupt. If I hadn't said anything to him, and if he hadn't told Harriet, Israel would probably be alive today."

"But you acted in good faith, Jane, within the bounds of all work expectations. What happened to Israel was Fate. In fact, as I understand it, you tried to make sure he stayed put at the mountain house, right?"

"Yes, I did try."

"But he didn't stay. He went out on his own."

"Why did he do that, Joe? Why did he go with Finn?"

"Maybe he wanted some fresh air. Maybe when Finn found Israel, he wasn't able to get away from Finn. You couldn't control Israel's life, his choices. None of us can control another person's life. At least not sanely and realistically."

"Good point. Controlling someone else's life...you remind me of how Israel barked at me about being a control freak. When we checked on that wandering catamaran that showed up in Walker Cove...after Honor Carleton called in. Did you hear about that, a year or so ago? Five people dead from too much fentanyl in some fake OxyContin party pills. Such a mess."

"I do know that case. Dave Tower's boat...he was a rotten apple as it turned out. And...you probably weren't told this, Jane, but apparently Tower was Israel's first handler in the corrupt cop hierarchy. It must have been hard for Israel when he saw the state Dave was in."

"What? What are you saying, Joe? Israel didn't say a word, and we were standing there when Tower died. And later, at our case follow-up, Israel said he didn't know Tower. But now you're saying they knew each other? That's...that's..., well, honestly, I'm shocked."

"Jane, I don't know what else I should or shouldn't say here. But it will probably all come out, and you'll be pissed if you didn't hear it from me now. The other thing you should know, which will give you the bigger picture, is that Finn was the one who became Israel's next handler."

"Finn? Finn?" Jane could feel the tears returning. "Oh my God. This is insane. No wonder Israel got so upset when I called him at the mountain house and told him I had talked to Finn about everything. Israel knew he shouldn't say anything outright, but he sort of fought me on my idea that Finn had been vetted and cleared."

"That would make sense."

"And earlier that day, how was it that Finn just happened to call me because he was doing chores on the mainland? Had he already heard about Israel?" Jane said, thinking out loud.

"Jane, enough. Don't beat up on yourself. You were trying to do your best. You're a good person. I wouldn't be here if I didn't think you were a good person."

Jane shut her eyes tight for a second. "Did you read the autopsy report, or talk to Dr. Kerner? Do you realize Finn and Harriet and whoever helped them treated Israel like they had bagged a deer. And then they put his clothes back on him. It's so sadistic! Why did they go to such trouble?"

"Well, Harriet and her collaborators have had little to say about those details," Joe said. "And yes, I did read everything related to the case. It seems to me the bad cops wanted to send a message to any of their recruits who might have second thoughts about cooperating with the whole sick scheme."

"I guess that's the only sense to make of it." Jane tried wiping her eyes. "Thanks, Joe. I'm sorry I'm crying like this. They really destroyed Israel, even while he was alive. It's all so sad. I feel so cold...and empty. Do you know that feeling?"

Joe stood up and went to her. "I'm here for you, Jane. Let me help."

....

Everyone was fast asleep...totally fast asleep, like they had maybe gone overboard half the night, from the broccoli onward...during and after the dinner of the century....

Joe had held Jane, tried to comfort her. It unleashed too much. Or did it begin to free her? Free her from sorrow and make her whole again? Make her feel like it might be OK to be with Joe Miller and not feel shame for feeling joy—not feel like it was wrong. To be *wild* again.

Good God...had she really lured him outside half naked to chase her around in the yard? In 40-degree weather?

Did they actually land on the kitchen table as she was spooning the Amarena cherries on top of his scrumptious homemade ricotta cheesecake?

Once they finally found their way to bed, all Jane could do was whisper *Heaven help me* as Joe pulled her halfway under him moments before they both konked out.

By 4 AM Mother Nature called and Jane was hobbling in the dark towards the bathroom.

What have I done?! How could I? Jane sat there, chastising herself and trying to do the trigonometry of Konstantin versus Joe...with Israel hovering somewhere above it all...not quite in heaven.

How do you love someone who isn't here? Is that really a relationship? Is it important to suffer when you're in love? Not to be able to give or receive what you fell in love with in the first place? Or am I simply selfish? Can you betray someone who is never with you? Shit. What does this make me? A wanton woman with no ego boundaries whatsoever? Maybe it was the cheesecake. Maybe I should send Joe home right now....

....

He quickly parked the rental car and slid more than jumped out. He was exhausted to the point of pulp after too many hours in toxic traffic jams in exotic countries and multiple flight connections through an outrageous number of decrepit airports around the world. To feel his feet on solid ground on a tiny Maine island should have meant Paradise. But he was too tired to care. Just a few more steps and he could collapse, next to her.

He opened the front door quietly and tip toed towards the bedroom. His bags were in the car. They could wait until tomorrow.

He walked into the dark room and could barely see her form beneath the covers. He loved surprising her. He loved hearing her sleepy ecstasy.

He lifted the thick down quilt and quietly slid in next to her warm sleeping body. This time he wouldn't try to waken her...but he couldn't resist a hug...one Big Hug.

"Mmmm, Jane, Jane?" came whispering out from the form under the covers, which rolled sleepily towards the affection-seeking arms, which suddenly seemed too muscular, too hairy....

"Hey!! WHAT THE HELL?!?!" Joe Miller threw the covers off his head and stared in the dark at the weary but amorous Konstantin Balankoff.

"Who are YOU?!?" Konstantin yelled as he sprang back. "And where's Jane Roberts?"

52

SAME NIGHT
Mending Bridges...Blowing Up Bridges

Jane dragged her feet back to bed. Why did her conscience have to bob up at the most inconvenient moments? It acted as though it were as tall as she was. And it was so insistent and pushy...bossy. Just like Jane. And did she hear yelling when she was holed up in the bathroom or was she dreaming?

Joe passed her in the hallway.

"Hey, Joe...slow down."

He brushed Jane away and aimed for the bathroom. *He's probably still feeling 100% proof. Let him be.*

She continued into the bedroom and flopped down on the bed. As she pulled her pillow closer, she felt the other body.

"AAAGGHH! HELP!!" Jane shrieked. "How did you get back into bed so quickly, Joe??"

"It's not Joe."

Jane screamed again. "WHAT??!! What is this?!"

She bolted out of bed and hit the wall light switch. Konstantin was lying there looking haggard and angry.

"Konstantin!!! What are you doing here?!"

"I might ask the same about Joe."

"Oh, shit. Oh, dear...I can explain everything," Jane rushed to assure him.

"No you can't."

Jane's eyes blinked large. "You're right. I can't." She grabbed his arm. "But let me try, OK?" she pleaded.

"One chance," Konstantin said.

296

"I suggest we all go sit down at the kitchen table and hash this out. We're adults, right?"

"At least one of us is," Konstantin answered. "And I don't think I need to warn you that I feel like you've ripped my heart out and tossed it to the sharks."

"Like I said, let's go to the kitchen. Let's sit up straight. We'll deal with this intelligently."

Jane went to her closet, pulled out a bathrobe, and wove her way towards the kitchen. She yelled back, "Come to the kitchen, Konstantin. It's the only way. You, too, Joe."

Konstantin caught up with Jane just as she and Joe entered the kitchen. Jane turned on the lights, which sent blinding flashes through their eyeballs. But that didn't keep them from seeing what Jane had forgotten entirely.

I LOVE SEX! SHAKE IT, BABY! was scrawled in Amarena cherry sauce all over the refrigerator door.

"Oh, my God. This isn't going to work," Jane said out loud, her face plunging into her hands.

"That's right, Jane. I'm leaving." Konstantin turned back towards the bedroom. They could hear him pulling himself together. Then he walked out and drove off—just like that.

"Let's head back to bed, Jane," said Joe, pulling her close to his side. "Maybe we'll fall asleep."

Maybe we won't.

DEEP FRIED FATE is the third Jane Roberts Mystery. Carol Chen lives in Camden, Maine.

Jane Roberts Mysteries in order:
LOBSTERS WITHOUT BORDERS
DON'T TOUCH MY COCKTAIL!
DEEP FRIED FATE

9 789898 643964 8